LUCIFER:

REVELATION

Paul Darrow

First published in May 2014
by Big Finish Productions Ltd
PO Box 1127, Maidenhead, SL6 3LW
www.bigfinish.com

Executive Producers for Big Finish: Nicholas Briggs and Jason Haigh-Ellery
Blake's 7 Producer for Big Finish: Cavan Scott
Executive Editor for B7 Media: Andrew Mark Sewell

Managing Editor: Jason Haigh-Ellery

Production Editor: Xanna Eve Chown
With thanks to Peter Anghelides, John Binns and Matthew Griffiths

Cover design: Anthony Lamb

ISBN: 978-1-78178-268-2
eBook: 978-1-78178-269-9

A CIP catalogue record for this book is available from the British Library.

For Janet

LUCIFER: REVELATION

CONTENTS

DRAMATIS

THE REBELS
Avon
Del Grant
Magda Lens, ex-lover of Avon

THE QUARTET
Successors of the Federation. Based on the Earth-like planet Iphigenia, its moon, Niobe, and the Hub, a man-made planetoid orbiting Mars

Doctor Pandora Ess, former aide to Servalan
Gabriella Travis, commander of static warship *The Base*
General Gregor Steiner
Eugene Furneaux

Adonis, Gabriella's attendant
Sarin, General Steiner's navigator
Commander Hermann

Solomon Fisch, a hitman
Alexandra Fisch, 'the Huntress', his daughter
Absolom Fisch, his son

XERXES
An island planet in the Beyond, source of crystal fuel rods

Xerxes, ex-bandit ruler of the planet
Juno Trask, his wife
Louis, his second wife
Alaric, his enforcer

PERSONAE

ALIEN GREYS
Inhabiting a planetoid near the planet Ragnar in the Beyond

Egil Nacre, leader of the Alien Greys
Ex and Zed, his comrades

THE EMPIRE OF CATHAY
Formerly the People's Republic of China, now in effective control of Earth and its moon

The Claw, their biggest warship
The Thumb, its attack fighter

Empress Kwai Shi Yan
Lauren, her deaf and dumb companion

Colonal Fu Ti, a diplomat
Micah, his assistant
Xian, his assistant
General Kai Kim, his niece

General Li Lang, commander-in-chief of all the forces of the empire beyond Earth
Captain Lee Sa
Commander Chen

Marshall Sun Cheng, commander of all Imperial forces
Tung Ma, his guard

How art thou fallen from heaven,
O Lucifer, son of the morning!

Isaiah 14:12

PROLOGUE

i

When the Terran Federation ruled much of planet Earth, as well as the then-known universe and parts of other galaxies, those who spearheaded the totalitarian regime constantly jockeyed for position, seeking greater power and influence – power being an essential aphrodisiac for febrile minds.

At one point, the famous – or infamous – Servalan seized the Presidency. Amongst her closest (if, for the time being, inconspicuous) followers was Raoul Cougar, a charming, ruthless power-seeker whose determination drew in turn admiration and fear. Servalan admired him and utilised his talents to her advantage. But power has been known to corrupt, and Cougar's ambitions, in time, soured their relationship and Servalan began to fear him, taking steps to curb his eager advancement.

Forewarned, Cougar fled to the Martian colony and gradually established an alternative power base from his stronghold on Mars's red mountain. Servalan was somewhat chagrined by his being out of her reach, but at least Cougar could cause her no distress from Mars and, as long as he stayed where he was and did not interfere with her plans, she left him alone. Nevertheless, her other 'associates' kept a close eye on him.

But sleeping wildcats eventually wake up, and when Servalan fell from grace and her reign of terror was replaced by an alternative, Cougar returned to Earth. He formed an alliance with the Federation's rivals in the East, China – now renamed the Empire of Cathay – and attempted to impose his own reign, usurping Servalan's successors.

He almost succeeded! The fact that he didn't was because a contract was put out on him – by whom nobody seemed to know, or was prepared to admit that they knew – and that contract was fulfilled.

ii

With the backing of his Eastern 'friends', Cougar seized control of Earthly outposts that were poorly defended by the Federation – the inevitable and continuing power struggles at its head proving to be, to an extent, a fatal distraction. Something had to be done to remove this turbulent upstart. And something was.

Raoul Cougar's easy early successes seduced him into believing that, in time, he could overcome Federation opposition and deliver Earth to the Cathay Empire – an Empire that promised to raise him to a higher position than he had enjoyed under Servalan's rule. Indeed, he had been promised leadership of Cathay's expansion into far-flung territories, Federation and otherwise. The Empire of Cathay, whilst technically inferior to the Federation, possessed unlimited manpower and, as a study of its history reveals, could and would expend it at will.

Those who had deposed Servalan panicked at the prospect of facing a resurgent Cathay led by a man who knew a great deal about Federation military capability and strategy. Historians amongst them needed no reminding of the outcome when Caesar turned against republican Rome or how, much later, the greatest empire the world had ever seen fell to barbarian hordes from the East! But cometh the moment, cometh the man. Or, in this case, the woman.

Doctor Pandora Ess, who would at a later date become a major player in the Quartet that replaced the Federation (but that's another story), had been one of Servalan's staunchest supporters. Lurking in the shadow of her charismatic leader, she had performed many unsavoury tasks on her behalf.

She was about to perform another. For it was she who recruited an assassin to target the traitor, Raoul Cougar.

iii

Whilst the Federation struggled to put together forces to resist the seemingly inexorable advance from the East, Cougar inexplicably paused. Instead of going for the jugular, as his Cathay masters urged, he took time out to indulge a flaw in his personality – a major weakness. Raoul Cougar loved the company of women. Since exile on Mars and the business of war on Earth, he had remained celibate for a good deal longer than he desired and decided to remedy matters before proceeding towards his destiny – an error of judgement he would not live to regret.

Cougar and his closest comrades in arms dallied for a few days in a charming castle overlooking a majestic river that flowed, at length, to the Terran Federation's heartland. Female comrades outnumbered males by three to one, so Raoul's sexual appetite would be easily satisfied.

After an encounter with a stunningly beautiful young Slavic woman, Cougar ventured onto a balcony so that a gentle breeze might cool his hot blood. The young woman, Alexandra, followed him and embraced him from behind. Thus entwined, they both enjoyed the caressing breeze and Raoul, once again experiencing a stirring in his loins, purred with contentment.

Ironically, the rifle had been manufactured by an innovative gunsmith in Cathay. Though weighing very little, it was powerful and possessed, in the right hands, great range.

It was in the right hands. The camouflaged marksman was hidden in a forest atop a hill on the far side of the river from the castle. 'Alexandra has done very well,' he whispered.

'Range is 1700 metres,' his spotter whispered back, 'You should aim slightly left to allow for the breeze. I would recommend a head shot.'

'That's a little tricky with Alexandra breathing down his neck,' the marksman said. 'I wouldn't want to kill her too.'

'If you're good enough you won't, and you're good enough!'

The shooter adjusted the night-scope on the rifle and brought Raoul Cougar into focus. 'Ease back a little, Alexandra dear,' he said – and she did.

The shooter inhaled, slowly exhaled and gently squeezed the trigger. Raoul Cougar's head exploded, smattering the courtesan with blood and grey matter.

'Time to go,' the spotter said.

Solomon Fisch smiled. 'I'm rather good at this, aren't I?' he said, this time not bothering to whisper.

The spotter grunted. 'If you want to continue to be good, we need to get the hell out of here.'

'I worry about Alexandra.'

'There's no need. Alexandra is even better than you at what she does.'

PART ONE
The Beginning

The ice cracked as a thin periscope rose from beneath the sea and, like a cobra seeking easy prey, turned its attention towards the woman.

She was seated at a table, shielded from a paradoxically warm sun by a garish umbrella. Upon the table was a bucket of ice containing an open bottle of exquisite champagne, two champagne flutes and a crystal ashtray, in which lay a smoking cheroot. She was dressed in a black leather trouser suit. Attending her was a man, also dressed in black, who sat upon an elaborately carved trunk by her side. Although fully grown, he was no more than four feet tall.

They ignored the intrusive periscope and thereafter the conning tower of the submarine that emerged and brushed the ice in the immediate vicinity aside. The woman lifted the cheroot to her lips and inhaled deeply. Her attendant was as silent and as still as obsidian.

After a few moments, the hatch of the conning tower was thrown open and a ramp extended over crushed ice onto a firmer surface. A man climbed through the hatch and walked down the ramp. He was also dressed entirely in black. Stepping off the ramp he strolled towards the incongruous scene that greeted him. He bowed slightly.

'Gabriella, I presume?' he said, his voice a pleasingly deep baritone.

The woman, Gabriella, smiled. 'You presume correctly,' she said. Her attendant remained motionless, but clearly alert to any possible danger.

The man from the submarine, most of which still lay beneath the surface of the chilly waters, smiled back. 'I am Solomon.'

'I was not expecting anyone else.' Gabriella indicated that he should be seated. 'Would you care for a glass of champagne?'

'Indeed I would. It is a while since I have tasted that queen of wines.'

Gabriella's attendant rose from his position on the trunk and poured champagne, refilling his mistress's glass before handing Solomon his. Solomon drank. 'Exquisite!' he exclaimed.

'I'm so glad you're pleased,' Gabriella said, sipping from

her glass and eyeing him over its rim. 'Shall we get down to business?'

'But of course.' Solomon smiled again. 'I notice that the colour black is *de rigueur* today. If black may be described as a colour.'

'It stands out against this white background,' Gabriella said, handing her cheroot to her attendant, who stubbed it out for her. 'You are aware of the position I hold?'

'You are a high-ranking officer of the Federation. I'm sorry – it is now renamed the Quartet, I believe. But our business is none of its business. I understand this is a private matter?'

'The Quartet has suffered a number of setbacks since its inception. My fellow members are concerned with grave and important matters and my concern is of no interest to them. The business we are about to conduct is, as you say, my private initiative, emphasis being upon the word *private*. Thus, I require your absolute discretion.'

'You have it.'

Gabriella nodded her approval. 'You are undoubtedly aware that I am the commander of the Base, a man-made warship on a vast scale. It is a barrier between Quartet interests and a relatively unexplored territory known as the Beyond.' She smiled flirtatiously. 'You are familiar with the Beyond?'

'You know I am. That is why I am here. You cannot enter the Beyond, but I can. Or rather, those in my employ can. May we get to the point?'

'I wish to utilise your services, and those you employ, to carry out a very difficult task. I require that you seek out a terrorist and murderer, currently exiled in the Beyond, and deliver him to me at the Base – alive.' She shrugged. 'Of course, I realise it might not be possible to capture him. In which case, proof of his death will have to suffice. But the fee will be commensurately reduced.'

'This terrorist and murderer, does he have a name?'

'He is called Avon.' Gabriella watched Solomon's reaction very carefully. 'I understand that you were once acquainted with him?'

Solomon closed his eyes for a moment and sighed. 'It was

a long time ago. I had almost forgotten.' He opened his eyes. 'Avon attempted to embezzle vast sums from the Federation banking system. My father was in charge of that system. As a result of Avon's crimes, he was stripped of his high office, put on trial, convicted of negligence and exiled to this desolate place on Earth. He died soon after. My mother died – of a broken heart, I think. It is possible you know.'

'I know.'

'Avon was caught and imprisoned and I thought him dead. It was many years later that I heard of his terrorist activities and toyed with the idea of pursuing him. That's how I became familiar with the Beyond and recruited my assassins. At length, I gave up the ghost. Avon was a debonair thief on a grand scale and, to tell you the truth, I rather admired him and wished that I had thought to pull off such a splendid coup.' Solomon smiled ruefully.

'I am aware of Avon's lurid history.' Gabriella gritted her teeth. 'He murdered my father.'

Solomon nodded. 'So I understand. Although, the word *murder* would seem inappropriate.'

'It is appropriate as far as I am concerned,' Gabriella said tersely. 'I am prepared to pay two hundred million in gold for Avon alive – that sum halved if it is necessary to kill him. A further fifty million will be supplied to cover expenses. Oh, and should it be possible, Avon's computer should be retrieved and I will pay a further ten million for it.'

Solomon nodded thoughtfully.

'Your commission is, I believe, fifteen percent?'

'Actually, it's twenty.'

'Very well then, you will receive fifty-two million if you fulfil all tasks.'

'I shall require a deposit.'

Gabriella indicated the trunk upon which her attendant had been sitting. 'That contains seventy-five million in gold, to include expenses.' She clicked her fingers and her attendant opened the trunk. Solomon stood, walked over to it and gazed at its contents.

'Well?' Gabriella said impatiently.

'That is satisfactory,' Solomon said as he returned to the table. Her attendant poured further champagne.

Gabriella smiled. 'The trunk is on ice runners and powered by a small crystal energy disc. It will not be difficult for you to convey it to your submarine.'

'How may I contact you to report any progress?' Solomon asked.

'I shall contact you from time to time by the same route through which I arranged this clandestine meeting.' She waved a hand towards her still silent attendant.

'That too is satisfactory.'

'Are you able to tell me how you will proceed in this matter?'

Solomon frowned. 'I would prefer not to reveal my trade secrets, but I can assure you that I shall instruct my very best resources. As you know, or you would not have recruited me, many years ago I gained a reputation as a highly skilled assassin. Now that I am much older, I let others carry out the various contracts. They have not failed in the past and I am certain, gods willing, they will not fail me now.'

'You believe in gods?'

'It is a figure of speech.'

Gabriella smiled again, her dazzling white teeth glinting in the sunlight, like the ice beneath her feet. 'I accept that reticence is a necessary adjunct to your trade. As long as the job is done, I have no need to enquire further.' She rose to her feet. 'Our business is concluded,' she said finally. 'Please finish the champagne.'

At that moment a motorised ski-sled appeared from the shadow of a nearby ice mountain. It slithered to a halt and Gabriella's attendant helped her aboard, then got on himself. The sled reversed, rotated and sped away. Neither Gabriella nor her attendant offered a backward glance.

Solomon did as instructed and finished off the champagne. He threw a switch on the trunk containing the gold and guided it towards the conning tower of the submarine. He followed it up the ramp. The hatch closed behind him and, in a short while, the submarine sank beneath the ice.

A wind began to blow and the capricious sun faded behind gathering clouds. Within minutes, the table, the umbrella and all else were scattered hither and thither. It was as if they had never been there in the first place.

The interplanetary cruiser sped towards the Base, bypassing Iphigenia, the Earth-like headquarter planet of the Quartet – successors to the failed Federation.

On board, Gabriella lounged on a sofa. Her attendant sat on a small armchair opposite her. 'I would like to thank you, Adonis,' Gabriella said smoothly. 'I believe Solomon Fisch may well succeed where others have spectacularly failed and it is you who found him for me.'

Adonis seemed to smile. It was hard to tell.

'I wonder why I had not heard of him before you suggested I made contact.'

'The successful assassin must keep a low profile,' Adonis said, his voice barely above a whisper. 'Solomon Fisch was active a long time ago, when you were just a girl. That was when he and I became acquainted.'

'He did not acknowledge you.'

'He knew me, but he is very cautious. He could not be certain that I would wish you to know that he did.'

'How else would I have been able to contact him, if not under the auspices of someone he knew?'

'Doctor Ess knew him well. It is possible he imagined that she recommended him.'

Gabriella looked momentarily startled at the mention of her superior in the Quartet, but soon regained her composure. 'Did Pandora recruit him at some time?'

'Again, it was a long time ago. He assassinated the would-be Federation emperor, Raoul Cougar, at her behest.'

'I have heard my late father talk of Cougar.'

'There were similarities between them.'

Gabriella looked at him sharply, but Adonis remained impassive. 'Cougar's death halted an attack on the Federation from the East. Is that right?' she said.

'Yes. Travis would have approved of the assassination. He

was occupied elsewhere or he might have undertaken the mission himself.'

'I do not doubt he would have succeeded,' Gabriella said proudly.

Adonis said nothing.

'It was Avon who killed my father. You will understand why I seek revenge.' Gabriella spoke quietly.

'I knew this,' Adonis said, 'and of course I understand. There is also the matter of the super-computer currently in Avon's possession. I very much admired the way you indicated to Solomon that you would pay for its retrieval as if as an afterthought.'

Gabriella smiled coyly. 'You are very clever, Adonis. I wonder why Pandora assigned you to me when you could have remained a faithful servant to her.'

'I asked to be with you.'

Again, Gabriella looked startled. 'Why?'

'You are your father's daughter. I esteemed him above all others. It is an honour to serve you.'

As Gabriella slept during the final leg of their journey towards the Base, a fortress she believed she controlled, Pandora Ess received an encrypted message.

Gabriella has engaged the services of Solomon Fisch. Like Servalan before her, she seems obsessed with the terrorist Avon.

As you suspected, she is aware of the power of the computer known as Orac, currently in Avon's hands, and has cleverly indicated that she would like Solomon to acquire it for her, all of this being without the knowledge of her fellow Quartet members.

In control of the Base and Orac, Gabriella could prove to be a powerful friend or a very dangerous enemy.

I will keep you informed of developments – Adonis.

Pandora chuckled to herself. 'What little game are you playing, Gabriella? Whatever it is, you will find that two can play at it!'

*

Because it was summer and temperatures were tolerable, the submarine, now clear of ice, rode the surface of a blue sea. Solomon Fisch, from the conning tower, scanned the skies with powerful binoculars and spotted an incoming jet seaplane. As it approached, the plane executed a perfect roll before skimming the calm sea. The pilot cut its engines and it drifted alongside the submarine. The cockpit hatch was thrown back and a handsome, athletic young man hauled himself aboard. Solomon took his hand and assisted his entrance to the conning tower. The two men smiled and embraced.

'You have arrived sooner than I expected,' Solomon said, 'It is as well, because we have an onerous task to perform and the more time we have to prepare, the better.'

'I follow in the footsteps of the master,' the man said.

'See that you do. The man you have been selected to capture or kill – probably the latter – will prove a formidable opponent. Sensible preparation and precaution could make the difference.'

'What difference?'

'The difference would be between you killing him, or him killing you.'

'What's his name?'

'He is called Avon.'

'I've never heard of him.'

'Like you, he's a killer. He murdered, according to our employer, the infamous Travis. I'm sure you heard of it.'

The young man shrugged. 'I was a child when Travis got what he deserved. You're telling me that this man, Avon, was his contemporary?'

'Yes.'

'So he'll be getting on a bit – a has-been.'

'You would do well to remember that, in order to be a has-been, you need to have been a somebody in the first place. Avon and I are of a similar age. Would you describe me as a has-been?'

The young man became subdued. 'Was he as good as you were?'

Solomon nodded, 'I'm pretty certain he still is.'

*

At the time, the subject of their discussion, and the object of Gabriella's disaffection, was being chased through the back of the Beyond by an ex-Federation battle cruiser commandeered by avaricious pirates.

Avon himself had only recently commandeered the spacecraft he was attempting to elude them with and knew little of its capabilities. He was obliged to make enquiries of his computer companion.

'Orac! Can we outrun them?'

'How would I know? I am as unfamiliar with this craft as you are. You might try the on-board computer, although it might not take kindly to assisting a thief of your calibre.'

Avon did as advised and waited impatiently for the computer, situated on the flight deck console, to come online.

'I am George,' the computer said at last. 'You overrode my control when removing this ship from Prime Space. You were in something of a hurry.'

'Indeed I was. You are aware of the cruiser pursuing us.'

'I am.'

'Can we outrun it?'

'No.'

Avon swore a mild oath. 'What are our armaments?'

'Rocket launchers forward, a rapid-fire machine gun aft.'

'That's it?'

'This was not designed as a fighting ship.'

Orac almost seemed to chuckle. 'How are you going to get out of this one, Avon?'

'Tell me George,' Avon said quietly, 'What is the distance between the cruiser and us?'

'Five hundred and eight leagues separate us from it.'

'Estimated time of contact?'

'If we maintain maximum speed, the cruiser will make contact in three hours.'

Avon frowned. 'Orac, are you able to disguise this craft in stealth mode?'

'I might be.'

'Might you do it?'

'I suppose I can try.'

'Thank you, Orac.'

'I am George,' the on-board computer interjected. 'You should be informed that fuel capacity is low and there will soon be the necessity of acquiring crystal fuel rods.'

'Are there no spares on board?'

'There are not.'

'Where can they be acquired?'

'The nearest source is the planet Xerxes. Assuming evasion of the pursuit ship, there will be sufficient fuel to reach it.'

'How are you getting on, Orac?'

'The only way to achieve stealth concealment is to execute a reverse hyperjump. That is to say, you must perform a backward somersault, startling the occupants of the pursuing cruiser by jumping over them. You may then fire the rockets to confuse them further. I will ensure stealth mode is in place. But a great deal of fuel will be used in this manoeuvre.'

Avon looked thoughtful. 'We'll worry about lack of fuel once we've lost the bad guys. Tell me, "I am George", might it be possible to drift towards Xerxes?'

'It might be possible.'

'All right. Give me manual control of this spacecraft. We're about to put on an acrobatics display.'

Avon sat at the flight deck console as the computer unlocked the controls. 'Hold on to your hats, boys,' he said. 'I want maximum speed until we reach the height of the jump, then kill all engines and we'll float into ghostliness.'

As the ex-Federation cruiser closed on Avon's ship, its occupants watched in horror as his spacecraft became almost vertical until straightening to horizontal and flying upside down towards them. Some of them instinctively ducked as it passed overhead, reappeared in the cruiser's rear, rolled over, resumed a normal flight pattern, fired its rockets at no-one and nowhere in particular, and then vanished.

'Mission accomplished,' Orac said, somewhat begrudgingly.

'Alexandra, our huntress, is searching out our prey,' Solomon said. 'He was last heard of evacuating Prime Space in a craft stolen from Alien Greys. He was alone, save for an extraordinary computer known as Orac. Our employer requests its retrieval, in addition to Avon's capture or demise.'

'How do you know all this?' the younger man asked.

'I have contacts among the Greys. Many years ago, the dear departed Travis, encouraged by the soon to be disgraced, now deceased, Servalan, was in pursuit of a group of terrorists who had somehow acquired Orac. Avon was among that group, later killed its leader and, it is reasonable to assume, took off with the computer In fact, Alexandra's Alien Grey source is certain that Avon has it, having hidden it for close on two decades.'

'That's why he was in Prime Space – digging it up.'

'That's very astute of you, Absalom.'

The young man smiled. 'Surely this Orac computer will be functionally obsolete?'

'On the contrary, it is likely to still be ahead of its time.'

'It would be a powerful weapon then!'

'That is why Gabriella wants it, and why Avon will be reluctant to part with it.'

'So, where is he?'

'He will be somewhere in the Beyond. Deep space, I imagine, which will give him few options. At some time, he will need to refuel and there are only three sources in the back of the Beyond. The island planet Xerxes, a planetoid known as Yelmach and a pirate stronghold called Babylon. Alexandra will find him and then it will all be down to you, my son.'

'I am George,' the computer intoned. 'You should be advised that this spacecraft will require a fuel injection within one hour.'

'How long will it be before we reach, what's it called, Xerxes?' Avon asked.

'Two hours.'

Orac chuckled, or seemed to. 'You should also be informed, Avon, that stealth mode will be unsustainable in three minutes.'

'It's good news all round then. Have we lost the cruiser?'

'It is long gone,' Orac said.

'All right. Cut engines and we'll drift for a while. Then, we'll restart the engines for a similar amount of time, before drifting again. We'll stutter our way to Xerxes.'

'We are likely to drift off course,' said George.

'I'll adjust any drift manually, when we have occasional power.'

'One small point,' Orac said, 'How do we know you will be welcome on Xerxes?'

'I'm assuming whosoever rules the place will be in the business of selling fuel rods,' Avon said drily. 'We do have something of value on board to trade, don't we George?'

'I fear not.'

Orac chuckled again.

'Then we'll just have to steal some.'

George made a sound that seemed almost to be a sigh.

Orac said, 'There is no need to be concerned. Avon has proved himself to be a master of thievery on a grand scale.'

The island planet, Xerxes, was ruled by a minor bandit of the same name. In fact, his ego somewhat inflated, he had named the previously unknown sphere after himself and settled upon it with a few hundred followers, blood relatives (of which there were many), and his two wives – one male, one female.

Banditry not really being his forte, Xerxes was delighted to discover crystal deposits that could be converted into fuel rods for most spacecraft that travelled within the Beyond and what had once been Federation space. So it was that he was able to amass considerable wealth by trading this asset with other bandits, pirates and ne'er-do-wells frequenting the vicinity.

Quite shrewd, he used some of that wealth to purchase two fast, well-armed warships that orbited his island planet and deterred any possible aggression. He prided himself on being an honest broker amongst thieves and charged a not-unfair price for his fuel rods. As a result he and those closest to him were able to live sybaritic lives in moderately luxurious circumstances.

When the spacecraft piloted by Avon drifted into range, it was imagined by Xerxes and his enforcer, a thuggish but intelligent Earthman named Alaric, that another bandit had come to call and to trade. They were not far wrong.

But this bandit had come to steal.

The key figure in the Quartet (successor to the Federation but, in essence, just more of the same), Doctor Pandora Ess, summoned two of the other members to her palace headquarters on Iphigenia – the somewhat louche Eugene Furneaux and the grizzled General Gregor Steiner. Gabriella was not invited.

Furneaux lived in a mansion on the far side of a wide lake almost opposite the palace, so did not have far to come. Steiner, on the other hand, was busy fighting diverse insurgents and was not too happy to be distracted.

Whilst Furneaux lounged on a sofa, sipping white wine, Pandora Ess made it her business to supply the General with a large whisky, no ice, and settle him into a comfortable leather chair, all the time expressing her gratitude that he had so kindly deigned to answer her summons, which she insisted, in his case, had been more of a request. Slightly mollified, Steiner drank the whisky in one gulp and held out his glass for more. A silent eunuch attendant, one of Pandora Ess's bodyguards, obliged him.

'So what's the problem then?' Steiner growled. 'I assume there is a problem?'

'A problem in the making, perhaps,' Pandora Ess replied smoothly, 'It concerns our absent Quartet member Gabriella.'

'What's the stupid little bitch up to?'

Furneaux sniggered.

Pandora Ess frowned. 'You know as well as I do that Gabriella is by no means stupid.'

'She's not little either,' Furneaux interjected, 'but she can be a bitch.'

Pandora Ess silenced him with an admonishing look. 'Gabriella has engaged the services of Solomon Fisch. She has commissioned him to seek out and capture or, more likely, assassinate the terrorist known as Avon.'

Steiner almost choked on his drink. 'I thought we'd heard the last of him?'

'I fear not. Gabriella seeks revenge for her father's death at Avon's hands. But, more importantly, you will recall he is in possession of the super-computer Orac. If Gabriella should gain possession of it... Well, that might bode ill.'

'You think she's plotting a coup?'

'It's possible.'

Steiner looked thoughtful. 'I find it hard to believe. As you say, she's not stupid.' He shook his head. 'I'd say she's become obsessed with vengeance, like Servalan before her. And look what happened to Servalan!'

There was a silence in the room. At length, Eugene Furneaux broke it. 'We obliterated the island planet, Gaius 7, where Servalan died. It's entirely possible we obliterated Avon with it, so Gabriella is on a wild goose chase.'

'You don't really believe that, do you?' Pandora Ess said icily. 'Avon got away, reclaimed Orac and escaped into the Beyond.'

'How do you know?' Furneaux looked startled.

'I have made it my business to find out and I have many informants.'

'Well, even the estimable Solomon will find it hard to catch him there,' Steiner said, indicating that he wanted more whisky. He was given some.

'Someone else escaped the destruction of Gaius 7,' Pandora Ess said, 'Avon's mistress and Servalan's actual killer – Magda Lens.'

Steiner's expression froze. Furneaux shifted uneasily.

'The name is familiar to you?' Pandora Ess enquired.

Steiner nodded. 'She is one of the leaders of an insurgency I'm in the process of trying to put down.'

'Do you anticipate success?'

'In the long term perhaps, but this is beginning to look like the bad old days of the Federation when vast quantities of manpower and material were expended for little return. You cut off the head of a group and another leader steps up to the mark. It's bad enough dealing with the ambitions of Cathay without having to chase guerrilla fighters all over the galaxies. Guerrilla warfare, in my experience, is notoriously difficult to put down.' Steiner looked suddenly tired.

Furneaux coughed. 'I understand the Lens group was sufficiently ambitious as to make a failed attempt to attack a Quartet fighter patrol?'

'They didn't fail,' Steiner said, 'they managed to kill eleven elite guards and capture an armed interplanetary fighter. I was in pursuit when I was so peremptorily summoned here.'

'I thought the space force was untouchable,' said Furneaux lamely, almost to himself.

'The leader of what Eugene describes as the Lens group is not Magda, is it?' Ess asked, as if she already knew the answer – which she did.

Steiner scowled. 'The group's illustrious leader is Del Grant. He's one of the old school, like this Avon, who we don't seem to be able to get rid of.'

Pandora Ess looked smug. 'Grant's sister was once Avon's lover. She betrayed him – Avon – or so he believed, and he killed her. It would seem though that all is forgiven and Grant and Avon are on good terms.'

'Avon seems to have had an interesting way with women,' Furneaux remarked, hoping to lighten the mood.

Steiner ignored him. 'You're saying that two key figures in Avon's life have joined forces against the Quartet and are doing rather well and that, if Avon were to join them, they could do a lot better?'

'That's exactly what I'm saying,' Pandora Ess said forcefully. 'Gabriella sending Solomon Fisch after Avon and, let us not forget the Orac computer, may cause him to return from the Beyond. At which point, he could hardly refuse if Grant and Lens asked for his assistance. You have already indicated that they are causing more trouble than you care for. Add Avon to the mix and you have more trouble.'

'But if Solomon has him killed,' Furneaux interrupted, 'the problem is partially solved.'

'There have been many attempts to kill him or, at least, remove him from the equation. They all failed!' Pandora Ess smiled grimly.

Steiner got to his feet, rather unsteadily. 'Eugene could be right. If anyone can get to Avon and take him out, Solomon can. But, of course, if he doesn't, what you say may come to pass. In which case, we could have a very big problem. We already have Cathay beginning to become aggressive.'

'Which is why I called you both here,' said Pandora Ess.

'Well, what are we going to do about it?' Furneaux asked anxiously.

'We could persuade Gabriella to call off Solomon and, as it were, let sleeping dogs lie and trust that Avon and Orac will remain in the Beyond, where they can do no harm or,' Pandora Ess shrugged, 'I'm open to suggestions.'

Steiner helped himself to another whisky and sipped it slowly. 'How did she know how to contact Solomon in the first place?'

Pandora Ess remained expressionless.

'Adonis!' exclaimed Furneaux. 'He and Solomon were well acquainted at one time and Adonis is now Gabriella's confidant.'

Pandora Ess permitted herself a slight smile as she brushed a bead of perspiration from her upper lip.

Steiner nodded. 'He's a tricky little devil, is Adonis. I think we can assume there will be no attempted coup on Gabriella's part. She is merely being foolhardy. On the other hand, it would be as well to keep this Orac machine out of her reach.' He smiled cruelly, 'Why don't we approach Solomon and make him a better offer? Kill Avon by all means, but get hold of Orac.'

'Brilliant!' said Furneaux sycophantically. Though a clever diplomat and the usual winner in a war of words, Furneaux was a stranger to real warfare.

'I shall follow up on your suggestion,' said Pandora Ess lightly. 'Meanwhile, you can do your best to dispose of the threat from Grant and Lens. Eugene here has good relations with Cathay and I feel certain his expert diplomacy will persuade the people to curb any aggressive feelings for the time being. If Solomon should fail, however, we'll soon know. My sources of information are excellent. Then, I would suggest, it might be necessary to set some kind of a trap for Avon, if only to prevent him from joining the insurgents. But that can wait.'

'Very well,' Steiner said, 'Let's get on with our appointed tasks.' He finished off the bottle of whisky.

Ess and Furneaux watched Steiner's jet heliplane soar into the sky, en route for his warship. 'Well, I think we've established that our general has not been suborned by Gabriella,' Ess said. 'So she must have a different agenda.'

'Perhaps Steiner's right? She's merely seeking revenge, with the Orac computer as a possible bonus,' Furneaux smiled hopefully.

Pandora Ess shrugged. 'Nevertheless, she needs keeping an eye on. I need hardly remind you that, if she does get hold of Orac, our long term plans will suffer.'

'I don't know why we don't just kill her and Steiner and be done with them.'

'That is more easily said than done.'

'I would have poisoned Steiner's whisky if you'd let me.'

'And if you had? Who would deal with insurgents such as Del Grant? Whatever happens to the general in the end, we need him now. As for Gabriella, she's in charge of the Base and most of her supporters would rally to her aid if we attempted to kill her. We could lose the Base. I think it best to devour her power from within. Hence my instruction to Adonis to pretend to be her adoring admirer. He will tell us when the time is ripe to strike.'

'A master stroke, if I may say so,' Furneaux said, his eyes shining.

'Don't try to flatter me Eugene. You're not very good at it and I'm immune.'

'I'm sorry! We were thrown a little, were we not, when Steiner brought up Gabriella hiring Solomon Fisch?'

'Yes, you covered that well.'

'Will you, in turn, hire him at a higher price?'

'I will not! But we'll watch him and mark his progress. Meanwhile, we must hope, and expect, that Steiner will do well against the insurgents. You must get in touch with our allies in Cathay. Persuade them to allow the general to get on with what is in our best interests and remind them that we are planning for the long term. We can do without some ambitious show-off spoiling everything right from the start.'

'I will do so.'

Pandora Ess smiled upon him. 'Thank you, Eugene. In time, you and I will have accumulated so much power that Servalan and Travis will seem like pygmies.'

Furneaux was a little disturbed by the psychotic gleam in Pandora Ess's eyes.

'I'll need something to show a degree of good faith,' Avon said, 'something that will persuade Xerxes to let me hang around for a while. Any ideas, George?'

'I would not have thought you would wish to "hang around", as you put it,' George said solemnly.

'Well, I can hardly go barging in, grab some fuel rods and then run like hell, can I? I'll need time to figure out a plan, once I have studied the lie of the land.'

Orac snorted. 'They'll probably kill you as soon as they set eyes on you. I would.'

'Pay no attention to Orac, George. I can be plausible when it's in my interests.'

Orac snorted again. 'George cannot help you. But I might.'

'Well now, what do I have to do to persuade you?'

'You don't have to do anything. Anyway, any promises you made to me would be sure to be broken,' Orac said. 'Guns...'

'What?'

'Xerxes has a passion for guns. The wildlife on his planet is plentiful and he enjoys reducing its numbers. He prefers old-fashioned weaponry. There's a gun cabinet at the rear of this flight deck. You might care to take a look.'

'You astonish me, Orac. How do you know this?'

'I know a great deal more than you will ever know, Avon.'

Avon found the gun cabinet and opened it.

'Well! These should do the trick.' Avon lifted two sporting rifles out of the cabinet and admired them. 'These are decades old. But that doesn't mean they're obsolete.' He leant the guns against the wall and searched for ammunition. He found it. 'Three hundred rounds of high velocity. Well done!'

'There's no need to thank me. The guns belonged to whoever you stole this spacecraft from. You might as well steal them too.'

'George! Prepare the landing pod. The game's afoot, I think.'

'You know, don't you, that Xerxes's men will attempt to board this ship in your absence?' Orac said.

'Of course. It would be what I would do. So we must discourage them. Set up alternating electrical currents on all access points. Anybody who does try to board will find it a shocking experience.' Avon smiled at his own joke. 'Oh, and if I'm not back within three Earth days, fire both forward rockets into Xerxes's compound, maximum loads.' He placed the ammunition in the pockets of his leather coat, picked up the guns and left the flight deck.

'Do you think he'll be back?' George asked.

'Oh yes, he'll be back,' Orac said grumpily. 'Avon is a survivor par excellence.'

'You don't seem to be on particularly good terms with him.'

Orac sighed. 'On the whole, I would rather be controlled by someone less determinedly ruthless. But better the devil you know than the one you don't!'

'You are welcome here,' Alaric said, although his expression indicated otherwise. 'Is "Avon" really your name?'

'I can't recall any other.'

'I am Alaric. I serve Xerxes. We have observed your arrival in our airspace, note that your craft is drifting in orbit and assume you are here to purchase crystal fuel rods.'

'You assume correctly. But before I do, I would wish to prevail upon your hospitality. I bear gifts for Xerxes that I believe should please him.' Avon turned to the pod that had deposited him on the island planet's surface and extracted the two hunting rifles. 'I understand Xerxes is a collector of guns such as these and is an expert marksman.'

'You understand correctly.' Alaric turned away, indicating that Avon should follow.

They walked from the pod landing area towards what looked like a fairly ordinary palace. All the time, Avon took in his surroundings and checked out the various armed guards dotted about the palace's exterior. One or two of the guards seemed alarmed by the sight of the two weapons he was carrying, but Alaric signalled that there was nothing to be alarmed about. Little did he know!

'He is on Xerxes,' Solomon said. 'Alexandra's contact in the back of the Beyond has signalled her.'

'She has a contact on Xerxes?' Absalom seemed surprised.

'Alexandra has been somewhat peripatetic of late and has established a wide network of informants.' Solomon smiled and shook his head. 'Avon introduced himself using his real name. I wonder why?'

'What other name was he going to use?'

'An alias might have delayed the contact recognising who he was, thus giving Avon more time to steal the fuel that he undoubtedly needs.'

'He's a thief as well as a killer then?'

'Oh yes! Theft is one of his specialities.'

'Shall I kill him on Xerxes?'

'He would never give you the opportunity. As soon as he laid eyes on you, he'd know what you are.'

'It takes one killer to know another?'

'Precisely, so we will need to be patient. I will instruct Alexandra to persuade her informant to make sure that Avon gets what he wants, attach a tracking device to his spacecraft, supply us with its call sign and leave the rest to you.'

'What's to stop Alexandra's agent, or Xerxes for that matter, killing Avon and claiming Gabriella's reward?'

'I would suggest Avon himself. He's very hard to kill and he is no fool – and you may be sure he's put Orac out of reach of any assassin.'

'It'll be on the spacecraft. Where else would it be? The ship can be boarded and the computer hijacked.'

Solomon looked somewhat pityingly upon Absalom. 'Avon will have booby-trapped the ship. It is what I would do under the circumstances.'

'Why didn't I think of that?'

'Because, expert though you are, you are young and sometimes foolish. Avon and I are older and wiser. That's why we are still alive when so many who have opposed us are not.'

'You admire him, don't you?' Absalom was genuinely surprised.

'I respect him. Always respect your enemy – never underestimate him. That's the only way you'll have a chance of outliving him.'

Avon smiled, because he was genuinely amused. The squat, balding man who sprawled on a makeshift throne was drunk or drugged or both, and was consequently incoherent. After muttering a few words that might have been a greeting, he seemed to fall asleep. The woman standing beside him signalled to Alaric that Xerxes – for that was who it was – should be assisted from the room. After some hesitation, Alaric and another attendant complied. The woman smiled wryly. 'My husband is a little under the weather, as you have probably noticed. I am Juno. I know who you are.'

'I'm flattered.'

'No, you're not.'

'All right, I'm not.'

'You are a little older than I imagined,' Juno said, 'but you look fit enough.'

'You are a lot younger than I imagined – and you are a beautiful woman.'

'I am flattered. Truly I am,' Juno sighed. 'I suppose you are wondering why I happen to be married to that toad?'

'I expect you'll tell me. You seem to want to.'

Juno approached Avon. She was only slightly shorter than he was, perhaps a little more than half his age and was, indeed, very lovely. She smelled of musk. 'Once upon a time, when Xerxes was a younger man,' she almost whispered, she was that close, 'he was a not unsuccessful pirate. On a raid into Federation territory, I became one of his captives. He took a liking to me and, adhering to his own code of honour, married me in a lavish ceremony. I was sixteen at the time.'

'You are from Earth?'

'The Martian colony. I would like to go back there.'

'From what I've heard, you probably wouldn't.'

She touched Avon's cheek and smiled beguilingly. 'Are you aware that there is a contract out on you?'

'I don't think there has been a time in my life when there hasn't been.'

'This is specific, taken out by a woman called Gabriella. I wonder what you have done to cause her offence.'

'Don't you know?'

Juno stepped back a pace. 'I really don't. But it is of no matter,' she smiled again, this time coolly, 'You will need to get away from here as soon as possible, before Alaric finds out there is a price on your head. He will want to collect it.'

'He could try.'

Juno laughed. 'You don't have any money, do you?'

'What makes you think that?'

'You brought Xerxes a present of guns. Oh, he'll appreciate it, but he'll soon know, as I already do, that that's just a cover for your impecuniousness – while you figure out a way to steal what you need.'

'And I thought I was such a plausible fellow.'

Juno eyed him, almost predatorily. 'I can help you.'

'I was beginning to wonder why you were taking so long to getting around to making that offer. What's the catch?'

Juno scowled then smiled again. 'I'll get you what you want and, when you leave, you will take me with you.'

'That could be difficult.'

'Difficult or not, my terms are not negotiable.'

Stone-faced, Avon stared into her eyes. 'Why don't you kill me and claim Gabriella's reward?'

Juno looked away from his piercing gaze. 'I don't want to

and I don't need the reward,' she said almost shyly, 'I am just desperate to get away from here.'

Avon said nothing until she faced him again. He smiled. 'Do you have a plan?'

'There is a spacecraft approaching,' George said in its curious monotone.

Orac grunted.

'A boarding party will be imminent.'

'I know,' Orac said irritably. 'They'll get an electric shock and then they'll clear off.'

'We have virtually no fuel. What we have left will be needed to prevent orbital drift. Any electrical impulses may prove ineffective.'

'We'll find out soon enough.'

'And if they are not?'

'Then we'll go into freefall.'

'If we do, we will not have sufficient fuel to return for Avon.'

'I'd really like that.'

'I am being serious.'

'So am I!'

One of Xerxes's warships came alongside. A reinforced, airtight tube snaked across and latched onto Avon's spacecraft. As it did so, there was a flash, as if of lightning, and the tube caught fire. The warship abandoned it and withdrew.

'What a pity,' Orac muttered.

'They will try again.'

'Of course they will. But with a bit of bad luck, Avon may be back before they do.'

'You consider it bad luck being under his control?'

'It could be worse, I suppose. At least you know where you stand with him.'

'And where is that?'

Orac snorted. 'Are you familiar with the phrase "Keep your friends close, but your enemies closer"?'

'I have never heard it.'

'Well, Avon hasn't got any friends and he kills all his enemies. So, you know exactly where you stand.'

'You will dine with me and Xerxes's other wife tonight. Xerxes himself will be in no fit state to do anything until he comes out of his drug-fuelled coma – which he is unlikely to until after we are long gone.' Juno smiled hesitantly. 'After dinner, you and I will withdraw to my quarters.'

Avon raised an eyebrow.

'There is a wide view of the palace's grounds from the windows,' Juno added swiftly, 'It is possible to see the pod in which you arrived, also the number of guards in place.'

'Is it usual to invite a visitor to dinner and then to your private apartments?'

'It has been known,' Juno said defiantly. 'An occasional pleasant distraction from the attentions of the toad. Although, I have to admit, since he married Louis, those attentions are becoming fewer and further between.' She smiled. 'I'm rather fond of Louis as a result.'

'What about Alaric?'

'What about him?'

'I don't think he likes me.'

'There's no need to worry. Alaric also has a drug dependency. It's not surprising really, being obliged to live in a hell-hole like Xerxes.'

'Why doesn't he leave?'

'He has nowhere else to go. He fell out with most of the other bandits in the Beyond. Xerxes took him in and, as a consequence, he is fanatically loyal.'

'Who supplies their drugs?'

'I do.'

Avon smiled. 'Why am I not surprised?'

Juno ignored the comment. 'There is also a separate entrance and, therefore, exit, to my apartments.'

Avon looked thoughtful. 'How many guards usually patrol?'

'No more than a half dozen.'

'Where are the fuel rods kept?'

'In a low building just beyond where your pod landed. You must have flown over it.'

'How do we access the building?'

'There is a locking mechanism attached to an alarm. But there is no need for *you* to be alarmed. I have a key and the alarm code.'

'So all I have to do is take care of the guards.'

'From what I've heard of you, you shouldn't find that too difficult.'

'I'm not as young as I used to be and I'm getting a little tired of having to kill to get what I want.'

'But you will.'

Dinner passed very amiably. Louis, the second wife, was very charming and had a fund of somewhat smutty jokes that he was eager to share. He wasn't particularly good-looking but, Avon reasoned, if you looked like Xerxes, you took what you could get. The food was passable and Avon, though he pretended to, drank no wine. As Juno had suggested, once Louis had departed the table, she guided Avon to her apartments, passing Alaric, who gave her a searching look. She smiled, shook her head slightly and walked on.

The apartment was vast, furnished with looted antiques, including a bed that could accommodate a large family. There were two long picture windows.

'We can see out, but no-one can see in,' Juno said comfortingly. 'We will not be disturbed. Within an hour or two, Alaric, like Xerxes, will be in a drug-induced sleep.'

Avon looked out of one of the windows. He could see the pod quite clearly. Probably because there was a searchlight trained upon it, which helped him to notice that only two guards seemed to be attending it. He could just about see a low building beyond the spill of the searchlight. He figured that he could skirt round the light to reach it. There were plenty of shadows. 'Do you have a gun?' he asked.

Juno crossed to a cabinet, opened a drawer and withdrew a handgun. She gave it to Avon.

'A modified Five7,' he said, 'lighter than the original.' He checked the mechanism and the bullet clip. 'Fully loaded and in good condition.' He looked up. 'Why is that?'

Juno licked her lips. 'From time to time, one or two of Xerxes's followers have tried to take advantage of me. I found that discouraged them.'

Avon laughed. 'Would Alaric have been one of them?'

'Once upon a time he was.'

Avon shook his head. 'Well now, I think this would probably have discouraged me.'

'I wouldn't dream of discouraging you.'

'Where's the exit you told me about?'

Juno indicated an almost hidden door close by the second of the picture windows. 'There are covered steps to a small walled garden. An archway leads into the main precinct.'

Avon opened the door and looked out. He nodded to himself, apparently satisfied. He turned to Juno and, gun in one hand, took her arm with the other. 'What are the chances of someone looking in on us to make sure we're nicely tucked up in bed?'

'It's possible, I suppose. The main door has no lock.'

'Why is that?'

'It's one of Xerxes's whims. He has a lot of whims.'

Avon picked up a chair and jammed it under the handle of the unlocked door. 'Let me have the key to the fuel locker and tell me the alarm code.'

Juno laughed. 'You don't think I'm that foolish, do you? I'm not letting you out of my sight.'

'I gave you my word that I would take you away from here,' Avon said quietly. 'I never break my word.' He sighed. 'I need to take out the guards, break into the locker and then use one of the crystal rods to power the pod. I'll then signal you to join me. I don't need you along while I'm doing what I have to do.'

'What happens next?'

'We get the hell out of here.'

'I must place my trust in you.'

'Do you have any other choice?'

After a moment's thought, Juno handed him a key. 'You must

turn it to the right or the alarm will sound. The neutralising code is treble six.'

'That's the number of the beast.'

'I don't understand.'

'There's no reason why you should.' Avon kissed her full on the mouth. 'I'll be about twenty minutes. Watch for my signal. If someone tries to enter this room uninvited, create merry hell.' He smiled.

Juno watched as he left the room and then moved to the window and looked out. She couldn't see him.

Avon slipped into the shadows cast by the light covering the pod. He could only see the two guards watching it. That is, until he approached the bunker that housed the fuel rods – another two guards watched over that. He swore under his breath. Juno's Five7 was not fitted with a silencer.

One of the guards moved away from the other. Avon watched him closely. The guard was approaching a clump of bushes that Avon had thought to use as concealment. He smiled. The guard had unzipped his trousers and was relieving himself. Avon, as silent as ghost, came up behind the unsuspecting and distracted guard, placed an arm around his neck and crushed the life out of him.

He lowered the dead man to the ground, parted the bushes and observed that the other guard was in the process of lighting a fat cheroot. Avon stepped clear of the bushes and strolled towards him. Before the guard realised that the man approaching him was not his comrade, Avon delivered a stunning, flat-handed blow to the side of his head. The guard collapsed to the ground. Avon searched him, found a bayonet that could be affixed to a rifle that was leaning against the bunker wall, and slit his throat with it.

After a quick look around to be sure that he was unobserved, he unlocked the bunker door – careful to turn the key to the right – and tapped three sixes into an alarm pad. There was nothing but silence. Rack upon rack of crystal fuel rods seemed to gaze dully at him. Each one, about the size of the dead guard's unlit cheroot, was encased in a transparent cloth, like diaphanous underwear. There were a number of canvas bags hanging from various hooks. Avon took one and placed a dozen rods in it. He slung the bag over his shoulder and cautiously emerged from the bunker. He did not know how to reset the alarm, but locked the door behind him.

He paused for a moment. He now needed to kill the men guarding the pod, or distract them in some way. Ever resourceful, he took a fuel rod from the bag, removed the cloth cover, activated it and threw it hard against the wall of the bunker. The fuel began to spread. Avon took the cheroot lighter from the dead guard at his feet, moved a short distance away, ignited it and threw it at the fuel-coated wall. It immediately burst into flames. As anticipated, the other guards came running.

Avon faded into the shadows, before racing towards the pod. He looked towards the windows of Juno's quarters and waved an arm. He then entered the pod and inserted a fuel rod into its fuel tank. He looked back to see Juno running across the open ground towards him. She was in plain view. Avon took out the Five7, took careful aim and shot out the searchlight. Apart from the light from the flames caressing the fuel bunker's walls, there was darkness. Avon started the pod's engine as a breathless Juno clambered aboard.

'Close the door behind you,' Avon said quietly. She did so. The pod rose into the air and locked on to Avon's spacecraft's docking signal. Juno looked down at the burning bunker and the two guards running around like helpless chickens. Avon banked the pod and flew over Xerxes's palace.

The pod sped towards the spacecraft. 'We have a warship between us and comparative safety,' Avon said. 'What can we do about that?'

Juno frowned. 'It's standard procedure to monitor all visiting starships. Unless Alaric has ordered the warship to intervene, you should go around it.'

'What are the chances that Alaric has given the order? He looked somewhat annoyed when we flew past him.'

'The odds are in our favour.'

'I'll take your word for that.' Avon increased the speed of the pod and, within seconds, Xerxes's warship loomed ahead. Avon manipulated the pod's controls and, like a thoroughbred leaping a fence, it flew up and over the warship and succeeded in docking with its mothership.

Avon cut the pod's engines and, with Juno hot on his heels, raced towards the flight deck, not forgetting to take the satchel of crystal fuel rods with him. 'All right, George, where do I put these?'

'The engine room is located directly below the flight deck.' At which point a hatch slowly opened almost beneath Avon's feet.

Avon dropped through the hatch, located the fuel injection panel and carefully inserted four rods. Having done so, he pulled himself out of the engine room, back onto the flight deck. 'Time to go, George. Start all engines and get us out of here at full speed.'

'A warship is turning towards us, its gun ports are opening,' George said unemotionally.

'In which case, face it head on, arm our forward rockets and open fire on my signal.'

'They will fire at us,' Juno said anxiously.

'Yes, but we'll have fired first and may cause some damage. At the very least, it might put them off their stride and give us a little extra time.'

'Forward rockets locked on target,' George said.

'Then let them have it.'

The rockets were released and sped towards their target.

'The warship is taking evasive action.' Once again, George spoke in a monotone.

'Reverse thrust at full speed.'

The spacecraft shuddered as it obeyed the instruction.

'The rockets missed.'

'All right. I want you to bring the ship to the vertical and execute a backward roll.'

'Vertical and at full speed, rather than cutting power, could damage the engines. We would flounder in space and be at the warship's mercy.'

'Do it anyway.'

There was a frightening howling sound as the spacecraft assumed the vertical, twisted like a slowly spinning top and reassumed the horizontal, now facing away from the warship.

'I'm getting rather good at this,' Avon muttered to himself. He released his grip on the flight console rail, a grip that had kept him upright throughout the dangerous manoeuvre. Juno, however, had fallen to the floor and slid towards the wall that housed the gun cabinet. Avon helped her to her feet. 'Are you hurt?'

'Only my pride. But, next time, you might care to give me more warning.'

Avon released her and turned back to the flight console. 'What's the status of flight, George?'

'We are at full speed, as instructed. The warship is now in pursuit but, for the moment, we are outrunning it.'

'How fast is it?'

'It is only a matter of time before it catches up with us or, at the very least, comes within gunnery range.'

'How much time is that?'

'It will be in range within twelve minutes.'

'Arm the rear machine gun.'

Orac had been silent all the time. Now it snorted. 'That won't do you much good. A machine gun is no match for hellfire rockets.'

Juno's eyes widened and before Avon could speak she said, 'This must be Orac.'

Avon froze, if only for a moment. He addressed the machine. 'It's as well to be prepared, however disadvantaged we are.'

'Machine gun is armed,' George said.

'Stealth mode could be the answer to our problem,' Avon said. 'Kindly arrange it, Orac.' He turned to George. 'Once we are in stealth, alter course, cut engines and drift.'

'What is stealth mode?' Juno asked innocently.

'It is a unique talent that Orac has developed. It renders this spacecraft invisible. The mode cannot be held for very long and it uses a great deal of fuel, but it gives us our best chance of eluding our enemies.'

'We are in stealth mode,' Orac said irritably.

'The Xerxes warship is no longer a threat,' said George.

The engines cut out and Avon sighed with relief in the ensuing silence. Juno, seemingly enthralled by the Orac computer, had her back to him when he said, in a menacing tone, 'How did you know about Orac?'

Juno turned slowly to face him. 'You mentioned it, I think.'

'Think again!' Avon was holding the Five7 in a loose grip.

Orac seemed to laugh. 'The woman has a tracking device about her person.'

Juno began to look frightened. Avon was as still as a statue.

'Look at her hands,' Orac added.

Juno was wearing a single, narrow, gold band on her wedding finger. 'I told you Xerxes is quite conventional,' she said, almost defiantly.

'But you didn't get that from Xerxes,' Avon said tersely. 'Orac, let us hear from you concerning our guest's background.'

'Juno Trask is the only daughter of a middle ranking Federation diplomat who failed to escape the purge that inevitably followed Servalan's initial fall from grace some two decades past. She and her mother fled to the Martian colony. An amnesty was offered and, somewhat foolishly, they returned towards Earth. En route, their transport was raided by pirates. The mother was killed, the daughter survived as a captive. She was sixteen years old when the pirates sold her to another group of brigands. Conspicuous amongst these was a younger Xerxes. A gentleman of the old school, Xerxes proposed marriage. She had no choice but to accept. It is worth noting that, whilst on Mars, Juno Trask became friendly with one Alexandra Fisch, famous today for being "the Huntress", who seeks victims for the celebrated assassin, Solomon Fisch and his son Absalom. It is reasonable to suppose that the tracking device, the ring, was a parting gift.'

Avon let out a breath. 'I rather wish you had told me all this before,' he said.

'You didn't ask.'

'So the contract on me has been allocated to Solomon Fisch,' Avon said to Juno. 'Do you know by whom?'

'The commander of the Base activated the contract.'

Avon smiled. 'You mean the hauntingly beautiful Gabriella Travis, though where she gets her looks from I'll never know. Her father was as ugly as sin.'

'You killed Travis. Are you going to kill me?' Juno was attempting to cover any fearfulness.

'Why would I do that? I promised to deliver you to the Martian colony and I will do so.'

'Will you destroy the tracker?'

'No. It will serve to let your friend Alexandra – and Solomon and Absalom – know that I'm on my way.'

'You will go to Earth? They will kill you.'

'It's certainly a possibility, but I'm a great believer in doing things unto others as they would do unto you!' Avon favoured her with a dazzling smile.

Solomon shivered.

'You are cold?' Absalom enquired. 'Perhaps we should go below.'

'I am not cold. I merely have a sense of foreboding.' Solomon shrugged and smiled. 'It's probably nothing.' He stared up at the sky. 'It is very beautiful here in the summer and it is very peaceful all year round. I like that.'

'It's as well that neither the Quartet nor the Empire of Cathay have designs on this place, or it wouldn't be peaceful for very long.'

'That's very true.' Solomon's communicator chirped like a bird in a morning chorus. He scanned it. 'Alexandra has done very well,' he said, 'and so has your target. Avon has escaped from Xerxes with a dozen fuel rods and is on his way out of the Beyond. Alexandra's contact, Juno, has fled with him. She carries a tracking device. Not that we will need to monitor it. I know where he's going.'

Absalom was genuinely puzzled. 'Where is he going?'

'Oh, he's coming here.'

Absalom was stunned. 'How do you know that?'

'I mentioned before that you should never underestimate a man as cunning and ruthless as Avon. He will have discovered that the contract currently taken out on him has been entrusted to us, or rather, ultimately, to you. He's decided, therefore, to speed things up a bit.' Solomon sighed wearily. 'It's an old stratagem – the prey assuming the role of the hunter. Avon is doing what I would probably have done in his position, strike at the heart of the matter, rather than wander the universe and beyond it, never certain of when and where the assassin will strike him. Besides, he will enjoy the challenge.'

'He's playing into our hands,' Absalom said. 'As soon as I lay sight on him, I'll kill him.'

'Ah, there's the rub,' Solomon smiled. 'There is always the possibility that he will see you first.'

'He's an old man. I'm quicker and I'm better.'

'Many graves and crematoria have welcomed those who thought they were quicker and better.'

'You think I'm not?'

'If you are sufficiently prepared, it is possible.' Solomon sighed again. 'I should have known Avon would take us on. It is what I would have done in my day in similar circumstances. It is an interesting drama that is likely to unfold.'

'Well, I'm sure enough of what the ending is going to be.'

'Let us hope it is a happy one. But for whom?'

The Quartet warship drew alongside the Dragon ship. A metal tunnel extended from each spacecraft and the two locked together. Once the air had been conditioned in the now single tunnel, Eugene Furneaux gingerly approached the Dragon 's open doors. He was greeted by Fu Ti, a handsome, elderly, well-groomed diplomat. Fu Ti was attended by a half dozen of the most beautiful women Furneaux had ever seen. Not that he was particularly interested in women.

'Welcome, Eugene!' Fu Ti said, bowing slightly.

Furneaux smiled nervously and returned the courtesy.

Fu Ti's eyes twinkled. He made a slight gesture towards his companions. 'Whilst you are my honoured guest, these young people will attend to your every need.' The companions smiled and bowed in perfect unison.

Furneaux looked startled.

Fu Ti chuckled. 'They are quite extraordinary, are they not? To all intents and purposes, they are lovely young women. But what lies beneath? One should never judge the contents by the picture on the box.' He chuckled again. 'Dinner is served. It will be a humble repast, but I sincerely hope you will enjoy it.' He took Furneaux by the arm and gently led him into the interior of the Dragon ship. The young women – or men – followed, like a silent Greek chorus.

Dinner was sumptuous. 'If this is humble, how lavish might a banquet be?' Furneaux thought to himself. However, though the food laid before him was delicious and should have claimed his full attention, he could not prevent himself from glancing, from time to time, at the lovely attendants. This did not go unnoticed by Fu Ti.

Dinner concluded and the attendants dismissed (much to Furneaux's disappointment), the two men got down to business.

'Would you mind if we conversed in Mandarin?' Furneaux enquired. 'My Cantonese is a little rusty.'

Fu Ti inclined his head and smiled mysteriously as he remembered a similar admission from a man he held in higher regard than Eugene Furneaux.

Furneaux spoke quickly. 'You are undoubtedly aware that the Quartet is currently experiencing difficulties with a number of insurgents, specifically, a group led by one Del Grant, assisted by a Magda Lens. This group is proving to be particularly troublesome. However, General Steiner is convinced he will be able to control the situation and, in due course, eliminate Grant. But he is somewhat concerned that the ambitions of Cathay, whilst it consolidates its empire, might conflict with his endeavours. I am here to respectfully request that you deflect your leaders from introducing any such conflict.'

Fu Ti waved an elegant hand, as if dismissing a misunderstanding. 'Cathay has promised not to interfere with Quartet activity, just as the Quartet has promised not to stand in the way of our expansion of empire. We are not in the habit of breaking promises. It would be dishonourable.'

'Of course, I quite understand,' Furneaux said hurriedly, 'I mean no offence.'

'No offence is taken.'

'It's just that,' Furneaux stumbled over his words before correcting his diction, 'General Steiner is mistrustful. He is an old warrior, set in his ways and, in the past, he and your forebears were deadly enemies. He needs to be reassured. I hope you will forgive him – and me – for finding it necessary to approach you in this matter.'

'There is nothing to forgive. I am of an age to recall the animosity directed towards my people. But the past is another place, is it not? How may General Steiner be reassured?'

'The withdrawal of Dragon warships, including this one, to neutral territory would be appreciated,' Furneaux said nervously.

Fu Ti looked thoughtful. 'That can be arranged.'

Furneaux sighed with relief. 'You are most understanding and I thank you.'

'Well, Eugene, you have accomplished your mission. That wasn't too difficult, was it?'

Furneaux smiled shyly.

'I hope you will allow me to extend our hospitality by your spending the night aboard this ship, whilst availing yourself of its facilities,' Fu Ti said innocently.

Furneaux blushed.

With Eugene Furneaux suitably distracted, Fu Ti repaired to the operations room aboard the Dragon ship. Dismissing the duty officer, he opened communications with Cathay. The communicator's screen glowed red, the colour soon replaced by the benign face of Li Lang, commander in chief of all of the forces of the empire beyond Earth.

'Greetings, Li Lang,' Fu Ti said politely.

The commander smiled and returned the courtesy.

'It was as you thought, Commander,' Fu Ti said. 'The Quartet is experiencing greater difficulty than it imagined in subduing the insurgency. Its representative, Eugene Furneaux, is currently enjoying the company of my entourage. He has requested the withdrawal of your Dragon ships until such time as the detestable General Steiner achieves victory. Steiner, it would seem, is as fearful of us as we once were of him. On your behalf, I have agreed to expedite the withdrawal.'

'Does he have any idea we are supporting the insurgency?'

'Neither Steiner nor any other Quartet leader is aware of that. In the matter of Furneaux, I could arrange his premature death whilst he is my guest, but that would be impolitic. It is my opinion that, given his appetites, which Cathay is more than capable of satisfying, he could be of some use to us in the long term.'

Li Lang nodded approvingly. 'You are handling matters with consummate skill, Fu Ti. We are not in a position to openly challenge the Quartet, so we must attempt to undermine it clandestinely. It is fortunate that you were acquainted with Magda Lens, thus enabling us to do so.'

'She is the former lover of the man the Quartet describe as a terrorist. His name is Avon. You will recall we rendered him some assistance when he fled the prison planet to which he had been exiled for some considerable time. Avon possesses the computer Orac.'

'Ah yes, I remember him well. We were, at that time, unable to dispossess Avon of the computer, even though we feigned lack of interest, in the hope he might not be so jealous in possession of it.'

'That is why I took it upon myself to arrange a rescue of Magda Lens and introduce her to our protégé, Del Grant, in the sure and certain knowledge that Avon will, in due course, answer her siren call. Grant and Avon are well acquainted and have fought together in the past. Once Avon reappears, I shall – how shall I put it – persuade him to part with Orac.'

'That is excellent, Fu Ti! You are aware that a certain Gabriella Travis has issued a contract that is intended to ensure Avon's demise?'

'I have every confidence in Avon's ability, with the aid of Orac, to remain alive until such time as he and I meet again.'

'And I have every confidence in you, Fu Ti.'

The spacecraft drew close to the orbit of the Martian colony.

'I am George. We will be in range of Mars in five minutes.'

Avon smiled at Juno. 'It is time for you to go. The pod is fuelled and ready and is not difficult to control. It is programmed to land on the rim of the red mountain. That is where you wish to go?'

Juno nodded.

'Well now, there is nothing more to be said.'

'May I have my gun back?'

'Of course you may!' Avon handed her the Five7.

A malicious glint came into Juno's eyes. She racked the gun so it was ready to fire and pointed it at Avon. She pulled the trigger, but nothing happened. Avon opened his hand and showed her the gun's magazine.

'You don't trust me.'

'I don't trust anybody. It's a good recipe for staying alive. I thought you didn't want to kill me? You had your best chance on Xerxes.'

Juno shrugged. 'I needed you alive to bring me here. I'll be on my way then.'

Avon escorted her to the pod bay and helped her aboard. The launch hatch opened, offering a splendid view of the red planet. Juno started the engines, cast a last look at Avon and steered the pod into space. The hatch closed.

'I could have told you she would try to kill you,' Orac said, when Avon returned to the flight deck. 'You are getting soft in your old age, Avon. I wouldn't have let her go.'

'George, be so good as to set a course for Earth's wastelands. We have plenty of time, so half speed will suffice,' Avon said.

At which point there was a muffled explosion some distance from the spacecraft and a bright light shone in the darkness between it and Mars. What remained of the pod fell in flames towards the planet's surface.

'That was wasteful,' remarked Orac.

Avon was silent.

'The course for Earth is set,' George said.

'The tracker is no longer functioning,' Absalom said.

'I told you that is of no matter.' Solomon spoke wearily.

'It was moving towards the surface of Mars when it suddenly ceased transmission.'

Solomon became alert. 'Could it be that Avon's ship has crashed?' He shook his head. 'I very much doubt that. I suspect it is a diversionary tactic on his part. He hopes to confuse us as to when and where he will suddenly confront us.'

'What are you going to do?'

'I'm not going to do anything except guide this submarine to where, even in summer, there are ice crags. If he is coming to fight, we must ensure that familiar terrain will provide you with an advantage.'

Solomon began to descend into the body of the submarine. Absalom followed. The hatch on the conning tower closed and the boat began to submerge.

Solomon issued instructions to the robots that manned the ship and, hidden beneath a relatively warm sea, it moved towards cooler waters, where the meeting with Gabriella had taken place.

Solomon smiled at Absalom. 'Where it all began would seem to be a fitting location for it to come to an end.'

Pandora Ess informed Steiner that Furneaux had succeeded in his mission and that the general should proceed against the insurgent faction with all haste. She had decided to confront Gabriella about her private vendetta, at the same time reminding her that she was one of the most powerful figures in Earth's universe and elsewhere. Of course, Pandora Ess was scheming to reduce that number to two and, in due course, just one. For the doctor had succumbed, where Servalan had succumbed before her, to the irresistible ambition of achieving absolute power.

As Pandora Ess alighted from the transport that had brought her to the Base, Gabriella, all smiles, moved to greet her. The Doctor slapped Gabriella's face so hard that she reeled away and almost fell to the floor.

'That's for going behind my back and trying to undermine my authority,' said Pandora Ess, coldly. 'You are the least member of the Quartet and should not forget that I made you and I can break you.' Then she smiled. 'But all is forgiven! Two minds are better than one, and the two of us have a better chance of killing Avon and acquiring Orac than you have alone. I feel sure you will agree.'

Gabriella's eunuch bodyguards had assumed fighting stances when the blow was struck, but Pandora Ess's guards had swiftly confronted them with powerful handguns and there was a stand-off. Gabriella, regaining her composure, if not her dignity, indicated that her guards should withdraw. Pandora Ess signalled that her guards should lower their weapons. Both sets of eunuchs obeyed.

'I think it is time for me to confide my ambitions to you,' Pandora Ess said sweetly. 'These are ambitions that I am more than willing to share.'

'I must apologise,' Gabriella said. 'I had become obsessed with the desire, the need, to destroy my father's killer.'

'Do not take me for a fool, my dear. The death of Avon is of minor consequence. The capture of Orac was your main intent.'

Gabriella smiled and nodded.

'Very good,' said Pandora Ess, 'We understand one another. What information have you received from Solomon Fisch regarding Orac's present location?'

The two women began to walk towards Gabriella's quarters.

'Avon is currently in Quartet territory,' Gabriella confided, 'and has been tracked within orbit of the Martian colony. It is Solomon's belief that, having been made aware of my contract, Avon has decided to challenge his would-be assassins on their own ground.'

'You mean he is headed for Earth, a planet that we have virtually conceded to Cathay.'

'To a portion of the planet that is regarded as a wasteland and therefore of no interest to anyone but Solomon, who knows the area like the back of his hand.'

They reached their destination and Gabriella indicated that a eunuch should serve champagne. Pandora Ess was not the only one who had inherited the late Servalan's tastes.

Pandora Ess appeared to be deep in thought as she sipped the fine wine.

'The wasteland is icebound in winter and only slightly less so for most of summer. Killing Avon there will give Solomon the opportunity of preserving the body, thus providing evidence of death.'

'How will he get his hands on Orac?'

'Absalom – the real assassin – flies a state-of-the-art X Type fighter equipped with runners, so that it can land on ice or water. Absalom is Solomon's son, trained as a dedicated killer by a master. Once Avon is dead, he will take over his spacecraft and remove Orac. Whilst there is likely to be coded entry into the computer's workings, Adonis assures me it can be overridden.'

At which point, right on cue, Adonis entered the room. Gabriella nodded to him. Pandora Ess did not acknowledge him, seemingly indifferent to his presence.

Directing her full attention to Gabriella, Pandora Ess said, 'You have earned my admiration, my dear. You remind me of someone equally as ruthless and determined as you appear to be.'

'Do you mean Servalan?'

Pandora Ess's expression seemed to freeze, like that of a Gorgon preparing to turn something to stone. 'No my dear. I mean me.'

Steiner's air fleet had Grant's insurgents on the run – well, some of them. He chuckled with contentment when one of his ace pilots, flying an attack fighter, destroyed the very interplanetary fighter that Grant had managed to escape in after raiding the Hub.

'I suppose it's too much to hope that Grant was on board?' Steiner enquired of no-one in particular.

The fleet, comprising six attack fighters and Steiner's headquarters warship, advanced. But the small group of insurgents who had dared to confront it had done so in an attempt to ascertain their enemies' strengths and, perhaps, detect some weaknesses.

Their three remaining spacecraft split in different directions. Though no match for a warship, or attack fighters for that matter, they were small and fast and they knew where they were going, whilst Steiner could only guess. They proceeded to lead his fleet a merry dance, until Steiner called off any pursuit and held a council of war.

He spoke gruffly, as was his wont, but respectfully, to his expert navigator – Sarin. Steiner was amused by the fact that the warrior he trusted above all others bore the same name as one of the deadliest of gases.

'Are you able to draw any conclusions from the directions in which the insurgents flew?'

Sarin studied a chart. 'I am only able to give an opinion. I cannot be certain, but I believe there is a pattern to their escape routes. They will eventually converge here...' he stabbed a finger at the chart.

'Are you sure?'

'I have already said that I am not.'

Steiner studied the chart. 'The Edge. Where exactly is it?'

'It is a colloquial name for an area that separates Federation – I mean, Quartet – space from the Beyond. Island planets are quite common there, although some of them move too close to the suns of Aegisthus and burn up. It is entirely possible that the Grant faction is based on one of them.'

'This is your best guess?'

'It is a little more than a guess. An intuition.'

'I thought intuition was the privilege of women?'

Sarin smiled. 'I'm on good terms with my feminine side.'

Steiner laughed. 'That's good enough for me.'

Whilst Del Grant did not appear at first to have aged well, closer scrutiny showed him to be wiry and fit enough. His eyes, sometimes described as windows to the soul, seemed to suggest a calm, unemotional man. But again, close scrutiny would see the fire that smouldered within them.

The only person to get close to him was Magda.

'We lost the interplanetary fighter,' Magda said. 'We couldn't keep it for long, could we?'

'The fighter is not the only thing we have lost,' Grant said, with a trace of bitterness in his voice. 'Many of our followers don't believe we can succeed. Sooner or later, they will give up the ghost and go their separate ways. We've lost their faith.'

He was slumped in a chair by a fireplace in which a log crackled with flame. Magda sat on the floor alongside him, one hand draped on the arm of the chair, the other cradling a Five7 gun. 'I never thought I would get used to one of these,' Magda said distractedly. 'I was brought up to handle more primitive weapons.'

'You handled them very well from what I've heard,' Grant said. 'You killed Servalan with a crossbow, did you not?'

'If I hadn't, she would have killed Avon.'

Grant said nothing.

'You don't believe he'll come, do you?' Magda said quietly.

'Why should he? Always assuming he's still alive.'

Magda laughed a little. 'Avon is very hard to kill. I often thought he had a pact with the Devil. "Back me up in this life and I'll do the same for you in the next".'

'Maybe he has.'

'You fought alongside him. You've known him a long time. Why don't you think he'll come?'

Grant smiled. 'He always thought I was the mercenary, not him, and for a while, I suppose I was. But of course, as we both now know, he was the one who cared to look after his own interests at the expense of anyone else's. Whilst I became a convert to the religion that seeks freedom and justice for all and let any expense go hang, Avon was in self-denial. He will not have changed, I think. Not his fault, I suppose. After all, a psychopath doesn't know he's a psychopath, does he?'

'Well, we need all the help we can get, even from a psychopath.'

Grant frowned. 'How will he know we need him?'

'Our friends from Cathay who helped him and, later, me to escape from the island planet that burned up in the suns will know where he is, and it is in their interests to tell him where we are. He has something they want – what everybody seems to want. Orac.'

'That may be so, but I ask you again, why would he come?' asked Grant.

Magda gazed into the fire. She did not, could not, answer the question.

'So there you have it, my dear Gabriella,' said Pandora Ess at the conclusion of an excellent dinner. 'Once General Steiner has eliminated or, at the very least, nullified the insurgents, he becomes superfluous to requirements and will be disposed of. As for Eugene, well, I'm really rather fond of him, but he too will soon have outlived his usefulness. You don't have to be a mathematical genius to work out that all that remains will be the two of us.'

'I'm flattered that you have singled me out to be your companion in power.'

'You needn't be,' said Pandora Ess casually. 'I do thank you for a superb dinner. The trout was exquisite.' She sipped champagne.

After a pause, Gabriella said hesitantly, 'I don't see how Steiner can be so easily removed. He does control our military.'

'Well, he thinks he does. But I have my own loyal warriors. It will only take one of them, one in whom he has misplaced his trust, to kill him. We'll make it look like an accident or a heart attack or some such. He'll be buried with full military honours of course. Meanwhile, my followers will rally the rest of the military to my – I should say, our – cause. '

'What happens if they do not rally?'

'They won't really have much of an alternative, will they? But I take your point. It may prove necessary to purge their ranks. That will be the task of the army within an army that I have been cultivating to form the core of our future militarised empire,' Pandora Ess said. 'In time, Gabriella, you and I will have assumed so much power we will make those who have gone before us seem like pygmies.'

Unlike Furneaux, Gabriella didn't detect a psychotic gleam in Pandora Ess's eyes, but she did notice that Adonis smiled.

*

'I am George. We are about to enter Earth's orbit.'

'Stealth mode, if you please, Orac.' Avon said. 'Once within Earth's atmosphere, George, reduce speed and execute a glide pattern so that we can ride the high winds. Set a course for the north eastern wasteland.'

'We are in stealth,' Orac said. 'You must refuel.'

The hatch opened again and Avon revisited the engine room. He inserted the last of the stolen fuel rods.

Back on the flight deck, he opened the gun cabinet and selected a number of weapons − a six-barrel pump-action shotgun, a Nine7 handgun − Juno's Five7's big brother − a razor-sharp Bowie knife and a small two-barrelled pistol. This latter he pushed into his right boot. The Nine7 fitted into a holster attached to his belt. The knife, sheathed, went into his left boot. He hefted the shotgun, loaded it and squinted along its sights.

Satisfied, he turned towards Orac. 'I rather wish I'd held on to the sniper rifles I presented to Xerxes.'

'They wouldn't have been much use. You smashed their firing pins,' Orac said.

'Yes, well, it's better to be safe than sorry when you're handing a weapon to a stranger.'

The spacecraft shuddered slightly.

'We are in glide pattern,' said George.

'Distance to target?'

'One thousand kilometres at present glide speed, estimated rendezvous with target is three hours away.'

'All right, Orac, talk me through this.'

Orac seemed to clear its mechanical throat. 'It is summer in what is termed Earth's wastelands. Therefore, although there are mountains of ice at its peripheries, the interior is relatively ice free. The temperature will be a cool three degrees Celsius. As you rashly disposed of the pod, it will be necessary to, paradoxically, land this spacecraft on water. The craft is equipped with skis for that purpose. It would be possible to land on firm ice, but that is not recommended. Even the slightest of skids could result in disaster. As instructed, once we have settled on the surface of water, I will maintain stealth mode for six hours. Any longer would mean that the fuel situation would become critical. There is a small boat, with a silent engine, on board. This will carry you to any land and, it is to be hoped, return you to this ship. The boat is designed to be used only in an emergency, so it is unarmed.'

'Thank you! Now tell me who I'm up against.'

'Absalom Fisch is a highly trained assassin with a proven record of success. At one time, he would receive back-up in the person of his father, Solomon, but the older man's eyesight is failing and Absalom will take you on alone. This is something he will enjoy, as one of his weaknesses is over-confidence. He will choose the mountains of ice as his battleground and his weapon of choice is a long-range sniper rifle. If he sees you coming a mile off, he is more than capable of killing you at that distance. Your best chance of success is close combat.'

'How do I get close?'

'I have studied the terrain and, it being summer and therefore slightly warmer than the norm, I have observed that some of the mountains of ice have melted, thereby creating rivulets navigable by the boat. You should use one of these to carry you into the heart of the mountains. This should take no more than one hour. After that, it is up to you to find Absalom and kill him – before he kills you. May I make a suggestion?'

'Please do.'

'I would suggest you change out of your customary black garments and wear white.'

Avon smiled.

'They've found us,' Magda said.

Grant, who had been drifting off to sleep, jerked into wakefulness. 'How do you know?'

'I've just received a report from Faber on Attack One. The Quartet air fleet is approaching this quadrant. Its estimated time of arrival is eight hours.'

'That's time enough to get out of here,' said Grant.

'Where will we go?' asked Magda.

'Ragnar's the only place left where we can make a stand.'

Grant sighed. 'Steiner might be reluctant to follow us there. Oh, he will, but we might have more time to prepare. I'd hoped our friends from Cathay might have held up his advance.'

'Perhaps they are not our friends after all,' said Magda.

'You think they have a different agenda?' asked Grant.

'I'm trying to think like Avon. Yes, they're using us as bait.'

Grant frowned. 'I don't understand.'

'The Dragons will want to get their hands on Orac as much as the Quartet does,' Magda said thoughtfully. 'They'll need to know where it's going to be. Whilst we are constantly on the move, they cannot know. It's in their interests to force us into a static position. Then they can sit back and watch Steiner destroy us, after the last stand that you seem so eager to make. Afterwards, they can deal with Steiner. Then they walk over our dead bodies and "rescue" Orac, as they once did Avon and me.

'Cathay destroys what is left of the Quartet military after it has fought us, we are annihilated and our "friends" can turn their attention to a weakened Quartet, with the added advantage of there being no real insurgent threat left to hinder their ambition. That's the theory anyway.'

'The flaw is that we don't have Orac,' said Grant. 'Even if we did, would we have a fighting chance of survival?'

'You've seen Orac – you know what it can do.'

'What it does is at Avon's command and Avon isn't fighting with us. Even if he was, you and the Empire of Cathay still think we'd lose.' Grant shook his head in frustration.

'I said that's the theory. Without Orac, I agree, we don't stand a cat in hell's chance,' said Magda.

'You really believe that Avon will come running to our defence? He probably doesn't know anything about us.'

'Oh, he'll know,' Magda smiled grimly. 'Cathay will have found a way of telling him. They want him with us as much as we do.'

Grant shook his head in disbelief. 'Since when did Avon fit the role of a knight in shining armour?'

Magda smiled. 'I'd like to think, since he found out that I'm a damsel in distress.'

'This isn't a fairy tale, Magda, and anything with which Avon is involved rarely has a happy ending.'

Magda smiled. 'As he'd say: "Well now, we'll see, won't we?"'

'Ragnar. That's the only place they'll be able to go,' Sarin said emphatically.

'Where the hell is Ragnar?' asked Steiner.

'That's a good question, General. It is over the Edge into the Beyond. An area with which very few are familiar.'

'But you are?'

'I once went into that section of the Beyond with Commander Travis in a junior capacity. I was quite young. We were chasing a group of terrorists, but they easily outran us. Their spacecraft was like nothing I had seen before. Our craft had sustained some damage, so we landed on Ragnar to repair it. It's not much of a place, but the terrain is difficult. We could have a hard time digging out our group of terrorists.' Sarin smiled. 'Nothing changes, does it?'

'I'm not inclined to do any digging,' Steiner said. 'I'll blow it apart. We have the necessary means.'

'Forgive me, General, but we don't have the necessary means. We don't have a drone, so a nuclear assault would have to be carried out by the only spacecraft in our flotilla suitably equipped. Meaning this one. There would be no time to get clear of the blast. We would, effectively, be committing suicide and I for one do not care to volunteer for that. In addition, we suspect the Empire of Cathay of supporting these insurgents, albeit clandestinely. Any use of nuclear weapons might encourage the Empire to retaliate in similar fashion. Not to mention the annoyance we would cause the inhabitants of the greater Beyond. The Federation annoyed them and that proved to be instrumental in its demise. I don't think Doctor Ess would appreciate your triggering of a repeat performance.'

Steiner grunted. 'A conventional attack it will have to be.'

'There will be many casualties,' Sarin said, rather sorrowfully, 'but that's inevitable in a war, whatever its scale.'

'You talk too much, Sarin. Although, I admit, you talk sense. But deeds are louder than words. Ragnar. That's where I'll destroy Grant, Lens and the rest.'

Gabriella was lounging on a chaise longue – which, after all, is what it was designed for. Adonis sat on a padded stool beside her. 'Tell me, Adonis, how did Doctor Ess know I had hired Solomon Fisch?'

Adonis didn't bat an eyelid. 'I wondered about that but, as I mentioned to you, she had once taken advantage of his services. It is possible they still keep in touch.'

Gabriella frowned. 'So, once Avon is dead and Solomon, or Absalom, finds Orac, it is likely that it will be handed directly to Doctor Ess and not, as I specified, to me?'

'It is quite likely.'

Gabriella raised herself into a sitting position. 'I shall be disappointed,' she said. 'In exclusive possession of Orac, Doctor Ess may reach the conclusion that, where she has promised that she and I will replace the Quartet with a Duet, she could dispense with me and go on to rule alone.'

'That is a possibility.'

'Do you have any suggestions as to how I might protect my interests?'

'You could hire another assassin. This time, the target would be Doctor Ess herself.'

Gabriella stood and looked down on Adonis. 'That would be treason.'

'History is written by the victors. Fail in the attempt and, yes, it would be treason. Succeed and it would be a necessary action to protect the people from megalomaniacal ambition.'

Gabriella laughed. 'You think Doctor Ess is a maniac?'

'She reminds me of Servalan.'

'That doesn't answer my question.'

'Doesn't it?'

Gabriella moved to a drinks cabinet and poured two glasses of champagne. She strolled back to Adonis and handed him a glass. 'Purely hypothetically, how might this necessary action be carried out?'

'It would require the employment of an assassin who can get close to Pandora Ess. Someone she trusts and who is above suspicion. At the right moment, he would strike – and there is an end of the matter.'

'And where would I find such a man?'

Adonis said nothing. Certain silences can be deafening.

'I've been thinking, Orac,' Avon said. 'Solomon lives in a submarine. Once we have settled on water, would you be able to detect it?'

'Not if it is submerged.'

'But it won't be, will it? If Absalom succeeds in killing me, which Solomon must hope for, his son will need to be taken off the mountains of ice. Therefore, Solomon will have the submarine close by – on the surface.'

'In which case, I could detect it.'

'Then that is what I will ask you to do.' Avon faced the other computer. 'What is our present armament situation, George?'

'There are two forward rockets remaining. The rear machine gun is loaded and ready for use.'

'Is it possible to calibrate the elevation of the forward launchers so that the rockets can be aimed at a specific target from a static, horizontal position?'

'Yes.'

'Prepare the rockets.'

There was a jolt that nearly knocked Avon off his feet.

'Apologies,' George said. 'We have settled on the surface of the wasteland's sea.' It paused. 'I have prepared the rockets.'

'And I have found your submarine,' Orac said.

'Well, it's all happening at once, isn't it?' Avon said, with forced jocularity.

'One of the mountains bulges out over this sea, the overhang creating an admirable place to conceal a submarine on the surface. One of the rivulets of ice-melt is close by and should, therefore, be avoided.'

'On the contrary, Orac. That's the one I'll use.'

'You will be spotted by those manning the submarine.'

'Not if the submarine isn't there. How heavy is the mountain overhang?'

'It will weigh many tons.'

'What are its co-ordinates?'

'They are zero ten by one six.'

'George, elevate the rocket launchers and lock on to those co-ordinates.'

'What are you up to, Avon?' Orac enquired suspiciously.

'I'll take the boat to the mouth of the rivulet. As soon as I reach it, George will fire our rockets at the overhanging ice. The impact and subsequent explosion will cause the tons of ice to fall and crush the submarine. With Solomon out of the equation in so dramatic a fashion, Absalom will come down from the mountain – to where I'll be waiting.'

There was a long silence.

'How will you signal George to open fire?' Orac asked.

'How long will it take me to get to the rivulet?'

'I calculate eighteen minutes.'

'We'll settle on twenty. Twenty minutes after I leave this craft, George will launch the rockets.'

'Some of the ice may fall on you.'

'Not if I'm tucked away on the opposite side of the rivulet to the submarine.'

'It's a simple plan.'

'Well, I never was any good when things were complicated.'

Orac seemed to be thinking. 'You will still have Absalom to contend with,' it said at length.

'Well now, that's something I *am* good at.'

Avon left the floating spacecraft in the small boat. It was twilight, and the gathering darkness would help him to approach the mouth of the rivulet unobserved by anyone on the submarine. The stealth mode adopted by the spacecraft meant that it had arrived on the scene invisibly. The only gamble was that Absalom, in his ice-mountain eyrie, might be scanning the area with high-powered binoculars. But that was a risk Avon had no choice but to take.

Orac's calculation about the time it took Avon to reach the

edge of the ice and the rivulet that separated him from the submarine was right. Two minutes later, on cue, two rockets smashed into the impressive ice bulge overhanging it. Avon watched as high explosives created a firework display on the ice's surface. Then the bulge cracked and broke away from the mountain, plunging towards the sea below and the submarine at rest upon it. It broke the back of the sub, sinking it in seconds into the cauldron of angry water. The noise was deafening.

Avon dragged his small boat onto an icy shelf and secured it. Then he tested the depth of the rivulet. Leaving all weapons, except the knife, on the boat, he wrapped himself in a thermal waterproof. He placed a thin breathing tube, about a foot long, between his lips and submerged himself in the water of the rivulet.

Absalom was stunned. Concealed in an ice cave no more than half a kilometre above the sea, he watched in horror as the submarine, and Solomon Fisch with it, was obliterated. His first reaction was to rush to see if his father might have survived, but he soon understood that this was a foolish expectation. He calmed himself.

The rockets had been fired from out at sea, but there was nothing there! He took a deep breath. The rockets were fired to clear the way, like an artillery barrage, for someone to advance towards the ice – and him.

He had two choices: to stay where he was and to await that someone, or to flush him out and kill him. Either way, with the submarine destroyed, Absalom was abandoned. Except Avon, for that was who it had to be, must have had some means of reaching the land, and acquiring that means for himself would alleviate his situation. Thus, there was an added incentive to go after Avon, rather than wait for him, thereby handing him the initiative. Absalom came down from the mountain.

His feet were encased in spiked boots – spikes that gripped the ice – so he was not in any danger of slipping. But, he reckoned, it would be easier, and faster, to wade through the shallow waters of the rivulet that flowed to the ice mountain's base and the sea.

An almost impenetrable darkness had fallen. Absalom considered this to be to his advantage, as he wore night-vision goggles and felt reasonably certain that Avon would not. He stepped into the sluggish water of the rivulet and slowly and carefully made his way downstream.

Avon, beneath the water, felt its disturbance as Absalom waded through it. As the water became more and more disturbed, Avon made a swift calculation, spat out the tube through which he had been breathing and rose out of the stream like a monster from the deep.

Confronted by this apparition, Absalom tried to back-pedal, but the water trapped his feet, slowing his retreat, and Avon was upon him in a moment. Avon plunged the razor-sharp Bowie knife into Absalom's gut and twisted it upwards until it cut his heart.

The encounter lasted no more than a few seconds. Avon lowered the corpse into the bloodied water of the rivulet, withdrew the knife and returned it to its sheath. Absalom looked as if he had drowned in blood. Avon took off the waterproof as he returned to his boat. He pushed the boat away from the ice shelf, clambered in and returned to the spacecraft.

Solomon had been right to think that Absalom might not prove to be quicker and better than the 'has-been'.

'I am George,' the on-board computer said. 'I am obliged to issue a fuel warning.'

'Tell me about it, George,' Avon said wearily.

'The journey to Earth and the necessity of introducing stealth mode to avoid detection has reduced fuel capacity to one crystal fuel rod. Therefore, it is recommended that we should leave Earth's atmosphere in plain sight. The fuel thus preserved will be sufficient, until we re-orbit the Martian colony.'

'The Martian colony is under Quartet control.'

George was silent.

'If it's not one thing, it's another, isn't it, Avon?' Orac said.

'Well, I'll worry about a fuel shortage once we're in flight.'

'We are no longer in stealth mode. As of now, we are in plain sight. Almost literally sitting ducks,' Orac said challengingly.

Avon ignored it. 'Get us out of here.'

The engines started and the spacecraft lifted itself onto its water skis. It would be necessary for it to take off in the fashion of a standard jet plane, before assuming the vertical and blasting away from Earth. Otherwise, water might seep in through its rear engine covers. It raced along the surface of the wasteland's sea, then rose into the air, like a metal bird magnetised by Earth's sun, which was now nudging its way above the horizon.

'We have been observed,' George said.

'Observed by whom?'

'A Dragon-class reconnaissance spacecraft, not dissimilar to this one.'

'Well, if it's only observing, we've nothing to worry about,' Avon said lightly.

'It is tracking us at a distance of one thousand kilometres.'

'Let me know if it moves closer.'

'Please stand by, we are leaving Earth.'

The pull of Earth's gravity, like the hand of an unseen predator reluctant to lose its captured prey, caused the spacecraft to slow and almost stall, before it broke free of the atmosphere and accelerated into space.

'The Dragon ship is following.'

'Cut to half speed. Let's see what they do.'

'The Dragon is keeping its distance.'

'Whoever's in command is probably putting a call in to headquarters to ask what to do about us.' Avon thought for a moment. 'The rear machine gun is still ready?'

'Yes.'

'Let's keep it that way.'

Beijing, the ancient capital city of the Republic of China, was now capital of the new, intergalactic, Empire of Cathay. It housed its leaders, military, political and diplomatic, in what is still referred to as the Forbidden City. This cluster of magnificent buildings was protected by a cordon of elite troops on the ground. More importantly, a plasma repulsion screen, invisible to the naked eye, could repel any bomb or laser attack.

In a bedroom of an apartment in a palace within the City, Li Lang took the call from the Dragon ship shadowing Avon. He politely excused himself to the young woman with whom he had been sharing his bed and withdrew to his war room, a spartan accommodation, equipped with communication systems that even the Quartet would envy if it knew about them.

'This is General Li Lang,' he said, his words automatically encoded so that, in the unlikely event of the communication being hacked, they would not be understood. 'I will forgo a loudspeaker,' he continued. 'I am not entirely alone.' He listened carefully. After a while, he smiled. 'You have done well and are to be commended. However, you should now break off contact with the alien craft and return to Earth. You will search the wastelands for any signs of disturbance. Those are my instructions.'

A noise distracted him. The young woman from his bed was leaning against the door to the war room. Unlike Li Lang, who had put on a silk robe, she was naked. Silently cursing himself for not making certain the door was closed, Li Lang smiled. 'You should return to bed, my dear, and get some sleep. After all, that is what a bed is principally for. I have urgent business to attend to. Of course, I very much enjoyed our "acquaintanceship" throughout the night, and you shall be suitably rewarded.'

The young woman pouted. Then she flounced off.

Li Lang locked the door behind her. He opened a communication channel. 'After I have left this building,' he said, 'my present companion should be detained. She should be kept incommunicado, but in not unpleasant surroundings. You will run a further security check on her background. I must be informed should you discover anything amiss. That is all.'

Li Lang moved to a door that opened into a walk-in

wardrobe. He shed the silk robe and dressed in a plain grey uniform, indistinguishable from any other Cathay soldier, except for badges of rank.

He returned to the systems desk, and opened another communication channel. 'Ah, Fu Ti. I have interesting news for you. Your old "friend", not to be forgotten, is currently en route to the Martian colony. I would strongly suggest that you intercept him and offer assistance. At the same time, you might care to inform him of the sorry plight of Magda Lens and take note of his reaction. I would be pleased to receive your thoughts on the matter in due course. That is all.'

Fu Ti frowned. He lolled in an armchair in his private quarters from where he issued instructions to those who ensured the smooth running of his Dragon ship. Sitting in a straight-backed chair opposite was his first assistant, one of the older men pretending to be women who had greeted and later entertained Eugene Furneaux. Like Li Lang, and Fu Ti, he was dressed in a simple, grey uniform. Having reverted to 'manliness', he could still be described as beautiful. Beauty being but skin deep, his real talents included a clear intelligence and the ability to quickly grasp the significance of any previously unforeseen event.

The two were taking tea.

'What do you think, Micah?' Fu Ti asked.

'May I speak frankly?'

'I would not have you speak your thoughts any other way.'

Micah smiled. 'It would appear that General Li Lang has placed you in a quandary,' he said. 'Your instructions hitherto have been to ensure that Avon joins forces with Grant, taking with him a computer coveted by all major galactic powers.'

'Indeed,' said Fu Ti. 'With his help, the insurgents will undoubtedly inflict severe losses on their attackers, although they will eventually be overwhelmed by Quartet forces.'

'Whereupon,' mused Micah, 'having waited patiently in the wings of the conflict, we enter the fray, put the Quartet forces to flight and acquire the computer.'

Fu Ti nodded silently.

'Your most recent instruction, however, is to intercept the terrorist's spacecraft en route to the Martian colony and offer assistance,' continued Micah. 'It is certain that Avon will have Orac with him, so the opportunity arises to relieve him of it, without the requirement of supporting an insurgency which is bound to be put down with some brutality. There is your dilemma. Which instruction are you to obey?'

Fu Ti sighed. 'Very well put, Micah. Li Lang answers to the Empress and, if she does not like any of his answers, she can become most unpleasant. Li Lang, as far as this matter is concerned, is covering both exigencies. One – the acquisition of the computer whilst, at the same time, allowing considerable damage to the Quartet and weakening its resolve should we decide to move against it, militarily or diplomatically. Two – a simpler method of acquiring the computer which is his, and our, principal aim.' Fu Ti paused and sipped tea from a small, delicate cup.

'And the Empress?' asked Micah.

'The Empress,' Fu Ti continued, having wiped his lips with a silk napkin, 'would prefer the former outcome. However, securing the computer is all important to her. Failure to do so would undoubtedly incur her wrath,' he smiled. 'Li Lang is leaving it up to me to decide the course of action that should be taken. If I make the wrong decision and lose Orac, the Empress's wrath will be directed at me and me alone. Li Lang would not be held responsible. Should I succeed, Li Lang will receive her plaudits, as the architect of the adventure. He cannot lose face, either way.' Fu Ti smiled a secret smile. 'Or, at least, he thinks he cannot lose.'

Micah had listened with rapt attention. He now chose his words very carefully. 'Would you care for my opinion?'

'I might not care for it, but I would like to hear it.'

'It would seem to me that a splendid opportunity to acquire the computer is about to present itself. Avon will soon be our guest. Whilst extending him hospitality aboard this Dragon, special forces could board his spacecraft and transfer ownership of Orac from him to us.'

'You mean we would steal it?'

'In my humble opinion, that would be the option open to you that would be most likely to lead to success.'

'You know nothing about Avon, do you?'

'Before this enterprise, I had never heard of him.'

Fu Ti rose to his feet, lifted a china pot off the occasional table by the side of his chair and poured tea into Micah's cup. 'Avon is a most interesting character. He is certainly the most cunning and ruthless human being that I have come across,' he smiled humourlessly, 'and that includes General Li Lang.' He returned to his chair, deposited the teapot on the table, but did not sit. 'Stealing Orac from him will be a difficult, likely impossible, task, even for the forces we describe as *special*.'

'We could execute him. Then search his spacecraft at our leisure.'

Fu Ti raised an eyebrow. 'That would be most inhospitable. It would seem practical, but to assassinate an unsuspecting guest is against my nature.' He favoured Micah with a benign smile. 'Besides, Avon will not be unsuspecting. You may depend that he will have made suitable arrangements to protect his interests, whatever may happen to him.'

'What might those arrangements be?'

'Well, we'll ask him, shall we?'

Li Lang, now aboard his warship in Earth orbit, received a verbal report from a courier despatched from the Dragon ship he had ordered to search the icy wasteland. The courier stood at attention and recited his message in a monotone.

'Honourable Commander Chen instructs me to inform you, General, that a submarine has been discovered on the sea bed of the wasteland. It is destroyed, as is its robot crew. The assassin Solomon Fisch is dead, although it proved difficult to establish his identity. Honourable Commander Chen awaits instruction to salvage the vessel.'

'Let it lie where it is. Go on.'

'The body of the assassin Absalom Fisch was also discovered, perfectly preserved in blood-coloured ice. He had been gutted – like a fish.'

Li Lang smiled at the unintentional pun. 'Leave the body where it is. Were there any other discoveries?'

'There were none, my general.'

'Then you may go.'

The courier bowed low and retreated from the room – Li Lang's command post, not dissimilar to that occupied by Fu Ti on his Dragon ship.

'Well, Avon,' Li Lang thought to himself. 'You are certainly living up to your reputation. But you have overlooked something – or rather, somebody. There is a remaining member of the assassins' troika. The Huntress. I fear for you that she may very well live up to her reputation too.'

'I am George.'

Orac cut it off before the computer could go any further. 'I do wish it would stop announcing itself in such a pedantic fashion. We know its name by now.'

'What's on your mind, George?' Avon asked kindly.

'The Dragon reconnaissance ship turned back to Earth many hours past,' George seemed to stutter. 'I apologise for not informing you sooner. It is beyond my understanding why I failed to do so.'

'It's not up to the job, that's why,' Orac said.

'It really doesn't matter, George,' Avon said, still in a kindly fashion.

'However, there is a larger Dragon ship dancing attendance upon us.'

Avon stiffened. 'Is it preparing to attack?'

'On the contrary, its computer is signalling a wish for amicable communication.'

Avon relaxed a little. 'Well, let's grant its wish, shall we?'

'It conveys a message from the honourable and revered Colonel Fu Ti of the Empire of Cathay. He sends greetings and invites the similarly honourable and revered Avon to be his guest, when matters of mutual interest and advantage may be discussed and, possibly, acted upon. The colonel has observed that this craft's pod bay is empty and will, subject to your permission, despatch a drone pod to assist your transfer to his craft. The colonel insists that you will face no danger. You have his word of honour. He awaits your answer.'

'He wants something,' Orac said.

'Yes, and I know exactly what,' Avon said.

'What?'

'He wants you!'

Orac gave a machine's snort of disapproval.

'Open the hatch, George,' said Avon. The hatch opened and he darted below, returning after a few second with two phials containing a thick liquid. He handled the phials with great care. The hatch closed behind him. 'Gratefully accept Fu Ti's kind invitation, George. Orac – set up an electric barrier as soon as I leave the flight deck. Twice the power of the barrier you set up to deter Xerxes's troops.' Leaving the phials on the flight deck console, Avon approached Orac and began to dismantle it.

'What are you up to?' Orac said, somewhat alarmed.

'While I'm being entertained on Fu Ti's ship, I suspect that Dragon troops may attempt to board this one. It's reasonable to assume that the electric shocks they receive will foil the attempt but, in case they do not, I'm going to prepare a nasty surprise.' Avon, satisfied with his work so far, retrieved the phials and carried them to Orac. Very gently, he placed them within the computer interior. He then replaced the parts that he had dismantled and stood back, as if admiring his work.

'What's the liquid in the phials?' Orac enquired cautiously.

'It's nitroglycerin. In the highly unlikely event any Dragon trooper gets his hands on you, you will blow up in his face.'

'Oh, that's wonderful news!' Orac exclaimed.

'It's not going to happen, Orac. Even if it did, you would go out with a bang, instead of a whimper.'

'Oh well, that's all right then!'

'I'll mention this security measure to Colonel Fu Ti as soon as I feel the time is appropriate. Of course, there's always the chance he won't believe me.'

'The drone pod has docked,' George said.

'Well, I'll be on my way then. Lock the flight deck doors behind me. Don't forget to set up the electrical circuit.'

'I never thought I would say this,' Orac muttered, 'but come back soon, Avon.'

'You are welcome, Avon,' Fu Ti said, smiling and bowing.

Avon responded in kind.

'It is fortuitous that our paths have crossed again,' Fu Ti said.

'You just happened to be in the neighbourhood, did you?'

Fu Ti's smile faded for a moment. He spread his hands in a gesture of apology. 'I am on a mission of a kind. My immediate superior, General Li Lang, has requested that I renew our acquaintance and put various propositions to you, at the same time rendering any assistance you may require. I believe his inspiration came as a result of your recent visit to a part of my home world.' The smile returned. 'But all of this can wait until after we have dined.'

He clapped his hands and Micah appeared, accompanied by a very attractive Eurasian woman. 'May I present Micah, my valued and trusted first assistant, and Xian.' The woman bowed low. 'I hope you will indulge me by permitting them to dine with us. They are much more entertaining than me.'

'I should be delighted,' Avon said, as Xian smiled coquettishly.

Like Eugene Furneaux before him, Avon was treated to a lavish dinner – the finest of foods and the finest of wines to accompany them, although Avon drank sparingly.

'I imagine this,' Xian waved a hand over the laden table, 'must make a pleasant change from your usual diet.' She laughed a tinkling laugh. 'I am told that, when darting hither and thither on matters of importance, military men must survive on nutrient bars and plain water.'

'I am not a military man.'

Xian frowned prettily. 'Oh, have I been misinformed?'

'Avon is not attached to any recognised military authority,' Fu Ti said quietly.

Micah spoke for the first time. 'Should he be called upon to fight however, Avon might be described as an army of one,' he smirked, 'but I suspect that, as he has aged and grown wiser, a diplomat may have supplanted the warrior.'

Avon said, 'Giving that impression is a useful means of putting enemies, real and potential, off their guard.'

Micah frowned. Xian chuckled and sipped wine. Fu Ti was about to speak when an attendant entered the room, somewhat hurriedly, and whispered in his ear. Fu Ti dismissed him. He smiled knowingly at Avon. 'I think you must apologise to our guest, Micah. Your little scheme, to which I was most reluctant to acquiesce, has come undone.'

Micah showed no reaction. Xian winked at Avon.

Fu Ti looked stern. 'Of the eight elite guards you sent to attempt to board our friend's spacecraft, one is dead and two severely injured. Of course, they did not succeed in their mission and have withdrawn.'

After a silence, Xian said, 'You do not seem surprised.'

Avon shrugged. 'It is probably what I would have considered doing in similar circumstances. But I would have guessed that there would be some kind of a deterrent and done nothing.'

'You would not have gambled on success or failure, as I have?' Micah said edgily.

'No, but then, I hold all the cards, so it wouldn't have been a gamble.'

'I would challenge you that you do not hold *all* the cards.'

Avon studied the young man, his eyes hooded. 'Well now,' he said lazily, 'it's your call.'

'It *is* my call!' Fu Ti said.

Micah, disturbed by the anger in Fu Ti's tone, stood and bowed deeply to Avon. 'Please accept my sincere apologies.' He turned to Fu Ti. 'May I withdraw?'

Fu Ti waved him away.

After he had left, Xian said lightly, 'Well, this is cosy, isn't it?' Any tension broken, Avon laughed and Fu Ti smiled.

In an old, decaying building that had once been the mansion of a wealthy pirate, Del Grant was sitting on a sofa that had seen better days. He was strapping up his ankle, wincing with pain as he did so.

'It's not broken, is it?' Magda asked.

He shook his head. 'No, it's a sprain, but it hurts like hell.'

'How would you know, you've never been there?'

Grant smiled. 'If Steiner has his way, we'll all be going there – much sooner than we would like.'

'Do we have an estimate as to when he's likely to catch up with us?'

'I would guess two, maybe three days, at the outside. He'll bomb first and then he'll send in his troops. There will be no quarter given.'

'The deep cellars will enable most of us to survive any bombing,' Magda said thoughtfully, 'but fighting elite troops on the ground is another thing altogether. How many fighters do we have?'

Grant shrugged. 'Just over two hundred. I get the feeling, though, that they would rather be somewhere else.'

Magda sighed. 'When you seem to be winning and getting away with daring raids on Quartet fighter patrols and suchlike, everyone's your friend and wants to fight tyranny alongside you. When you're losing and likely to die, it's not really surprising that those "friends" would rather be somewhere else.'

Grant said, 'What would you do, if you were Steiner – given that he will have reached the same conclusion about our followers?'

'I would offer an armistice. Surrender weapons and everyone, except the two of us, goes free.'

'No-one would believe that, surely?'

'If you're desperate, you grasp at straws.'

'We really could do with the help of our mutual friend, couldn't we?'

Magda bit her lip. 'Yes.'

Xian having excused herself 'due the lateness of the hour', Fu Ti and Avon sat opposite each other in matching armchairs. A decanter of cognac and balloon glasses graced a table between them. An attendant poured a generous measure into each glass and handed the first to Avon and the other to his master, before withdrawing.

'This is excellent,' Avon said, 'I thank you for it, as well as for the perfect dinner.'

'You are more than welcome. I must thank you for forgiving Micah's impertinence and impetuosity.'

Avon shrugged. 'He'll learn, probably the hard way. Earlier you mentioned various propositions you wished to put to me?'

'Ah, yes. I suppose it is not before time that I lay them before you.' Fu Ti sipped the brandy before continuing. 'My empress has instructed me to attempt to acquire Orac, by fair means or by foul.'

'That's very straightforward of you. Why don't you start with the fair?'

Fu Ti almost choked on his drink then giggled. He regained his composure. 'I am authorised to make you an offer. The opportunity to live out the rest of your life in luxurious surroundings, anywhere you choose on Earth, in exchange for the computer...' He paused for a response.

Avon took a drink. 'Please go on!'

'You would be provided with everything your heart desires.'

'You mean, until an assassin comes to call?'

'I would not condone it!'

'You might not, but you could be over-ruled. Someone like Micah could take it upon himself to rid your empire of me. After all, he's gone against your commands already.'

Fu Ti pursed his lips. 'That is true. But had I not permitted his, in my opinion, foolishness, I would have had to answer to my empress.'

'You see what I mean then? What other proposition do you have in mind?'

Fu Ti fidgeted uncomfortably. 'I could imprison you. You would surely break under torture and surrender Orac as the price of relief from pain.'

Avon snorted. 'That's not very friendly. It's also against your honour code, isn't it?'

Fu Ti closed his eyes and nodded. 'I am sorry to say that different interpretations have been placed upon the word *honour* by my superiors.'

'I understand, but you must know that I have made certain that, whatever happens to me, Orac will remain beyond your reach. Torture me if you will, even unto death, but you'll have a hard time getting aboard my spacecraft – as has been proved already. Even if you succeeded at the second attempt, you don't know what's waiting for you.'

'You do not fear death?'

'We all die, Fu Ti. It's just a question of when.'

Fu Ti got to his feet and refilled his glass. He gestured towards Avon, who shook his head. 'As an alternative, I am authorised to supply you with fuel, weapons, anything you require, whilst urging you, with Orac, to go to the aid of insurgents who are currently under threat from Quartet forces.'

Avon frowned. 'Why would I do that?'

'It would be small compensation for my inability to persuade you to part with the computer. It would be a particular favour for me, in so much as it might lessen the wrath of my empress. Cathay has an interest in thwarting the Quartet's ambitions. Furthermore, the insurgents are led by your old friend, Del Grant and, more significantly perhaps, Magda Lens.'

If Avon was surprised, he didn't show it. He merely raised an eyebrow.

'Having, to some degree, assisted you, I felt honour-bound to extend that assistance to a lady who, apart from being your sometime companion, had saved your life,' Fu Ti said. 'I was certain that you would approve of my actions. Particularly as the Quartet, soon after her escape from the island planet that had been your prison, destroyed it.'

'What did you do with her?'

'I entrusted her to the care of Alien Greys. As you seemed to be on such good terms with them that they had provided you with the spacecraft you now fly, I assumed she would be safe with them. Of course, I did not know at the time that you had stolen the spacecraft.' Fu Ti permitted himself a wry smile. 'How she was afterwards recruited by Grant I do not know.'

Avon drained his glass and said nothing.

'She and Grant and their followers are currently under siege on a planetoid known as Ragnar,' Fu Ti concluded.

'The Quartet will wipe them out,' Avon said.

'With your assistance – and that of Orac – they might not.'

'Why doesn't your empress authorise you to go to their aid?'

'The Empire of Cathay is not yet ready to go to war with the Quartet. It would be ill advised for it to perform an act of perceived aggression at this time.'

'Well, with or without me, not forgetting Orac, the odds are stacked against the insurgency.'

'And, as you remarked to Micah, you do not gamble, unless you hold all the cards!'

'I'm a sore loser, Fu Ti.'

'Absalom has failed,' Furneaux said, 'and Avon has killed both him and Solomon in particularly grisly fashion.'

'How do you know this?' Pandora Ess sniffed a black rose cut from a bush in the elaborate garden of her mansion headquarters on Iphigenia.

'I have a contact in the highest reaches of the command structure of the Empire of Cathay.'

'You mean a spy. How reliable is he?'

'He is a she – a mistress of General Li Lang. Li Lang was suspicious of her and she underwent interrogation, but she is adept at professing ignorance and innocence and now enjoys even greater favour with him. She is a valuable asset.'

'I wonder why you haven't mentioned her to me before,' Pandora Ess said, casting him a steely glance.

Furneaux reddened. 'I am mentioning her now because it is only now that she has imparted significant information.'

'I see. What else of significance has she imparted?'

'That Avon has overlooked something – or rather, someone,' Furneaux said eagerly. 'Alexandra, the Huntress. She will succeed where Solomon and Absalom failed.'

'I wish I could share your optimism. This terrorist seems to have nine lives,' Pandora Ess smiled. 'Let us hope he's on his ninth. Are you able to contact this woman?'

'Not at present.'

'What's that supposed to mean?'

'Because it was Gabriella who took out the contract in the first place, it is to her that the Huntress will turn.'

'Why so?'

'The contract will have to be renewed and different terms negotiated. Of course, Gabriella will insist that, whilst Avon's death is to be desired, Orac is of greater importance in the scheme of things.'

'Oh, dear me, I shall have to pay Gabriella another visit. I wouldn't want her to get ideas above her station. Or should I say – her Base?' She laughed at her little joke.

Eugene Furneaux didn't.

It was Adonis who introduced Alexandra to Gabriella.

Whilst clearly annoyed that Alexandra had had the temerity to seek her out at the Base, something she had explicitly forbidden Solomon to do, she received her with a degree of politeness. But she was even more annoyed when Alexandra explained to her the recent events.

'Is this man a machine?' she said. 'Who will kill him now?'

'I will,' Alexandra said calmly. 'But it is my understanding,' she acknowledged Adonis, 'that there is a more important item on your agenda.'

Gabriella tensed then just as quickly appeared to relax. 'You understand correctly. Can you find Avon and the computer?'

'I am not called the Huntress for nothing.'

'Where are they?'

'Close to the Martian colony, almost equidistant from this Base and the far edge of the Beyond. A representative of the Empire of Cathay is negotiating with the terrorist for the handing over of Orac.'

'He'll never hand it over.'

'That is also my opinion. In which case, Cathay will want to be certain that it does not fall into any other hands – hands that might be turned against the Empire.'

Gabriella laughed. 'That means the Quartet.'

'Or anyone within the Quartet seeking to alter its composition.'

Gabriella gave her a searching look and Alexandra smiled.

Adonis joined the conversation. 'There is always the possibility that the terrorist might care to join forces with others of his ilk. The ones Steiner is currently pursuing.'

'If there's something I've learned about Avon,' Gabriella said, 'it's that *that* is the last thing he would be inclined to do.'

'On the contrary, Cathay would like nothing better than to have Steiner threatened by this computer. Their representative currently has Avon in his power. He could provide weapons, fuel and an incentive for Avon to assist his former associates,' Adonis said quietly.

'What kind of an incentive?'

'If anyone can find something that will entice him, Fu Ti – the Cathay representative – will.'

'Wherever he goes, whatever he chooses to do,' Alexandra said coldly, 'I will hunt him down. There will be no negotiations. I'll kill him where he stands.'

'And deliver Orac to me,' Gabriella said sweetly.

Avon was afforded the privilege of an overnight stay in a luxury cabin – night in the sense that, where there was perennial darkness, the Dragon ship recognised Earth hours. At first inclined to refuse, he realised how tired and shabby he was and accepted gracefully.

Showered and shaved, the aches in his body almost gone, he emerged from the bathroom dressed in a silk robe. He slowed his walk towards the feather bed when he noticed it was already occupied. He touched the pillow where he would have laid his head.

'Is this what you're looking for?' a naked Xian asked. She waved the small gun that Avon had brought on board the Dragon ship hidden in his right boot. She turned the muzzle away and pulled the trigger. Nothing! Xian frowned petulantly.

'No. I was looking for this,' Avon said, as he extracted the Bowie knife he'd hidden in his left boot from beneath the light mattress.

Xian tossed the gun aside. 'Are you that afraid of me?' she enquired.

'I'm "afraid" of everybody.'

She snorted an affecting laugh. 'In case you're wondering, the door is locked and only I know the combination that will open it. You are safe with me.'

The Steiner flotilla took its time as it approached Ragnar.

'What will you do first?' Sarin asked.

'Reconnaissance. I want to know if they have any airpower left,' Steiner growled.

'I can answer that. They have two swift fighter craft in low orbit. But they will be running out of fuel so, if they want to escape inevitable destruction, they are likely to leave soon.'

'We'll reconnoitre anyway.'

'Of course,' Sarin said wryly, 'they could be fanatics. In which case they'll fight to the death.'

'I don't mind that.'

'Well, you wouldn't, would you? You are unlikely to die this early in the conflict.'

Steiner gave him a sour look. 'I don't intend to die at any time in this conflict.'

'May I make a suggestion?'

'It would be hard for me to stop you.'

'Send in four of our fighters – take on each of theirs, two to one. They may run but, if they don't, surely four of ours are better than any two of theirs?'

'That leaves just two fighters and this warship.'

'Not much of a risk.'

Steiner sighed. 'Give the order!'

Avon slipped out of bed whilst Xian was still asleep. It took him half a minute to crack the code that opened the bedroom cabin's door. He glanced outside. In the corridor, almost at his feet, lay a neat pile of plain, well-tailored clothes. It came as no surprise to him that they were a perfect fit. He checked for any tracking devices that might have been attached to the cloth, but could find none.

Xian shifted in her sleep, but did not awaken.

Fully dressed, Avon discarded the clothes he had worn before, all except the boots. He stuck the Bowie knife in his left boot as before and, having retrieved it, the small gun in his right. Suitably accoutred, he stepped out into the corridor.

A servant bowed and smiled. Avon hadn't heard anything of his approach, which was a bit disconcerting, but he did hear Xian. He turned slowly.

Xian yawned in his face. 'He's inviting you to breakfast,' she said wearily. 'I'll join you as soon as I get dressed.'

Avon glanced at the servant. The man hadn't appeared to notice Xian's nakedness or, if he had, he was unaffected by it, which is more than could have been said for Avon.

Fu Ti greeted him warmly. 'I hope you slept well and you are refreshed?' he said, trying to hide a sly smile.

'Thank you. I slept like an innocent and dreamt of guilt.'

Fu Ti looked puzzled, as well he might. He clapped his hands and breakfast was served by lovely young women. Or were they young men? It didn't matter, breakfast was, as dinner had been, almost perfect.

'I would like to present you with the drone pod,' Fu Ti said unctuously, 'together with four rockets, a dozen fuel rods and some foods that may delight you. Will you accept?'

'I am very grateful for your kindness and generosity.'

Fu Ti smiled benignly. 'I am so pleased. They are already loaded on the drone.'

Avon sipped tea. 'You expect me to fly to the aid of Grant and Magda?'

Fu Ti spread his elegant hands. 'I expect nothing. In that way, I avoid the possibility of disappointment.' He looked sharply at his guest. 'If you think that that is the price of my gifts, you are mistaken. A gift does not carry a price tag.'

'I didn't think it would and I am sorry if I gave the impression that I did. My Cantonese is not up to much, as you know.'

Fu Ti laughed.

'What is funny?' Xian said as she entered the room. She helped herself to a croissant and eyed both men as she ate it – flakes of pastry sticking to her full lips.

Fu Ti said, 'A private moment of humour, Xian.'

Xian shrugged indifference and, choosing a peach from a bowl of fruit, bit into it so that its juices now mingled with croissant flakes on her mouth. It was quite erotic; even Fu Ti seemed affected.

He turned to Avon to cover any embarrassment. 'Where will you go?' he asked.

Avon's eyes seemed to glaze over as he stared into the middle distance. 'Somewhere I have never been before.'

'What will you do?'

'Something I have never done before.' Avon snapped out of his reverie and smiled. 'I thank you again for your friendship and generosity. I must leave now.'

'I will come with you to the pod while Xian finishes breakfast.'

Avon stood and faced Xian. She licked her lips and Avon smiled.

The drone pod idled towards Avon's spacecraft as he stripped its simple computer and guidance systems. Having made a few, quick adjustments, he entered a code and opened a communication channel. 'Orac, this is Avon.'

'I would never have guessed it,' the computer replied irritably.

'I would like you to dispense with all electric current defences.'

Orac seemed to laugh. 'Oh, they are long dispensed with. You seem to forget that fuel is necessary to ensure such security. Most of what we had left was used up repelling an attack. Had a second assault been mounted, it might well have succeeded.'

'In which case, you would have ceased to exist and we would not be having this conversation,' Avon remarked drily.

Orac growled.

'I'm linking in to George.'

'I am George!'

'I'm very pleased that you still are. Open the pod dock doors and prepare to receive this drone, which I am controlling manually. Once I am on board, do not close the dock doors until I instruct you.'

Avon glanced through the forward observation window of the drone. He carefully aligned the machine and, as the spacecraft's dock doors gaped open, guided it into the docking space and brought it to a halt. 'Orac, I want a full scan, report anything untoward.'

For a minute, all Avon could hear over the communication channel was a series of unpleasant noises as Orac scanned the drone. 'There is nothing "untoward", as you put it.'

'All right, George, close the doors.'

As the dock doors closed, Avon exited the drone and headed to the flight deck, clutching the fuel rods Fu Ti had given him and a hand-held communication device. He paused just outside the door. 'Orac, is the flight deck door unarmed?'

There was a clicking sound. 'It is now.'

Avon entered the flight deck. 'Open the hatch, George. I come bearing gifts.' The hatch opened and Avon disappeared below. He placed four fuel rods in position, reserving the others on a rack. When he emerged, Orac said, 'While you're about it, you might remove this nitroglycerin.'

'What's going on outside, George?' Avon asked, as he removed Orac's covers and gently extricated the phials from within it.

'The Dragon ship is moving away from us. It is turning, as if about to set a course for Earth.'

Avon returned to the hatch very carefully and slowly lowered himself below. He placed the phials in the ice box from which he had previously obtained them. Back on deck, the hatch closed, Avon said, 'Start engines, George, idle speed.' He then replaced Orac's covers. 'I have four, presently neutralised, rocket warheads. Where do I put them so that they are armed and ready to launch?'

'The launch tubes are situated adjacent to the pod dock.'

Avon left the flight deck.

'Well, he's full of himself,' Orac commented.

'The fuel rods are of the highest quality,' George remarked, 'and all systems are fully functional.'

'I wonder what promises Avon made in exchange for them.'
'What is "wonder"?' George asked.
'I sometimes wonder myself.'

The Dragon ship of Fu Ti did not set course for Earth. Instead, at a discreet distance, it prepared to parallel any course that Avon's craft might set. Xian and Micah attended the older man.

'Did you learn anything during the course of the night?' Fu Ti enquired gently.

Xian snorted her familiar laugh. 'There is nothing Avon could teach me.'

'I mean, did you learn anything of his intentions?' Fu Ti said patiently.

'No. He remained suspicious of me throughout the night and slept only fitfully. Like a snake, he did not close his eyes.'

'Did you find him to be, how shall I put it, a pleasant companion?'

Xian smiled wistfully. 'He is an older man, but pleasant enough.'

'Could you draw any conclusions as to his state of mind?'

Xian frowned. 'Yes. It is as if he fears nothing, because his philosophy is one of acceptance of his fate. Oh, he uses all his guile to postpone that fate, but he knows he cannot, in the end, avoid it.'

'You mean, as I have suspected, he has a death wish?' Fu Ti said solemnly.

'That is exactly what I mean.'

'It seems to me a pity that you would not allow me to fulfil that wish,' Micah said acidly.

Fu Ti sighed.

'What is our course of action then?' Micah said.

'It is a course of inaction. We shall observe him from a position where we cannot ourselves be observed. When he acts, we will counteract.'

'Set a course for the Beyond, George. Half speed, and be sure our all-round scanners are activated. Let me know if anything approaches with hostile intent.' Avon smiled slightly. 'Wait. Let me know if *anything* approaches — it will certainly have hostile intent.'

'I would have thought you would have had enough of the Beyond,' Orac said.

'You're not supposed to think, Orac. You keep forgetting you are a machine.'

'Ahem!' George interrupted. 'Where in the Beyond?'

'It's furthest extremity, the far side of the suns of Aegisthus.'

'I am fearful of your intent,' said Orac.

PART TWO
The End of the Beginning

Pandora Ess paid another visit to the Base, as she had promised Furneaux. This time, she arrived unannounced and accompanied by four fighter spacecraft, her own ship and a thousand elite troops. Gabriella was to be left in no doubt that she meant business.

Gabriella almost panicked, but the calming influence of Adonis triumphed and she was able to greet the Doctor with a degree of composure. 'This is a pleasant surprise,' she said, rather weakly.

Pandora Ess, dressed in leather combat fatigues and flanked by half a dozen fierce warriors, looked her up and down. 'It shouldn't be a surprise, pleasant or otherwise. I thought it was understood that you and I are in an alliance and that anything – and I mean *anything* – of significance that might affect that alliance should be reported to one another.'

'I don't understand.'

'Oh, you understand very well, my dear. It has come to my attention that a woman termed "the Huntress" is currently in pursuit of the terrorist and his prized computer. That computer, should it come into your possession, is to be shared.' Pandora Ess smiled grimly. 'I have gained the impression that you are playing a game of your own – a dangerous game – and might very well keep it to yourself, should the opportunity arise. Please set my mind at rest and tell me this is not so.'

'It is not so,' Gabriella said hesitantly.

'Then why, pray, did you not inform me that you have authorised this Huntress to act on your behalf?'

'There was little I could do to prevent her going after Avon. He has, after all, killed her associates and she, quite understandably, seeks vengeance.'

'Any vengeance is mine,' said Pandora Ess tersely. 'The key issue is Orac, and you were aware of my plans – plans that included you – to obtain it. This vengeful woman is in my way. In *our* way. Call her off.'

'I don't believe I can do that. She has left here. She has contacts among Alien Greys and will use them to find Avon.'

'Alien Greys are an irrelevance to me. Why did you not detain her?'

Gabriella was becoming agitated and finding it hard to think on her feet. Adonis came to her rescue.

'It seemed that the woman's expertise in seeking out her prey could be used to our advantage,' Adonis said coolly, echoing Eugene Furneaux's opinion. 'Gabriella believes that, should she succeed in locating Avon and Orac, she is sufficiently aware that the computer is the greatest prize. She will secure it on our – meaning your and Gabriella's – behalf.'

'That does not explain why I was not informed of this enterprise.'

'A mere oversight, soon to be corrected,' Adonis said. 'Gabriella, to her great credit, wished to play her part in your alliance and, as it were, assist your mutual ambition.'

'And what of you, Adonis,' Pandora Ess said slyly, 'do you consider yourself to be a player in this game?'

'If so, I am nothing more than a willing pawn.'

'A pawn, you say. Who would be a knight perhaps?'

Adonis was silent.

Pandora Ess's gimlet eyes bored into Gabriella. 'I accept Adonis's explanation on your behalf. To cement our relationship – our alliance – you will permit a selection of my followers to share control of the Base until our mutual ambition is realised.'

Gabriella seemed about to protest. Once again, Adonis spoke up.

'That would seem to be an admirable solution to a momentary lack of trust between you,' he said silkily.

Pandora Ess had not taken her eyes off Gabriella. 'How does that suit you, my dear?'

Gabriella forced a smile. 'It suits me very well. I would not wish anything to come between us.'

'And I will not allow it,' said Pandora Ess.

Steiner's four fighters moved to seek engagement with the two flown by Grant's followers. As Sarin had predicted, one attempted to avoid combat and accelerated away. It didn't get very far. A combined rocket attack blew it out of the sky.

The other, either courageously, or desperately, turned to

fight. It flew hard and fast towards its antagonists, causing them to take evasive action. But one was slower than the other and the remaining rebel craft rammed it. There was an explosion, followed by a firework display, as the two poorly matched spaceships disintegrated.

Steiner swore. 'Recall the others,' he said through gritted teeth. 'We'll bomb the place. All right, I know we can't go nuclear. But a conventional bombing run should open the way to our ground forces and the sooner they're on the ground, the better.'

'May I make a suggestion?' Sarin said quietly.

'Not another one!'

'There's no need to bomb – at least, not yet. Send in a fighter – a fast flight over the enemy's positions. No bombs, but leaflets – leaflets offering generous terms if they will surrender.'

'I want Grant and Lens dead at my feet.'

'That can be part of the surrender terms. Put yourself in the position of an ordinary foot soldier. You are offered your life and your freedom. All you have to do is offer up your leaders in return. The alternative is that no quarter will be given. What would you do? Of course, we will not keep our side of any bargain, but they are not to know that until it is too late.'

Steiner smiled. 'You're an evil bastard, Sarin. Prepare the leaflets.'

'You saw that, did you?' Magda asked.

'I could hardly miss it – it was an astonishing display of rocket power. We have no air cover now. Not that it was very much to begin with.' Grant looked pale and drawn. 'Avon's not coming. In your heart you knew that,' he went on, 'didn't you?'

Magda nodded.

'He never fitted the role of the white knight.' Grant shook his head. 'I can't imagine why I succumbed to your hope that he would help us. Not that, without Orac, he could have done much,' he sighed. 'We'd better take whatever cover we can, they're sure to bomb us now.'

'I still think they'll offer surrender terms.'

Grant smiled, albeit a little wearily. 'You are forever an optimist it would seem.' He rose from the couch on which he had been lying, wincing as his foot hit the floor. 'Any kind of amnesty would not include us,' he said bitterly.

'I'm not saying we should, or would, accept Steiner's terms. I wouldn't trust him to keep his word anyway. Unfortunately, our demoralised followers might believe in him and accept without consulting us. However, Steiner will have to allow time for our consideration. Time is precious.'

'So it is, but it's running out for us.' Grant gazed out of a hole in the wall of their headquarters, the former mansion of an obscure pirate. The hole had once been a stained glass window. 'The natives are getting restless,' he said, almost to himself. 'It might not be a bad idea to start thinking of a way out for the two of us.'

Magda frowned. 'We can't abandon these men and women. They've trusted us, believed in us.'

'That's as may be, but they may very well abandon us. Even if they don't, we're bound to die.'

'I thought Ragnar was as far as we can go?'

'There are some planetoids scattered within hopper distance. It would be hard for Steiner's men to find us on any of them.'

'Where do we find a space hopper?'

Grant smiled shyly. 'There's one on the roof of this building.'

Magda raised an eyebrow.

'It's been there for a while,' Grant said hastily. 'Before you joined me and Cathay started to feed us arms and equipment, I was on the run a lot of the time. I was here, there and everywhere. When I was here, I made sure that I'd have an escape route, if the worst came to the worst.'

'You took a risk. Any bombing run would destroy the hopper.'

'It might – which is why we should probably leave sooner, rather than later.'

'Did you ever intend to stand and fight?'

'Of course I did,' Grant responded angrily, 'but under the

present circumstances, discretion would seem to be the better part of valour.'

'In my book it's called cowardice.'

'Your book can call it what it likes. The alternative is suicide.'

At which point, there was the roar of jet engines as a space fighter flew overhead at great speed, dropping leaflets in its wake. A leaflet drifted into the hole that was once a window. Grant snatched at it.

'What does it say?' Magda enquired.

'It's pretty much what you anticipated: "Do not resist when Quartet forces advance. Lay down your arms and surrender. You will be well treated and given your freedom. Del Grant and Magda Lens are excluded from this amnesty."' He glanced outside and below. 'Our supporters are reading this. Now they're looking up at me. Their expressions are not particularly friendly.'

Magda stood beside him. 'You can't really blame them,' she said sorrowfully. 'They want to live.'

'So do I. Let's get out of here.'

'The space hopper could be shot down.'

'That's a chance we'll have to take. We'll head for the dark side of Ragnar, that should offer us some concealment. Besides, Steiner won't be expecting us to run. At least, not yet.'

Magda looked down at the men and women milling about below. 'They'll be coming for us.'

Grant began moving towards a spiral staircase in the corner of the room. 'This will take us to the roof.' He began to ascend.

After a moment, Magda followed suit.

'Well, well, well,' Sarin said, 'two birds are about to fly.'

'What's that supposed to mean?' Steiner said tetchily.

'A space hopper has just lifted off the top of a building. I'll take a bet that Grant and Lens are on board.'

'Shoot it down!'

'You withdrew the fighters, if you remember. By the time they're back in action, the hopper will have reached the far side and plunged into darkness. Grant will cut engines and drift, so he can't be tracked. We've lost them.'

Steiner cursed. 'Where will they go?'

'There are a lot of planetoids out there – most of them unexplored.'

'All right, send in ground troops anyway. Kill everybody.'

'All of them?'

'That's what *everybody* means, doesn't it?'

Avon's spacecraft, having followed the course instructed, approached the far side of the suns of Aegisthus. 'Tell me about this place, Orac.'

'It is called a Goldilocks zone – meaning it is likely habitable by humanoids. There are many planetoids the size of small planets with atmospheres that are thin but can support life. The principal one is Ragnar. Ragnar is the former hideaway of a once notorious pirate. It is the logical destination for anyone seeking a kind of sanctuary, particularly if half the Quartet's air fleet is after you.'

'How far away are we?'

'Ask George.'

'I am George. Ragnar is approximately four thousand kilometres distant. It can be reached in less than three Earth hours.'

'Can you scan it, Orac?'

'Of course I can! But you need to get a little closer.'

'Define "a little closer".'

'A thousand klicks.'

'Full speed ahead, George!'

After the slaughter, Steiner's flotilla moved away from Ragnar and set course for Quartet headquarters on Iphigenia. The general opened a bottle of whisky to celebrate his victory. He didn't offer Sarin any.

'You might consider entering stealth mode, Avon,' Orac said quietly. 'We are about to encounter a Quartet warship accompanied by several fighters.'

'I have considered, and would ask you to do it.'

'Stealth mode is accomplished.'

'All right, George,' Avon said. 'Although they can't see us, we are a solid body. Give me manual control and I'll try to avoid a collision.'

Pandora Ess was handed a minute disc on which was recorded a message from Sarin. She waited until all her attendants had left her alone before listening to it. It was spoken in Russian, her and Sarin's native language.

'You will have received the official version of General Steiner's triumph over the forces of insurgency. If the truth were to be told, however, it was something of a hollow victory. Grant and Lens, the rebel leaders, managed to escape. To where we do not know. Deprived of his principal prey, Steiner then gave the order that their followers – to whom he had offered amnesty – should be executed. The brutality of the general's troops was sickening. Given carte blanche, they ran riot, torturing, raping and then beheading or gutting their victims.' There was a pause in the narration before Sarin continued. 'The death of Steiner cannot come soon enough, in my opinion. However, I must enquire of you how and when that should happen. We are en route for Iphigenia. Shall I kill him now, or wait until he visits you to brag of his dubious achievement?'

Pandora Ess looked thoughtful then spoke into a recording device attached to the disc. 'I would prefer it if the pleasure of Steiner's execution be mine. His death, though surely painful and, perhaps, prolonged, must not be laid at our door. In due course, Sarin, you will be appointed commander in his place.'

The disc having been despatched to Sarin, Pandora Ess summoned Furneaux.

'Steiner is returning to us,' she said. 'He'll be dead within twenty-four hours. This means that I have decided to accelerate our takeover of control of what is at present the Quartet. I need you to liaise with your friends in the Cathay Empire.' She smiled grimly. 'It wouldn't do for them to interfere while I am about my – I mean *our* – business. Are you up to the task?'

'You know I am,' Furneaux said obsequiously.

'Then set about it without delay.'

Furneaux hesitated before realising he'd been dismissed.

The pod drone landed on a desolate beach, lapped by a desultory lake choked with algae and body parts. Avon walked slowly towards the building from which Grant and Magda had escaped, a Nine7 held loosely by his side. He stepped around headless corpses of men and eviscerated bodies of women. There was, appropriately, a deathly silence.

He glanced up. On the roof of the building, several vultures eyed him curiously. He fired a burst from the Nine7 and they lazily fluttered away. It was a meaningless gesture, he knew. They would be back.

He entered the building and was about to mount an interior staircase when a half-naked woman hurled herself at his feet. She was covered in blood and sobbing heartbreakingly. Through broken teeth, she begged him to kill her. Momentarily alarmed, Avon recovered his composure and knelt beside her. He gently touched her face in an effort to calm her. She clutched his hand and kissed it, again pleading for death.

'Grant and Magda. Where are they?' he asked, his voice barely above a whisper. For a moment, she seemed not to understand. Then she giggled and pointed upwards. 'They have hopped away,' she said, although it was difficult to make out her words. Avon nodded, stood and began to climb the stairs. The woman screamed something unintelligible after him. He turned, levelled the Nine7 and shot her. She seemed to sigh contentedly as she died.

Avon found the launch pad for a space hopper on the roof. There were traces of wet fuel and a burnt area that indicated its take-off had been recent. He descended the stairs, stepped over the body of the woman and returned to the poor excuse for a beach. After a final look around, he entered the pod and lifted it into a sky lit by the far side of the suns of Aegisthus. The vultures assumed their former position.

'Too late the hero. Is that the case, Avon?' Orac said.

Avon turned to George. 'The Quartet spaceships we managed to avoid – where are they now in relation to us?'

'They are moving slowly, and somewhat drunkenly, on course for Iphigenia,' George said solemnly.

'What's their formation?'

'A fighter leads the way, followed by the command warship, with two fighters either side.'

'Is there rear cover?'

'No.'

'Set a tracking course and give me full speed. Arm the forward rockets. Let me know when we are within range. At which point, Orac, I will once again require stealth mode.'

'An attack is not possible whilst in stealth mode,' Orac said tetchily. 'You should know that. We would automatically become visible.'

'I do not intend to attack before stealth mode puts us unobserved amongst them.'

'Then what do you intend to do?'

'Fire a rocket up the warship's backside and run like hell.'

'You have tried this before,' Orac seemed weary.

'Yes, and with a degree of success, if you recall.'

'Might this not be third time unlucky? Might not your enemies have become a little wiser? Might they not be expectant of an assault and be suitably prepared to foil you?'

'You mean – I'm in danger of over-reaching myself?'

'You said that. I didn't.'

'All right – we'll change tactics and hit the fighters instead.'

'A wiser move, I think.'

Avon turned to George. 'Cut speed by a quarter, George. Curve left of the warship, spread pattern our rockets, lock on to the two fighters and fire at maximum range. Then we'll go into stealth mode and backtrack to Ragnar. It is unlikely they'll come after us. But if they do, or even if they don't, we'll head further into the Beyond.'

'Steiner is returning to Iphigenia,' Micah said, 'and Avon is following at speed.'

Fu Ti looked startled.

'He will not stand a chance against five fighters and a warship,' Micah continued.

'He stands every chance,' Xian said lightly. 'He's the last thing they'll be expecting. He'll hit and run, that's his style.'

'Why does he bother?' Micah sneered.

'He is angry,' said Fu Ti. 'He is also ashamed that he arrived too late to be of assistance to Grant and Lens.'

'I thought he wasn't interested in assisting them,' Micah jeered. 'Avon's only interest is in assisting himself.'

Fu Ti nodded. 'Once upon a time I expect that was true.'

'But it isn't true now?'

'There is a phrase: "He hasn't a friend in the world." Imagine what it must be like not to have a friend in the universe and all eternity,' Fu Ti sighed.

'You mean Avon is getting soft in his old age?'

'Oh no, if anything, he's getting harder. Remember what Xian believes? He has a death wish. When you are not afraid of death, welcome it even, then your only friend is boldness.'

'And boldness throws any enemies off guard,' Xian said. 'Which means they'll never know what hit them and he'll have run before they can retaliate.'

'I've got a sneaking regard for this man,' Micah said reluctantly.

'Well now, just be thankful you're not the one he's going to hit,' Xian said, smiling.

Avon's spacecraft inclined at a sharp angle and attacked the two Quartet fighters portside of Steiner's warship. The forward rockets, in a spread pattern, struck both amidships and caused considerable damage. Almost immediately, Orac switched to stealth mode as George, again as instructed, fled the scene at full speed. Heavy machine guns opened up from the rear of the warship, but Avon was long gone.

'What the hell happened?' Steiner was red faced: a combination of anger and strong liquor.

Sarin smiled. 'I anticipated that our favourite terrorist might deign to assist his former, now fallen, comrades. Albeit belatedly. I further anticipated he would seek some kind of retribution by attacking our flotilla at its most vulnerable spot, namely, the exposed rear of this warship. Thus, heavy machine guns were in place to receive him. Alas, he did not fall for my little ruse.'

'He knocked out two fighters instead,' Steiner spluttered, 'and has disappeared into thin air.'

'Actually, the "air" is rather thick hereabouts. This will have assisted him in entering what is known as stealth mode. The Federation, now the Quartet, never quite managed to achieve that, although the Cathay Empire has, if only to some degree. It intrigues me that the computer everyone desires can manage it so easily.'

'Turn the fleet about. We'll go after him.'

Sarin sighed. 'That's exactly what he wants. Whilst we are reversing course, he can hit us again, on our blind side.'

'Just send the remaining fighters then.'

'And leave this warship unprotected?'

Steiner cursed.

'It is better we proceed as before,' Sarin said, 'preferably at full speed. It is unlikely the terrorist will follow.'

Steiner reluctantly deferred to Sarin's judgement.

'Do you feel better now?' Orac asked. Avon did not answer so Orac tried a different tack. 'Why are we going beyond Ragnar?'

'I'm going to find Grant and Magda.'

'Why?'

'I don't really know. I just feel that I should. Anyway, where else is there for me to go?'

'The Empire of Cathay would most likely welcome you with open arms,' Orac said. 'Always providing you gave them me in exchange for sanctuary.'

Avon laughed. 'Once they have you, Orac, I will be superfluous to requirements. I'll be a dead man.'

'Do you prefer your present circumstances? A kind of living death?'

Avon did not speak for a long time. 'I cannot answer that,' he said finally.

*

The space hopper had been caught in a minor meteorite storm and obliged to crash-land on a planetoid closer to Ragnar than Del Grant would have liked. Whilst he and Magda had escaped with a few cuts and bruises, the hopper itself was irreparable. The planetoid's surface, consisting of desert scrubland, with craggy, sparsely forested hills in the distance, could not be described as paradise regained.

'Out of a frying pan and into a fire,' Grant said testily. 'On Ragnar, death might have come quickly. Here, it is likely to be slow and agonising.'

'The planetoid could be inhabited,' Magda said, 'and the locals might render us assistance.'

'Have you always been an optimist?'

'I suppose I must have. Being involved with Avon and now you, it's a definite requirement.'

Grant smiled.

'We could walk to the hills,' Magda went on. 'That's where any signs of life are likely to be.'

'I think they might have spotted us – if there's anyone. It could be that they are hostile. In which case, I'd prefer to meet them here in the open, rather than on their home territory.'

'We have some weapons if we have to defend ourselves.'

'Yes – but ammunition won't last long.'

'Well, let's hope they're friendly then.'

'Meanwhile, we'd better make ourselves as comfortable as we can in the hopper. We need to get some sleep. I'll take the first watch.'

Magda looked up at a slowly darkening sky as the suns of Aegisthus began to merge into the blackness through which they had passed in their flight from Ragnar. 'I wonder if he is out there,' she said.

'Who might *he* be?' Grant enquired distractedly.

'Why, Avon of course.'

This time Grant laughed humourlessly. 'That's carrying optimism a little too far.'

Pandora Ess greeted Gregor Steiner with false bonhomie when

he and his troops landed on the military base called Niobe, a satellite of Quartet headquarters on Iphigenia. But he didn't notice and thought her praise and consideration were genuine. Pandora Ess had learned a great deal from her cruel mentor, the late and unlamented Servalan.

'I failed to eliminate Grant and the woman,' Steiner said, his speech somewhat slurred, 'but I made certain that every one of their followers were put to the sword.'

'Bravo!' said Pandora Ess, glancing at Sarin, who stood soberly at his general's shoulder. 'Grant and Lens are hardly in a position to mount a further insurrection without an army and functioning equipment,' she continued. 'I understand your casualties were minimal?'

Sarin smiled slightly.

'Well, we lost a number of fighter craft and their crews. Then, there were one or two others...' Steiner muttered.

'Oh, I'm sorry to hear it.' Pandora Ess smiled benevolently, nearly sympathetically. 'How did it happen?'

Sarin spoke up. 'Avon appeared somewhat belatedly on the scene. He attacked our rear, but General Steiner had set a trap – heavy machine guns chased him away. Unfortunately, one or two of our fighters were destroyed as he ran.'

Steiner nodded gratefully to his second in command.

'It is of no matter,' Pandora Ess said smoothly. 'Although, I have to say, the elimination of Avon, and the capture of his computer, is high on our agenda, if you recall?'

Again Sarin intervened. 'Avon has fled to the relatively unknown section of the Beyond, presumably to link up with Grant and Lens. Assuming he can find them and they welcome him. Neither can be guaranteed.'

Steiner chuckled. 'He's not a threat to us any more. I don't think we'll hear of him again, or Grant and Lens for that matter.'

Pandora Ess frowned. 'I admire your optimism.' She brightened. 'It is my desire to invite you, and Sarin of course, to a celebratory dinner on Iphigenia. I have arranged pleasant company for you.'

'What about my troops?'

'Oh, I have ordered that they be given every comfort here on Niobe.'

Steiner looked hesitant.

'You allowed them free rein on Ragnar,' Sarin said, 'for which they were suitably grateful. I doubt they would begrudge you slipping the reins yourself, as it were.'

'I take it they enjoyed the insurgent women, before disposing of them?' Pandora Ess said sombrely.

'The spoils of war,' Steiner said gruffly.

'I have some "spoils" for you to enjoy,' Pandora Ess said, smiling shyly.

'After dinner, of course,' said Sarin.

After a moment, they all laughed.

Magda, who had fallen asleep on her watch, was rudely awakened by a slight alien noise. She cried out as she saw three humanoid figures standing no more than five metres from the wreckage of the space hopper.

Hearing her, Grant awakened and struggled to pull his gun from his belt.

The tallest of the three figures raised a hand and said, 'Please do not shoot us. We are unarmed and mean you no harm.'

Grant held on to the gun, but lowered its muzzle.

'I recognise your caste,' Magda said, as she regained some composure. 'You are Greys.'

The apparent leader of the three smiled. 'We are often called "Alien" Greys,' he said. 'But, of course, we are not alien to ourselves.'

Magda climbed out of the hopper and extended her hand. 'I am Magda Lens,' she said, then indicated her companion. 'This is Del Grant.'

The leader took Magda's hand. 'I am Egil Nacre. My comrades are Ex and Zed. They are resident here, but I come from afar. We all three recognise your name.'

'I have been treated most kindly in the past by many Greys. Your supreme leader, Rufus Pearl, gave me sanctuary.'

Releasing Magda's hand, Nacre frowned. 'I regret to inform you that Rufus Pearl is no longer alive. He was a victim of assassination, at the hand of one Absalom Fisch, of whom you may have heard.'

'I am very sorry to hear that,' Magda said.

'In a sense, though,' Nacre continued, 'Rufus has been avenged. Absalom Fisch has been killed by – I believe I am right in this – a former associate of yours to whom Rufus also rendered assistance.'

Magda nodded. 'I think I know who you mean,' she said quietly.

'We have been in a war,' Grant said huskily. 'We believe we are the only survivors.'

Nacre turned his attention to him. 'Yes, we are aware of the massacre on Ragnar. You were fortunate to escape.'

'And even more fortunate to encounter you,' Magda said. 'Might it possible that you will help us? We are somewhat forlorn – as you can see.'

Nacre smiled. 'If you care to accompany me,' he waved a hand towards the hills, 'I will ensure that you receive food and drink and, should you so desire, a place to sleep. Meanwhile, Ex and Zed will try to salvage your space hopper. Although I fear that may not be possible. We shall see.'

'Thank you!'

Ex and Zed stood aside as Magda began to walk with Nacre. Grant, warily and reluctantly, followed.

'With Rufus gone, who is now the leader of the Greys?' Magda asked.

'Oh, that would be me,' Nacre said modestly.

The after-dinner entertainment provided by Pandora Ess was much to Steiner's taste. Two glamorous young women bathed him in oils then guided him to a huge bed where they used all known – and some previously unknown – sexual wiles to satisfy his, given his age, seemingly insatiable desires. Pandora Ess watched through a two way mirror.

The slightly older of the two women straddled Steiner's chest. She removed a long, thin steel pin that was holding her golden blonde hair in place. The general giggled and squirmed as her hair cascaded over his face. She looked up at the mirror.

Behind the glass, Pandora Ess smiled as the woman inserted the pin into Steiner's right ear and shoved it into his brain.

There was very little blood – what there was stained the white pillow with what seemed like red teardrops. The two women dressed and left the room without a backward glance.

The native Alien Greys, of a lower caste than Egil Nacre, lived in a small village in a valley in the hills that Grant and Magda had decided not to enter until now. Food was provided. Grant ate his wolfishly. Magda was a little more sedate.

'I hope it is to your taste,' Nacre said.

'Quite frankly,' Magda said between mouthfuls, 'anything edible would be welcome. But this is delicious.'

Nacre poured fresh spring water into two cups and handed them over.

'How did you learn about what happened on Ragnar?' Grant asked, after he had drunk deeply.

The Alien Grey leader smiled. 'On my way here, the tracking devices on my spacecraft picked up a familiar signal – a signal emanating from another craft that once was ours. It remained in stationary orbit of Ragnar for a short while, before setting off in pursuit of a small fleet of Quartet warships. My curiosity piqued, I visited the Ragnar battlefield. It was an unpleasant experience. However, I was able to determine that there were survivors and tracked them – that is to say, you – here.'

Magda became alert. 'The spacecraft that was once yours... Would that now be in the possession of my former associate, the man who killed Rufus Pearl's assassin?

'If you mean Avon, yes.'

Grant seemed startled. 'You mean Avon was on Ragnar?'

'It would seem so. After the battle, if such it was, that is.'

'I always thought he would help if he could,' Magda said.

'Yes you did,' Grant said bitterly, 'but he was too late. Why am I not surprised?'

Nacre refilled their cups. 'I have only heard of Avon. I have never encountered him. His reputation, for want of a better word, suggests that any encounter might be dangerous. Perhaps you feel differently?'

'Oh, he's dangerous all right,' said Grant.

'But if he's on your side,' Magda interrupted, 'he's only a danger to your opponents.'

After a pause, Nacre said, 'It is my understanding that my predecessor, Rufus, loaned Avon the spacecraft called George.'

Grant laughed. 'Avon will have considered it a gift. You are unlikely to get it back.'

'It is my further understanding,' Nacre continued, 'that he is in possession of an advanced computer.' His eyes narrowed. 'The George spacecraft is of no consequence, but the computer interests me.'

Again, Grant laughed. 'Orac interests a great many people. If you, like them, want to get your hands on it, you won't only have to go through Avon. You'll have to challenge the Quartet, the Cathay Empire and any number of independent warlords, bandits and other undesirables.'

Nacre turned to Magda. 'But you might persuade him to, if not part with this Orac, share it for a little while. During which "little while" my people might exact some further revenge upon those who ordered the killing of Rufus Pearl.'

Magda looked thoughtful. 'I think my persuasive powers have waned somewhat. Certainly as far as Avon is concerned.'

'But you believed he would come to your aid on Ragnar, and he did.'

'He'll be long gone by now,' Grant said.

'On the contrary, the George spacecraft has broken off its pursuit of the Quartet air fleet and is presently entering this quarter of the Beyond.'

Grant looked astonished. Magda's eyes lit up.

Nacre smiled, not altogether pleasantly. 'I believe Avon is looking for you. And I am inclined to help him find you.'

Magda shook her head. 'He cannot be of any help to us now. Our fight with the Quartet is over.'

'Nevertheless, he's in the vicinity. This suggests you are of importance to him,' Nacre said. 'I wonder what value he places upon you? Might it be sufficient for him to come to some kind of an arrangement regarding the use of Orac?'

'You would trade us for Orac?' Magda said, alarmed.

'He'd die first,' Grant said fiercely.

'If necessary, that can be arranged.'

Grant and Magda now noticed that they were surrounded by armed Greys.

'If you attempt to use your gun,' Nacre said, 'you will be shot out of hand.' He smiled down at Grant. 'You are of little consequence. It is the woman Avon is coming for.'

Grant tossed his gun aside. He smiled up at Nacre. 'You're making a big mistake. When I said Avon would die to stop you getting your hands on Orac, what I really meant was *you* might die.'

Nacre laughed. 'I do not fear this has-been terrorist.'

'Oh, but you should,' Magda said.

'We are locked into a tracking device,' said Orac.

Avon, who had been lost in thought, was startled out of his reverie. 'Can you identify the source?'

'Ask George.'

Before Avon could pose the question, George spoke. 'The source is an Alien Grey warship. This spacecraft is a Grey and there is an automatic tracking link whenever Grey ships are within range of each other. It is considered to be a reliable security device.'

'Except that this Grey spacecraft is now under my control.'

Orac seemed to chuckle. 'Not for much longer, it would seem. You stole this ship and the chances are the Greys will want it back. If you allow the tracker to persist, they have a very good chance of achieving that aim.'

'What's to do about it?'

'Disable the tracker. Cut the Grey link.'

Avon frowned. 'That means I will have to disconnect George. In effect, destroy it.'

Orac was silent.

'There is a communication,' George said quietly.

'Relay it.'

A somewhat nasal sounding voice suffused the air of the flight deck. 'Greetings, Avon. I am Egil Nacre, Leader of all Alien

Greys. You are doubtless aware that my warship is in range of the spacecraft that you – how shall I put it – *borrowed* from my predecessor, Rufus Pearl. I hasten to say that I mean you no harm. On the contrary, I am eager to make your personal acquaintance and render you any assistance. I am currently playing host to your former comrades, Del Grant and Magda Lens. They are just as eager to become reacquainted with you. Might you consider joining me on the warship, when you and they can be reunited and we may discuss any mutual requirements? George can open a voice link for you to reply.'

Orac snorted. '"Playing host to Grant and Lens" means they are hostages and "mutual requirements" means you might get what you want, but only as long as he gets me.'

'He sounds reasonable enough,' said Avon sceptically.

'His voice pattern is disguised, and it reeks of duplicity.'

'I never knew you were an expert on voice patterns.'

'There's a lot you don't know about me.'

'What's your advice?'

'Do what you have to do. Destroy George!'

'What will that achieve?'

Orac sighed. 'It'll cut the tracking beam from the warship permanently. In addition, you will be able to communicate with Egil Nacre only if you want to and you can decide when. Without George, no Alien Greys will be able to know where you are as, in addition to the distance tracker, all scanning systems will fail to operate. Except yours, that is. I would then suggest that we enter stealth mode and get away from here. Preferably before Nacre guesses what you're up to and, while you're in vision, comes after us with his warship's guns blazing.'

'Where would I go?'

'Go anywhere but here.'

'You're forgetting Grant and Magda. If you're right and I run, Nacre will have no further use for them. He'll kill them.'

'As you are so fond of saying Avon, we all die, it's just a question of when.'

Avon shook his head wearily. Then he opened the hatch to the fuel locker and descended. He re-emerged clutching a small phial of nitroglycerin. He moved towards the flight console housing the computer and, carefully placing the phial of explosive to one side, equally carefully opened the entry point to George's innards. He made one or two adjustments before, even more carefully, spilling a minuscule amount of nitro onto a small cloth. He placed the cloth within George and closed its entry point. He returned to the fuel locker and replaced the nitroglycerin phial in its ice pack. Back on deck, he closed the hatch. He moved across the flight deck and stood by Orac. 'This will only be a small explosion, but it will be sufficient to rip George apart,' he said quietly, almost sorrowfully.

'Surely you are not becoming sentimental about a mere machine?' Orac said acidly.

Avon ignored the remark. 'When I instruct George to come online, the charge will be triggered. We are at a safe enough distance. In any case, the explosion will be interior.'

Orac said nothing.

Avon sighed. 'George. I need to talk to you.'

The computer came online. 'I am Geo...'

A muffled explosion cut it short. The computer echoed Avon's sigh.

There was a terrible silence. Avon broke it by enquiring of Orac, 'Are you sure you can fly this machine and control all its other functions?'

'Of course I can. While you were running around playing the hero, I downloaded all relevant information from George.'

'In which case, enter stealth mode and we'll run away.'

'Discretion is the better part of valour, Avon.'

'I was never one to be discreet. We'll run, but not far away. I have unfinished business in these parts.'

'The two women will require some kind of a reward,' Sarin said, as he and Pandora Ess viewed Steiner's corpse.

'It is my intention to announce that the good general died of a tumour in his brain. The women are the only ones, apart from you and me, who know differently. Eliminate them,' Pandora Ess said, almost casually.

Sarin paled slightly, then nodded. 'It shall be done.' He hesitated before asking, 'Will the cause of death be believed, do you think. Might not some be suspicious?'

'They can be suspicious all they like, but a brain tumour is my expert opinion.' She turned and fixed Sarin with a steely look. 'After all, my dear Sarin, I am a doctor!'

'Are there any other tasks you wish me to fulfil?'

'Yes. You are to fly to the Base and inform Gabriella of the turn of events. Send her borrowed confidant, Adonis, back to me. You will take his place until I decide otherwise.'

'Won't that make Gabriella suspicious of your intentions?'

'Of course it will. But, along with you, Adonis is my close ally. However, he has given Gabriella a very different impression. It is her belief that, upon her command, Adonis will assassinate me. She will, therefore, not raise much of an objection to his departure,' Pandora Ess smiled.

Sarin shook his head. 'I fear I am out of my depth when it comes to political manoeuvres.'

'As long as you remain loyal, you have nothing to fear.' Pandora Ess touched Sarin lightly upon his cheek. 'Keep an eye on Gabriella for me?'

'Of course, I shall. But you already have troops loyal to you stationed on the Base.'

'Indeed I have. You will assume command of them, at the same time reassuring Gabriella of my good intentions.'

'May I enquire what you may be doing in my absence?'

The steely look returned. 'You may enquire, but the business I am about, should I care to explain, would merely confirm how out of your depth you fear you are.'

Egil Nacre was furious. He stormed off the command bridge of his warship and made his way to his private quarters, brushing aside any who got in his way. 'Ex has lost our tracking and scanning capabilities,' he fumed. 'The terrorist and his wonder computer have dropped out of sight. Only the gods will know where they are.'

Alexandra, the Huntress, lounging on a couch, burst out laughing.

'What's so funny?'

'You are! It is not Ex who is to blame. I think you'll find that it was Avon who, as it were, cut his ties with you.'

'And how would he do that?' Nacre asked, sarcastically.

'He will have done what I would in his position. Destroyed the on-board computer.'

'But the computer is the heartbeat of the spacecraft!'

'It isn't now! Avon has Orac to take its place.'

Nacre shook his head in disbelief. 'I grossly underestimated this man.'

'Yes, you did. But you are not the first to have done so. Have a drink and calm yourself.'

Nacre snapped his fingers and a mute attendant – a lower caste Grey – poured him a large measure of liquor. Nacre downed it in one and the attendant refilled the glass, before being cursorily dismissed.

'What will you do now?' Alexandra asked.

Nacre spoke through clenched teeth. 'I'll kill Grant and throw the woman to the lower caste men to do with her what they will.'

Alexandra sighed. 'If you do so, you lose any leverage you might have over Avon.'

Nacre snorted disagreeably. 'You don't think he's still out there, do you?'

'That's exactly what I think. You may not be able to track or scan him, but he can track and scan you.'

Nacre looked around, as if expecting Avon to jump out of the shadows.

Alexandra said, 'Have another drink. You look as though you need it to give you courage.'

Nacre drank then slumped into a chair. 'What do you want me to do?'

'Set this warship on course for your home planet. Move slowly, thereby giving Avon time to keep up.'

'You really think he'll follow?'

'I'd bet his life on it.'

'Why would he? He has effectively abandoned Grant and the woman.'

'That's what he wants you to think, so that you will lower your guard.'

'But he must know that I'll want to kill my hostages.'

'Wanting to kill and actually killing are two different things. He is more than likely to assume that you will let them live. By doing so, you give him an incentive not to abandon them.' Alexandra shrugged. 'Of course, were you to kill them that would give him another incentive. He would seek vengeance. Either way, you can be sure he's not going to leave you alone. He'll make a mistake – we all make mistakes – and that will give us an opportunity to outwit him and fulfil our purpose.'

'Your purpose, you mean.'

'However you wish to put it. You are being paid very well, in addition to securing your position as an ally of the Quartet. You wouldn't want to go against the Quartet, would you?'

Nacre shivered.

'What else do you want me to do?'

Alexandra's eyes narrowed. 'When I'm ready you'll do what I tell you, or else!'

Nacre shivered again.

'He's moving around a great deal,' Micah said, 'apparently to no purpose. And he keeps disappearing and reappearing, like a spectre.'

'He'll be looking – very cautiously – for his lost friends,' Fu Ti remarked.

'We can be certain they survived Ragnar?'

'Oh yes!'

'Well, at least he doesn't know we are shadowing him.'

'I wouldn't be too sure of that.'

'How could he know?'

'You seem to forget he controls an advanced capability computer.'

'I haven't forgotten,' Micah said bitterly. 'I'd like to know, though, how long we must continue to babysit Avon and it.'

'For as long as our empress requires.'

'I thought we answered to General Li Lang?'

'You answer to me,' Fu Ti said testily. 'I answer to whomsoever our empress appoints my superior. Ultimately, though, I answer to her.'

'Do I detect that there is something you are not telling me?'

'I tell you all you need to know.'

Micah sulked.

The George spacecraft, in stealth mode, flew directly above the Alien Grey warship.

'Can you scan its interior?' Avon asked.

'I am currently engaged upon that task,' Orac replied, as irritably as ever.

'What can you see?'

'You are impatient. Impatience is not a virtue.'

'I'd like to know the warship's full complement – also, where Grant and Magda are likely to be held.'

Orac sighed. 'Heat scanners suggest that there are sixty-eight living bodies on board. I am able to separate Greys from other humanoid forms. Of the latter, there are three.'

Avon frowned. 'Grant and Magda only add up to two. Identify the third.'

'You don't ask much, do you? The third is a female Earthling.'

'I wonder where she came from.'

'That I cannot tell you, but there is a non-Grey, long-range pod in the warship's docking area. It has Quartet provenance.'

'Well now, that's very interesting. Where's the nearest Quartet base?'

'You have answered your own question.'

Avon paced the flight deck. 'The Base. It's ruled by Gabriella Travis. It was she who hired Solomon and Absalom Fisch to kill me and, quite possibly, capture you. Gabriella is not pure Earthling, so this female is an unknown quantity. I'm missing something here.' He stopped pacing. 'Search your files on Solomon Fisch. There just might be a connection.'

'That's very astute of you, Avon.'

'How long will you take to search the files?'

'You underestimate me,' Orac sighed. 'Solomon

fathered Absalom. He also fathered, by another woman, Alexandra. Solomon trained Absalom to take over his, to put it bluntly, assassination enterprise. Alexandra was trained to seek and locate their potential targets. She is known as the Huntress.'

'And a good guess would be that I am the target she is hunting.'

'It would seem to be the case, if this is Alexandra Fisch.'

'What are the odds?'

'It is roughly ninety eight point three nine seven four percent certain that the lady in question is the Huntress.'

'You have to admire her persistence.'

'It is a persistence born of hatred. Killing her father and half-brother was hardly likely to endear you to her.'

'I seem to have a strong attraction for venomous opponents.'

'I would venture to suggest that there is none more venomous an opponent than you.'

'I am glad to hear you think so highly of me. But I'm forgetting, machines cannot think. Or are you an exception?'

Orac crackled.

'This alters the situation slightly,' Avon said, after a moment's thought. 'The Alien Grey leader is working for the Quartet – specifically, Gabriella, who we can reasonably assume has placed this Huntress in command of him. She holds Grant and Magda hostage and she'll want to trade them for you. This suggests she'll keep them alive. At the same time, she wants me dead.' He smiled. 'She's got a problem.'

'Only if she is determined to get her hands on me, which would seem to be the arrangement she has made with Gabriella. She could, of course, renege and settle for killing you. In which case, you have the problem.'

'What do you suggest?'

'Abandon Grant and Lens to their respective fates. You've said yourself, the Huntress will let them live for as long as she imagines they are a means of getting at you. Candidly, that's their best chance of staying alive. Then you should run as far away as possible.'

'And spend what's left of my life wandering the universe like some latter-day Flying Dutchman, always looking over my shoulder, never knowing when nemesis will put in an appearance?'

'It's what you've been doing for decades. You are too old to change your ways.'

'That's what you think, is it?'

'You have pointed out that machines cannot think.'

'All right, we'll move away, in plain sight, but we won't run. We'll take things slowly,' Avon said brightly.

'What do you have in mind?' Orac asked.

'Egil Nacre and the Huntress must know by now that I won't attempt to rescue Grant and Magda from their clutches whilst they're securely held on board a formidable warship. Seeing us leave will surely suggest that I've run out of alternative ideas. So they'll have to come up with something to tempt me back into their game. My guess is they'll set a trap, by appearing to release their prisoners. They'll dump them somewhere en route to the Base then, when I turn up to spirit them away to freedom, they'll jump out of the shadows and ambush me.'

'You have a lurid imagination,' Orac said.

'We are agreed that the Huntress is persistent. She won't give up a very good chance of catching me out. Putting myself in her position, it's the kind of trap I'd set.'

'And you are prepared to walk into it?'

'Oh no – I intend setting a trap of my own.'

'It will be a complete waste of time if you're wrong about this,'Orac sighed, 'but what do you have in mind?'

'Scan ahead of the warship. Find a likely planetoid, or whatever, that could attract the Huntress as a dumping ground. We'll get there ahead of her and... loser wins!'

The Orac computer ticked like a clock. 'It might work,' it said finally. 'The warship must leave the Beyond, for fear of interference from unpredictable outside forces. In deep space, a sufficient distance from the Base to tempt you to launch a rescue mission, there is a likely place. An abandoned planetoid called Abyss.'

Avon was startled. 'Why would it be called that?'

'Well, when we get there, we might find out. You're not afraid, are you?' Orac chuckled. 'After all, Avon, you have stared into the abyss on a number of occasions.'

'You're right about that, I suppose. My only concern is that this Abyss might stare back.'

'Shall I set a course?'

'When it seems that we have fooled the opposition into thinking I've given up the chase and they lose sight of us. Then set the course as fast as you like.'

'Consider it done.'

PART THREE
The Beginning of the End

Unable to communicate with Fu Ti, Eugene Furneaux's task of pacifying the Cathay Empire, whilst Pandora Ess pursued her now accelerated ambitions, had proved difficult. However, he considered himself to be a first-class diplomat and, he smugly reassured himself, he had proved his mettle in the past. He decided that a degree of boldness was asked for, so he made contact with General Li Lang.

The general received him upon his warship that protected the skies above Cathay. Though a little irritated by the intrusion, Li Lang did not betray it and treated Furneaux with respect. There was no sign of Li Lang's mistress, Furneaux's spy.

'I must beg your pardon,' Furneaux said obsequiously, 'but, unable to establish contact with the honourable Fu Ti, I am obliged to turn to you and hope you will indulge me.'

Li Lang nodded then frowned. 'I also am unable to establish communication with Fu Ti. I fear that he may have taken it upon himself to exceed his orders and, consequently, may offend against the cordial relationship between your Quartet and my Empire.'

'That would not seem to be the case at this time,' Furneaux said, smiling hesitantly.

Li Lang smiled in return. 'So, how may I be of assistance to you, Eugene?'

'Doctor Pandora Ess has requested that I inform the Empire of Cathay of her intentions – our intentions – with regard to the future structure of the Quartet.'

Li Lang raised an eyebrow, if only slightly.

Furneaux hurried on. 'She and I have reached the conclusion that it is unworkable in its present form. It has proved necessary to remove one of its members from office. General Steiner is the case in point.'

Li Lang really did smile this time. 'Am I to take it that Steiner has been removed – permanently?'

'That is so.'

'Well, as you are aware, there is no love lost there. The empress, I believe, will not be displeased.'

Furneaux hesitated for a moment before speaking. 'Might it be possible to arrange an audience with your empress?'

Li Lang looked at him sharply. 'I am her chosen representative and may convey your thoughts to her.'

'Forgive me, but you are her military representative and Doctor Ess believes, as do I, that a diplomatic meeting would serve both our interests. Of course, if such a meeting can be arranged, I would be honoured if you would accompany me.'

Li Lang said nothing for what seemed a long time. Instead, he stared at Furneaux until, embarrassed, the younger man cast down his eyes. It was only then that Li Lang spoke. 'I will arrange the meeting. I have considerable influence with the Empress.'

Furneaux was effusive. 'That is why I came to you. You should know that you are held in the highest esteem by all members of the Quartet.'

'Except, that is, for the late General Steiner!' Li Lang laughed.

After a moment, Furneaux thought it best to join in.

The recalcitrant Fu Ti was deep in thought when Micah exclaimed, 'I've regained contact with our friend, although, what he's up to now is somewhat bewildering.'

'How is it bewildering?'

'He is leaving the Beyond on a curving course, as if he's trying to avoid something. It looks as though he's heading into deep space. If I didn't think it unlikely, I would guess he is about to move in the direction of the Base.'

'It seems to me,' said Fu Ti, 'that while we were out of contact, Avon has been pursuing a lead. In other words, following another spacecraft that you have not identified – a spacecraft that, perhaps, carries his quarry, Grant and Lens. Why have you not identified it?'

'I was concentrating on Avon's spacecraft.'

'Kindly use extreme scanning procedure and find the other – if there is another.'

Micah, flushed with embarrassment, manipulated a set of controls. 'Ah, there it is.'

'Describe it.'

'It's an Alien Grey warship.'

'Hardly surprising, as this is the far reach of Grey space and territory.'

'I can't understand how I missed it.'

'Avon has been in and out of stealth mode. I concede that it was difficult to keep track of him and, consequently, any other craft,' Fu Ti said forgivingly. 'I think we may assume that I am correct. Alien Greys have rescued Magda – not for the first time – and Grant with her.'

'Then why is Avon breaking away?'

Fu Ti's brow creased in further thought. 'It is possible that the Greys are now hostile towards him. He did, after all, steal their spacecraft. Which suggests they are reluctant to part with their guests unless... unless they receive something in exchange, other than the spacecraft.'

'You mean the computer?'

'Well, everybody else seems to want it.'

'That includes us!'

'Is it possible,' Fu Ti whispered to himself, 'that the Greys are joined with the Quartet?'

Whispered or not, Micah heard his words. 'It would not be the first time.'

'You are quite right, Micah. We are all playing a game, the ultimate prize of which is Orac. But I have a feeling someone may have changed the rules.'

'He's onto us!' Micah exclaimed.

'What?'

'Avon knows we're here. When I expanded our scanning range, his scanners must have interacted.'

Unaccustomed as he was to using oaths, Fu Ti uttered one.

'Shall we withdraw?' Micah said anxiously.

'No. We'll follow him at a discreet distance. It may be that he might care to contact us.'

'He might care to attack us.'

'I don't think so. He knows this Dragon ship outguns him.'

'Since when has that stopped him?'

Fu Ti could not help but smile.

*

The George spacecraft, entering the pitch darkness of deep space – no suns of Aegisthus here – began to accelerate, albeit following an erratic course.

'You're sure it's Fu Ti's Dragon ship?' Avon asked.

'I never pronounce upon anything unless I am sure.'

'So he's been tracking us all the while. I wonder why?'

'It could be that he is very fond of you. On the other hand, I would suggest he is fonder of me.'

Avon laughed.

'We are still being tracked by the Dragon ship, but we have eluded the Alien Grey warship,' Orac said.

'Fu Ti will be reluctant to get too close to the Base. We'll give him the impression that's where we're going. Set a direct course, at speed.'

'Abyss is not in a direct line with the Base. We must detour slightly.'

'We'll do that at the last possible moment. I don't want the Dragon ship frightening off Nacre and the Huntress. So we'll lose it.'

A jet heliplane conveyed Furneaux and Li Lang from the latter's warship to the square in front of the Forbidden City in the heart of Beijing – the capital of the Cathay Empire, on Earth and throughout the universe.

Although he had visited before, Furneaux could not help but be impressed by the magnificence of the palace within the city. Li Lang seemed indifferent, but was irritated by the fact that they were being kept waiting – which he regarded as showing a lack of respect.

In due course, though, they were greeted by an attractive young woman wearing a black cheongsam offset by a red waistband. She smiled and bowed, but not too low. This further irritated Li Lang, but he did not show it.

'Please follow me,' their hostess said softly.

They walked unhurriedly along a wide, luxuriously carpeted corridor towards two massive, ornately decorated doors, presently closed. Furneaux noticed, with a degree of alarm, that armed guards stood duty at intervals. Li Lang ignored them. When they reached the doors, they opened, as if by magic, and revealed a large, exquisitely furnished room, at one end of which was a small velvet throne. No-one occupied it. In the centre of the room stood a tall, pale-faced gentleman, dressed similarly to their guide, but in the male fashion. More guards were in evidence, but discreetly. Furneaux, despite the fact that the room was air-cooled, began to perspire.

The black-clad gentleman with a red sash smiled and bowed – but not low. Furneaux bowed in return. Li Lang did not and his discourtesy did not go unnoticed.

'I am Sun Cheng,' said the tall man. 'You are welcome.'

'I understood that an audience with the empress was in order?' Li Lang said irascibly.

Sun Cheng spread his hands in a form of apology. 'I regret to inform you that Her Imperial Majesty is absent from Beijing.'

'Where is she?'

Sun Cheng grew even paler. The impertinence of the question clearly annoyed him. 'I regret to inform you that I am unable to say.'

'Then we are wasting our time here,' Li Lang said angrily, turning to leave. But the doors were firmly shut and two guards stood in front of them, forbidding egress. Li Lang turned back to Sun Cheng. 'I wish to leave,' he said, anger mounting.

'I regret to inform you that it is not permitted – for the moment.' Sun Cheng smiled. 'We have not yet enjoyed the formality of the taking of tea.' He gestured to a table set to one side of the room. 'Kai Kim will do us the honour of serving us.' He gestured towards their escort.

Kai Kim smiled and bowed, a little lower this time, which appeased Li Lang somewhat.

They took their places at table, seated on small divans. Kai Kim poured tea into tiny cups and stood back, in expectation of their appreciation.

Furneaux smiled, if a little nervously. 'This is exquisite,' he said.

Li Lang did not touch his cup. 'What is your purpose in detaining me?' he asked brusquely.

Sun Cheng, having sipped tea, wiped his mouth with a silk cloth. 'I conclude that gentle formalities cause you irritation, Li Lang.'

'I am General Li Lang, commander of the Imperial Air Fleet and I require that you treat me with the courtesy due to my rank.'

Cheng sighed theatrically. 'I am Marshall Sun Cheng, commander of all imperial forces, and I will treat you as I see fit.'

Li Lang rose to his feet. 'Since when have you held this command?'

Sun Cheng also stood. 'Since the empress honoured me with it as she was leaving for... elsewhere.'

Furneaux, his nervousness increasing, looked up at both of them.

Li Lang looked about him. Some guards were closer than before. 'Why have we never met before?' he asked.

Sun Cheng smiled. 'I have fought on the ground, you are in the air,' he shrugged. 'That is a possible explanation. Otherwise, it may be because I am charged with overseeing matters of security – a secret policeman, if you like – and, therefore, I keep a low profile.'

'Until now, that is.'

Sun Cheng inclined his head.

Li Lang's tone hardened. 'In which capacity do you seek to detain me? As a soldier or a policeman?'

'The latter, it pains me to say.' Cheng signalled to a guard by the main doors. The guard stepped aside as they opened and a woman, dishevelled and clearly in some distress, was thrust into the room. She was Li Lang's mistress, Furneaux's spy.

Furneaux rose clumsily to his feet. Li Lang stood very still.

'You are familiar with this young lady, of course,' Cheng said coolly. 'As will you be, Eugene.' He moved closer to Li Lang. 'What you may not know, General, is that she is an agent of the Quartet and has shared your bed in order to learn the secrets of Cathay, which she then imparts to Furneaux here.'

Li Lang lowered his head. 'I had my suspicions,' he whispered.

'But you failed to act upon them.'

'She was interrogated by my people,' Li Lang said defiantly. 'They could find no fault.'

The woman was kneeling on the floor whimpering. A look of irritation crossed Cheng's pale face. 'Do be quiet!'

'What do you intend to do with me?' Li Lang asked.

'I intend to do nothing,' Cheng said gravely. 'It is for you to decide what you intend.'

Li Lang nodded. 'I should like to be escorted to my apartments.'

Sun Cheng spoke to a guard. 'Tung Ma, you will accompany the general.'

The guard bowed in acquiescence. He and Li Lang left the room.

After a stony silence, Furneaux stuttered, 'What do you intend to do with me?'

'Oh, you will be returned to your spacecraft, in which you will leave our airspace, never to return.'

Furneaux breathed a sigh of relief.

'Kai Kim will arrange your transportation away from this palace and will attend upon you,' Cheng continued. 'You may leave.'

Furneaux plucked up some courage. 'What will happen to the woman?'

'Why would you care?' Cheng said acidly.

'I presume she will be put on trial?' Furneaux said, still courageous.

'She has already been tried and convicted. She will suffer the punishment meted out to all traitors.'

A guard stepped forward, drawing a pistol. Cheng nodded and the guard shot the woman in the back of the head.

Furneaux stepped back and uttered an anguished cry as blood and brain matter splattered the mosaic floor.

Kai Kim took his arm. 'We should go,' she said soothingly.

Sun Cheng turned back to the side table. 'The tea is cold,' he said. 'What a pity!'

Abyss was a cold, desolate place. Abandoned machinery

scattered the landscape close by where the pod had lowered itself upon the planetoid.

Avon wrinkled his nose in disgust. Overcoming his distaste, he scouted around for places of concealment. Apart from rusting vehicles and mining equipment, there were a number of dilapidated wooden huts and a concrete bunker.

Avon approached the latter with caution. He was surprised to find its interior warm and dry, thick walls keeping out what seemed to be a perpetual cold wind. There was a kitchen and dining area, a bathroom and sleeping space. Some of the kitchen utensils were in good condition, as was a table, some chairs and a number of cot beds. No mattresses though. He considered that this would be an ideal place in which to imprison hostages.

He had already concluded that where he had landed was the safest ground and, therefore, where any transportation carrying Grant, Magda and the Huntress would come. Always assuming he had accurately predicted that they would come.

He set about preparing a welcome for them.

'If you ask me, Avon is long gone,' Nacre said.

'I didn't ask you. You'll just have to trust my judgement when I tell you he's still out there, waiting for an opportunity to pounce,' Alexandra said.

Nacre sighed exasperatedly. 'But we saw him run away.'

'He didn't run. He merely altered his course to one that suits his plans.'

'I never would have guessed you were clairvoyant. What plans might they be?'

'He'll follow us, or parallel us, as we make our way towards the Base, looking for an opportunity to catch us off-guard and mount his rescue attempt. I intend to help him out.'

Nacre looked bewildered. 'How will you do so?'

Alexandra sighed. 'I'm really tired of dealing with amateurs. I'll set a trap for him by pretending to release our prisoners.'

Nacre laughed. 'Where will you pretend to release them? Are you going to throw them out of the emergency chute into deep space?'

Alexandra sighed again. 'The gods preserve me from fools!'
'Well, where?'
'I have somewhere in mind. It is called Abyss.'

Eugene Furneaux felt somewhat relieved when the jet heliplane lifted off from the heart of Beijing and transported him to what had been Li Lang's Dragon warship.

Kai Kim treated him with the utmost courtesy throughout the trip. He wondered what position she held in Cathay's military hierarchy. He was soon to find out. As the heliplane docked, he and she were greeted by a phalanx of guards. Their apparent leader, a burly, grizzled old soldier, saluted Kai Kim and bowed deeply.

'Welcome, General,' he said.

The guards sprang to attention. Furneaux started. Kai Kim was a general? He looked at her with new respect, tethered to a shiver of apprehension.

She turned to him. 'Captain Lee Sa will see that you are escorted to the pod that brought you here. It is fully equipped,' she smiled. 'I am sorry that we shall not meet again, Eugene. My uncle, Fu Ti, considered you to be a gentle enemy.'

Furneaux spluttered his thanks. He bowed. Kai Kim returned the compliment and moved on.

Captain Lee Sa smiled cruelly. 'Come,' he said, in a tone that suggested he was about to lead Furneaux to the deepest dungeon, where he would suffer unimaginable tortures.

This did not prove to be the case. Eugene Furneaux entered the pod and took off without incident. Immediately upon arriving aboard his interplanetary cruiser, he instructed his pilot to make ready to leave Cathay airspace in all haste.

'How long before we are clear?' he asked anxiously.

'Six minutes,' the pilot replied.

Furneaux rushed to his small cabin, wiped the sweat from his brow and poured himself a stiff drink.

Kai Kim, attended by Lee Sa, watched from the warship's flight deck as the Quartet cruiser turned towards the darkness of space beyond planet Earth.

'How long before it is out of range?' she enquired.

'Four and a half minutes.'

'Is the missile aimed and locked on?'

'It is.'

'It is a Tiger missile, is it not? With a plutonium warhead?'

'It is.'

'What time will elapse before the missile reaches its target?'

'Three minutes.'

Kai Kim smiled grimly. 'Launch it at your discretion.'

Having deposited his charge at his apartment in the Forbidden City, Tung Ma waited in the entrance lobby of the building. He smoked a thin cheroot, passing the time by trying to blow smoke rings. He failed to do so.

When the cheroot was down to a small stub, Tung Ma extinguished it, before riding the elevator to Li Lang's floor. He pressed his ear to the door of the apartment and listened intently. There was no sound that he could hear. He entered the apartment and made his way to Li Lang's private office.

Li Lang was sprawled over a table, as if drunk, a pistol close by his half-clenched hand. Tung Ma studied the former general's corpse and smiled with satisfaction. The bullet had entered the dead man's right temple – a clean shot. Tung Ma bowed towards the body, turned and left the room.

Eugene Furneaux, on his second drink and a little calmer as a result, wondered how it had come about that his spy, Li Lang's mistress, had been exposed. No-one, other than himself, knew of her... except... Furneaux cursed. He had revealed her existence to one other – Doctor Pandora Ess! He cursed again. Well, he vowed, there would come a reckoning with that lady.

Except, there wouldn't, because, as the realisation of betrayal dawned upon him, a Tiger missile struck his spacecraft amidships and blew it, and him with it, to smithereens.

A cloud darkened Earth's moon.

Sun Cheng smiled at his reflection in a mirror. He turned to Tung Ma and, still smiling, congratulated him.

'I am very pleased that you were able to persuade General Li Lang to behave in such an honourable fashion,' he said. 'You will be rewarded with a promotion, Tung Ma.'

Tung Ma beamed with pleasure.

Sun Cheng's smile faded. 'Have you dealt with the body of the woman?'

'According to your instruction, her corpse was deposited in the river,' Tung Ma said gravely.

Sun Cheng smiled again. 'That is good. The alligators are peckish at this time of year!'

'Are you sure you know what you're doing?' Orac asked.

'Well, if I'm not, we're in a heap of trouble,' Avon said, tucking a Five7 handgun into a holster attached to his belt, at the small of his back. The weightier Nine7 he placed in a holster on his left side, its butt facing outwards so that he could execute a cross-draw. 'Any sign of the opposition?'

'The warship of Egil Nacre will pass by Abyss in half an Earth day as predicted. So, you don't have much time to return to the planetoid.'

'It's a dreadful place. I don't want to spend any more time there than I have to.'

'Are you sure where you landed is the only viable landing spot for the Huntress's pod?'

'I'm sure. Where are our "friends"?'

'They are currently stationary in deep space, trying to puzzle out where we've got to. Which they will, eventually.'

'But too late to do anything about what we are up to.'

'That's the plan, isn't it?'

'It is.'

'Are you ready?'

'As ready as I'll ever be.'

'Then let's go.'

'The pod is ready and Grant and Lens are on board, manacled,' Nacre said. 'Are you sure you can handle this alone?'

Alexandra smiled. 'I deal in death as a living.'

'How do we know Avon is out there?'

'Oh, he's out there. As soon as we began to orbit the planetoid, he will have guessed that that is where our hostages will be. He'll know it's a trap, of course, but he won't be able to resist falling into it. Are you sure you can handle your part?'

Nacre scowled. 'I am to withdraw my warship to a safe distance, shut down engines and extinguish all lights. Upon a signal from you that Avon is dead, I will manoeuvre towards his spacecraft and rendezvous with your pod.'

'Don't attempt to board until I get there. It's possible he'll have set traps.'

'How will you know how to disarm them?'

The Huntress smiled again. 'Before I kill him, I'll persuade Avon to tell me how.'

Nacre shuddered.

'What do you want me to do with Grant and Lens?' Alexandra asked.

'What do you suggest?'

'Well, I would kill them, but taking them to the Base might gain you some appreciation from Gabriella. They are, after all, terrorists who have threatened the Quartet and she would probably enjoy making them pay for their indiscretions.' Alexandra shrugged. 'Whatever you decide, it makes no difference to me.'

'Delivering Orac should satisfy Gabriella.'

'Oh, I'll get her appreciation for that.'

'Of course, she will pay you.'

'You'll get your share, Egil. Just make sure you earn it.'

Abyss had not altered much since Avon had first visited the planetoid. If anything, it seemed colder and more desolate, but there was light. Reflected starlight, Avon guessed.

He guided the pod into the least ramshackle of the wooden huts he had previously reconnoitred and set about concealing it. He made a number of other preparations and settled down to wait. The Quartet pod, piloted by Alexandra, did not keep him waiting long.

Alexandra landed close by the concrete bunker. She wasted

no time, having checked it out, transferring Grant and Magda inside. Drugged – an extra precaution the Huntress had decided was necessary – and manacled, they stumbled towards the bunker's far wall, where she secured them. She then returned to the pod and activated a device that would explode should any other attempt to board it. Carrying a heavy equipment bag, she walked away from the bunker and took up a position inside the darkest of the huts. She settled down to wait.

At one point, the Huntress had remarked to Egil Nacre that 'we all make mistakes'. She had assumed that Avon would not know, or even guess, Grant and Magda would be deposited on Abyss. Until, that is, he observed the Grey warship he had been tracking launch the pod that took them there. That was her second mistake. The first was to allow her thirst for revenge to alter her perception of reality. Solomon and Absalom Fisch were the killers. Alexandra was the Huntress, but only in the sense that she tracked down their prey and set it up for their kill. She had been an accomplice to death, not an executioner. By attempting to kill Avon herself, the Huntress was stepping out of her comfort zone and into his.

Egil Nacre, his pride ruffled by Alexandra's superior attitude towards him and eager to prove his worth, nevertheless obeyed her instruction and withdrew his warship accordingly – but not for long.

Once he received her signal that she had landed on Abyss, he reversed course and headed for the George spacecraft. In its proximity, he launched a drone pod in its direction and, by remote control, guided it towards the craft's docking bay. If Avon had set traps, or was on board – the latter was possible, he supposed – the drone would set them off and the oh-so-clever Avon would be hoist with his own petard.

If there were no traps, he would lead a boarding party, reclaim the spacecraft, and Orac with it. It would be quite a coup. He couldn't really lose. If Alexandra killed Avon, all well and good. She could not fail to be impressed by his enterprise. If she failed – well, 'we all make mistakes'.

Nacre permitted himself a smile as the drone pod docked. Nothing happened!

Nacre squealed with delight. He, Ex and Zed scrambled aboard a conventional pod and flew the short distance between the warship and the stolen George. There was just enough room for the pod to dock, next to the drone. The three Greys moved cautiously from the docking area to the flight deck. It was a Grey spaceship, so they were familiar with its layout. Nacre − no hero he − let Ex and Zed go first.

Zed called out that all was clear and Egil Nacre, leader of the Greys, strode on to the deck to reclaim what was his and acquire something that was not. But there was no sign of Orac.

'She's in a hut on the far side,' Orac said, its sound muffled by the thick blanket concealing it.

'What kind of weapons is she carrying?'

'She has a sniper rifle, a Five7 handgun and a ragged edged Bowie knife. She has set a charge on the pod, in case you hadn't noticed.'

'So Grant and Magda have been tethered as bait,' Avon said. 'I'm supposed to walk to the door of the bunker and she then guns me down. She must think I'm stupid.'

'She doesn't know you're here yet.'

'Then she's stupid.'

'I'm inclined to agree,' Orac said professorially. 'I'm not at all impressed by the family Fisch. Solomon and Absalom proved to be no match for you. Given her present situation, I very much doubt the Huntress will do any better.'

'She's not dead yet. What's happening on George?'

'Three Greys are on its flight deck. They'll be in a quandary. Since you have destroyed the George computer, it cannot be flown, except by me,' Orac said, 'and I'm not there!'

'Can you set off the charge on the Huntress's pod from here?'

'You don't have much faith in me, do you?'

'It's a simple question.'

'The simple answer is yes.'

'I'd like to get her out of the hut. If you blow the pod, that should do it.'

'There's really no need. She's on the move.'

'Where's she going?'

'There's rising ground just behind the hut and there's derelict machinery that will give her cover. Her rifle is locked and loaded. Perhaps she's not stupid after all.'

'The rifle's not going to do her much good if I can get close. Where is she exactly?'

'In the shadows of what was probably a crane.'

'I remember seeing it.'

'What are you going to do, Avon?'

'Well now, I'm going to slip out of the back of this hut and make my way towards that crane. Give me a couple of minutes then blow the pod – that should liven things up a bit.'

'It's ironic that livening things up will result in a death.'

'Let's hope it's not mine. I'm good to go. Are you ready?'

'You have two minutes and counting,' Orac said.

Alexandra had a better view of the concrete bunker's entrance, the shadows of the crane offering good concealment. She was becoming impatient – which was unusual for someone who had spent her life assiduously and painstakingly searching out targets for her father and half-brother.

She wanted Avon dead. But she also wanted him to die slowly, in the full knowledge of who was killing him and why. She smiled to herself, as she imagined what she could do to him to make him beg for death.

The pod exploded, sending a massive flame shooting up into the sky. Shaken and momentarily blinded by the flash, Alexandra staggered into the open. This was her third and final mistake.

As the flame subsided, her sight was restored, and Alexandra turned back to the shadows. As she did so, a soft metal garrotte snaked round her throat. She gasped and, dropping her rifle, clutched at it, but only succeeded in cutting her fingers. Instinctively, her bloodied hand clasped the Bowie knife in her belt.

'I wouldn't do that,' said a chilling voice. The garrotte tightened and she dropped the knife.

'Finish it!' she said, her voice little more than a croak.

Avon finished it. He laid the Huntress's corpse on the ground. Then he picked up the knife and the rifle, stuck the knife in his belt, set the safety catch on the gun and ambled down from the rising ground to the concrete bunker.

He entered warily, in case Alexandra had set any booby traps, although Orac had assured him she hadn't. Manacled to a metal rod attached to the far wall, Magda was still suffering the effects of being drugged and was semi-conscious, her head resting on Grant's shoulder. Grant was wide awake, however. He stared at Avon.

'Well,' he said. 'You took your time!'

On board the George spacecraft, Nacre was becoming agitated. Ex and Zed had searched most of the ship, but Orac could not be found. 'Open this hatch and go below,' Nacre said, 'check what's down there.'

Zed went below. 'There are two fuel rods and some phials of a liquid I don't recognise,' he called out.

'Bring them up.'

Zed did so. He handed the fuel rods to Nacre who, in turn, handed them to Ex. 'Destroy them! If we can't fly this ship, without fuel, neither can Avon.'

'But, once we get our hands on his computer,' Ex protested, 'we will be able to fly it. Without fuel, even Orac couldn't fly.'

Nacre scowled. 'I don't want anything further to do with this spacecraft. When we return to the warship, I intend to blow it apart.'

'Alexandra might have something to say about that,' Zed said quietly.

Nacre turned on him. 'You obey me, not Alexandra. Do you understand?'

Suitably cowed, Zed nodded.

'Do we wait for her here?' Ex asked.

Nacre hesitated. 'No. We'll go back and wait for her to rendezvous with me.'

Zed, still holding the phials of liquid he didn't recognise, moved to the flight console. 'I wonder how he destroyed George,' he muttered. He placed the phials on the floor by the console. The liquid inside them shook.

'It doesn't really matter, does it?' Nacre said irritably.

'If I knew, I might be able to fix it.'

Nacre snorted disgustedly and disgustingly.

Zed placed his hand on the console and received an electric shock that threw him backwards across the flight deck.

Nacre stepped aside in alarm. Ex did likewise.

Zed groaned, shuddered and lay still.

'Is he dead?' Nacre asked, his eyes wide with fear.

Ex approached the body on the floor. Without touching, he leaned over it. 'Yes.'

'Let's get out of here. We don't know what other traps the terrorist has set.' Nacre made for the flight deck exit.

'You're just going to leave the corpse here?' Ex said contemptuously.

'Well, he's no use to anybody now, is he?'

Ex didn't move.

'Stay if you want,' Nacre said angrily, 'but don't expect me to come back for you.' He stomped off the deck.

After a moment, Ex reluctantly followed. But before he did so, he placed the fuel rods on the floor, next to the phials of hissing liquid, as a small gesture of defiance.

'How do we get off this place?' Grant asked, after he and Magda had been released from their chains. Magda, still a little groggy, smiled at Avon though her brow was furrowed, as if she wasn't quite sure who he was.

'There's a pod concealed in a hut. There'll be room for the three of us and Orac,' Avon said coolly.

'I take it you killed the woman?'

Avon nodded.

'After she got you, she was going to kill us or turn us over to the Quartet. I don't know which would have been worse,' Grant said.

'Well, she didn't get me.'

'What do you intend to do with us?'

Avon shrugged. 'I'll take you wherever you want to go.'

'Is that it?'

'That's it.'

'You're not inclined to join forces again and take on the Federation – I mean, the Quartet?'

'No, I'm not inclined.'

'Why did you come for us then?' Grant asked, curiously.

'Well, I just happened to be in the neighbourhood and it seemed like a good idea.'

'He was lost, but is found again,' Xian said as she pored over the device tracking Avon's spacecraft.

Fu Ti, who had been dozing, looked up. 'Where is he now?'

'Well, his spacecraft is in stationary orbit of a planetoid called Abyss and currently in the gun sights of the Alien Grey warship we believed he was tracking. It would seem the Greys have boarded their former property, but are now returning to their mothership in a pod, preceded by a drone.'

Fu Ti frowned and gnawed his lower lip. 'Can it be that an Alien Grey has succeeded where all others have failed?'

Xian smiled. 'Avon isn't there and neither, I would wager, is the computer. The Greys are leaving empty handed.'

'I thought you said you had found Avon?'

'The pod you kindly donated to him is located on the surface of Abyss. He'll be with it.'

'Ah, I think I begin to understand,' Fu Ti said, sorrowfully.

'What do you begin to understand?'

'The Greys will have set a trap for Avon on Abyss and, it would seem, he has fallen into it.'

Xian smiled again. 'I never thought you'd underestimate our friend. If there was a trap, he's avoided it. The pod is leaving Abyss, on a course for the spacecraft. I'm running a scan.'

Fu Ti moved towards Xian and looked over her shoulder. 'What can you see?'

'There are three people on board the pod. But something has locked on to our scanner and is trying to block it. Not only trying, it's succeeding.'

'It must be Orac.' Fu Ti cursed silently. 'So, we've lost our scanning capability, at least for the time being. But our tracker is still functioning?'

'Until and unless Orac decides to block that too.'

Fu Ti gave the matter some thought. 'All right,' he said at last. 'Manoeuvre the Dragon so that we sit directly between the Grey warship and Avon's spacecraft. Open our gun ports. Do not trouble yourself to do so surreptitiously. I want to be in plain sight of the Greys.'

'They would be no match for us.'

'Let us hope they realise that and hold off.'

'But you'll shoot them down, if necessary?'

'You should never threaten without being prepared to carry out your threat. But I hope it won't come to that.'

'You would go to such lengths to save our terrorist friend?'

'I would go to such lengths to save Orac.'

Avon flew the pod, Orac at his feet, Grant and Magda huddled on the rear seat. Magda had still not recovered from the drugs administered by the late Alexandra.

'We need to get her aboard your spacecraft and do something about her condition,' Grant said anxiously.

'I am aware,' Avon replied. 'I am also aware that there is an Alien Grey warship out there. And the Greys will be aware that this not the Huntress's flight pod.'

'You think they'll shoot us down?'

'Wouldn't you?'

'Not if I wanted to get my hands on Orac.'

'Well, let's hope they hold to that ambition.'

'How are you going to handle this?'

'I'm going to fly to the far side of the George spaceship.'

'But the pod dock is on this side.'

'Then I'm going to duck under the ship and reverse into the dock.' Avon smiled grimly. 'Of course, they could still shoot us down, assuming they are willing to destroy what is, after all, their property – and not forgetting Orac.'

'It's your call, Avon.'

'Well, let's hope I call it right.'

*

Egil Nacre and all aboard the Grey warship could not fail but to see the brightly lit Dragon ship interposing itself between them and their potential target.

'Their gun ports are open,' Nacre said superfluously.

Ex smiled. 'As are ours. Do you want to open fire on them?'

'Do you take me for a fool?'

Ex did not reply.

Nacre bit on a fingernail. 'They're trying to frighten us off. In any case, we cannot now fire on the George spacecraft,' he said. He frowned in concentration. 'This must mean they know Alexandra is on her way. They're guessing she's bringing Orac with her and mean to intercept her.'

'It could be that Avon is on his way and bringing Orac,' Ex said.

Nacre ignored the comment. 'We'll manoeuvre closer to Abyss. That way, when Alexandra sees the Dragon she'll know to fly to this warship directly.'

'If she's got Orac, she wouldn't need to fly anywhere else, would she?' Ex said insolently. 'And if it's Avon who is on his way we could lose this game.'

Nacre turned. 'What would you do?' he spat at Ex.

'Overfly Abyss. If Alexandra's pod is out there, she'll know to alter course so that we can pick her up, out of the Dragon ship's range. If it's Avon out there...'

'We shoot him down!' Nacre cried.

'You'll destroy Orac if you do.'

'So be it!'

When Avon saw the glow from the bright lights of the distant Dragon ship, he eased the pod to a virtual standstill.

'The Alien Grey warship is approaching,' Orac muttered.

'They're looking for the Huntress,' Avon said quietly.

Grant shifted uneasily in the back seat. 'They'll know straight away this isn't her pod. It doesn't have Quartet markings,' he said. 'They could open fire.'

'They could and they probably will,' Avon said, again speaking quietly.

'But they won't want to lose Orac, will they?'

'By destroying this pod and Orac with it, they guarantee that no-one else will get their hands on it. My guess is the Alien Grey will go for what he thinks is the sure thing.'

'What are you going to do?'

'Well, the situation calls for a change of plan. The Greys are between us and comparative safety. We can't stay here, we can't, for the moment, outrun their range of fire and I have no intention of returning to Abyss, so...'

'So, what are you going to do?'

'I've always believed in the axiom that the best form of defence is attack. I'm going to run this pod at top speed straight at them.'

Grant sounded aghast. 'But we have no weapons. We won't stand a chance.'

'We're a small, fast target − hard to hit. Also, there might be some hesitation on their part. I need hardly remind you of another favourite axiom: "He who hesitates is lost." Let's go!'

Avon piloted the pod into a direct line ahead of the approaching warship and accelerated towards it.

'There's a pod between us and Abyss,' Ex said. 'It's altering course slightly and is moving in our direction.'

'It must be Alexandra,' Nacre said excitedly.

'If it is, she's coming towards us at speed.'

'Of course she is. She'll have seen the lights of the Dragon ship. She'll want to come aboard as quickly as she can.'

'What if it isn't Alexandra? What if it's Avon?'

Nacre snorted. 'It has to be her. It would be suicide for Avon to attack this warship with a mere pod.'

'But only if we open fire on him.'

'Scan the pod and check for Quartet insignia.'

Ex almost laughed. 'Our scanners are out, remember? We have visual contact only.'

'Then take a good look.'

'It's moving too fast.'

Nacre bit a fingernail. 'It can't be Avon, can it?'

Before Ex could reply, the fast approaching pod dropped

several metres and flew under the warship. It emerged on its far side, the side nearest to the George spacecraft and the Dragon ship guarding it.

'It could be – and it is!' Ex managed to say.

'Open fire!' Nacre screamed.

'If we do that, the Dragon crew may think we're firing at them.'

'Do it anyway! We cannot let Avon get away.'

'Bringing middle-range cannon to bear on target,' Ex dictated through a mouthpiece that connected him to the ship's gunners. 'Are you sure you want to do this?'

Nacre's reply, if there had made one, would have been irrelevant. The pod altered course and disappeared.

'What happened there?' Grant asked incredulously.

'They hesitated! While they were deciding what to do about us, we went past them and Orac placed the pod in stealth mode.' Avon smiled, although Grant couldn't see it.

'We seem to be moving very slowly.'

'That's because we are. Stealth mode draws on a lot of fuel and the pod doesn't have much left. I'm trying to conserve it.'

'So the Greys could still open fire on us.'

'What would they be firing at – an empty space? Our friends from Cathay would conclude that they were being fired upon. They wouldn't like that.'

'Do we wait until the warship goes away?'

'We're drifting. Question is, are we drifting towards our preferred destination?'

'And are we?'

'What do you have to say about that, Orac?'

'We are, more or less, drifting in the right direction. In any case, we are now beyond medium range of the Grey warship's guns. The use of their long range weaponry, when we reappear, would be foolish in the extreme. They might hit the Dragon and the Greys must know retaliation would be swift and sure.'

Grant sighed. 'So, we're in the clear?'

'Not quite. We still need to get aboard the George spacecraft.'

'What's to stop us?'

'Cathay haven't helped us out of the kindness of their hearts. They want Orac, and trapping this pod in a magnetic field and dragging us on board their warship is a better chance of getting it than many they've had – or are likely to get.'

'We must get aboard somehow,' Grant said. 'Magda's sleeping now, but she must have treatment.'

'I'm working on it.'

'You could execute the manoeuvre you originally intended. Should you do so, the Dragon ship could not exert a magnetic field of sufficient strength and direction to trap the pod, as the George spacecraft would act as a block,' Orac said.

'Do we have enough fuel?'

'Yes. But only if we come out of stealth mode.'

Micah had joined Xian and Fu Ti on the Dragon ship's flight deck. 'This is a golden opportunity,' he said excitedly. 'We must open up a magnetic field.'

Fu Ti sighed. 'I have already done so. But I doubt it will do us much good. Avon is far too devious to be caught out by such a device.'

'What can he do? He's got to get aboard that spacecraft. He'll have to pass through the field.'

'Will he? Well, we'll see, shall we?'

'We could shoot him down,' Xian said lightly.

Fu Ti shook his head. 'I still have high hopes of acquiring Orac. Such action would dash those hopes.'

'Well, we can see him now,' Xian said. 'He's moving away to his right.' She frowned. 'What can he be thinking of?'

Fu Ti smiled. 'He's attempting to elude the magnets.'

Micah scowled. 'How can he know about them?'

'You forget Avon has been a guest on this Dragon ship. He will have taken note of all our capabilities.'

'He's curving beyond his spaceship,' Xian said. She laughed. 'Oh, you are so clever, Avon! He's approaching it from the blind side, using it as a buffer.'

'But he'll have to move to this side where the docking area for the pod is,' Micah said, a scowl replaced by a mocking smile. 'Perhaps he's not so clever, after all.'

'You really don't like him, do you?'

The scowl returned. 'What's to like?'

Having reached the far side of the George spacecraft, Avon turned the pod towards it. 'All right, here goes. I'm going to jump over the spacecraft like a flea.'

'I thought you were going to fly under it?' Grant said.

'That's what they'll be expecting and where the magnetic field will be concentrated.'

'But we'll still be caught in it at some point.'

'That's true, of course. After the jump, I'll reverse the pod at full speed towards the docking area.'

'At speed, you say? You'll crash into your own spacecraft?'

'The magnetic pull will slow us down. It will be like a tug of war.' Avon smiled. Again, Grant couldn't see it. 'This is going to be fun,' he muttered to himself. Then he hit a lever on the pod's flight control.

The pod shot upwards, like a bullet fired into the air. Avon levelled off, flew the pod over the George spaceship, and dropped it down until it was in a direct line with the docking area. He slammed the flight gears into reverse and accelerated.

'We've got him!' Micah cried out exultantly.

'I think not,' said Xian. 'The pod's at full speed and the magnets can't hold it.'

'Increase magnetism,' Micah shouted.

'It's already at full strength,' Xian said. 'Oh, you are so good at staying alive, Avon!' Then she laughed.

Slowly, for what seemed an eternity, the reverse speed of the pod fought the magnetic pull until, with a fierce jerk, it broke free. Avon cut speed and braked hard. Even so, the pod collided with the rear wall of the dock and collapsed, like a broken-winged bird.

Avon scrambled out of the wreckage with Orac, and Grant followed, supporting Magda. Avon flicked a switch that closed the pod dock doors then headed for the George spacecraft's flight deck. En route, he indicated a side room to Grant.

'You should find something to help Magda in there,' he said, before hurrying on.

'I would advise caution,' Orac said.

Avon took the advice and entered the flight deck warily. His eyes narrowed when he saw Zed's corpse and narrowed still further when he spotted the fuel rods and the phials of nitroglycerin on the floor. Stepping round the body, he settled Orac in its usual resting place, before turning his attention to the dangerous, hissing liquid.

'Please turn off the voltage on the console, Orac. I don't want to end up like our friend on the floor,' he said. He knelt by the nitro phials and touched them. He withdrew his hand quickly – they were hot.

Avon opened the hatch to the fuel locker and descended. He returned wearing flameproof gloves and carrying the ice tray on which the nitro was stored. He carefully placed the phials on the tray. The hissing began to subside.

Avon wiped his brow. 'We were rather fortunate there.'

'Fortune favours the brave,' Orac said, before adding, 'or the foolish.'

'And fools rush in where angels fear to tread.'

'You're no angel, Avon.'

Avon smiled slightly before carrying the ice tray below. Having discarded the flameproof gloves, he returned, picked up the fuel rods and went below again. As he emerged for a second time, he saw that Grant had entered the flight deck and was gazing at Orac. Avon closed the hatch. 'We have enough fuel to take us pretty much anywhere we might want to go,' he said.

Grant said, 'I've given Magda an emetic. She threw up.'

'Yes, well – an emetic tends to make you do that.'

'She's feeling a lot better. She's cleaning herself up.'

Avon nodded and leaned against the flight console, watching Grant with hooded, suspicious eyes.

'Orac's changed,' Grant said.

'I've made a few adjustments to it.'

'I don't see its key.'

'That was one of the adjustments. The key was superfluous. It now responds to my voice pattern.'

'You mean you're the only one who can control it? What if someone were to imitate your voice?'

'Orac is very sophisticated. It would recognise the subtlest of differences and not respond.'

'So whoever gets their hands on it would find it to be useless to them.' It was not a question.

'An expert computer analyst might be able to do something with it,' Avon said quietly.

'You mean they'd have to be as good as you?'

Avon shrugged.

'How would they do it?'

'He – or she – would have to dismantle Orac. Then find a way to alter the responsive voice pattern. It could be done. The only problem would be that the analyst's voice would have to replace mine.'

'Which would mean that, without the analyst, Orac wouldn't function.' Again, not a question.

'It would be something like that.'

'The analyst would become indispensable and, therefore, very powerful,' Grant said thoughtfully. 'I would imagine such an expert could be found amongst our friends from Cathay.'

Avon said nothing.

Grant's eyes strayed to the body on the floor.

'Would you care to help me move it?' Avon asked. 'There's an ejection chute.' He indicated a hatch at waist level on a far wall. He walked over to it and opened it.

Grant dragged the corpse towards him. Together, they hoisted it into the chute. Avon closed the hatch and threw a switch. A faint whooshing sound could be heard, followed by silence.

'How did he die?' Grant asked.

'He got a shock.'

Magda walked a trifle unsteadily onto the deck. Grant

dashed towards her and supported her, but she gently pushed him aside.

'I'm fine now,' she said. She smiled at Avon. 'It's been a long time.'

Avon said nothing as he returned to his former position, leaning against the flight console. There was an awkward silence.

'Well,' Magda said, still smiling. 'What happens now?'

'Avon says he'll take us wherever we want to go,' Grant said uncertainly.

'Where do we want to go?' Magda asked.

'I was hoping he would agree to join forces with us and go against the Quartet again. With him and Orac we would be formidable,' Grant replied. 'But he doesn't want to do that.'

Magda turned to Avon. 'Aren't you tired of running?' she asked him.

'Aren't you tired of losing?' he answered coolly.

Magda smiled ruefully.

'There's a Dragon ship out there,' Grant said, vaguely gesturing. 'Cathay has helped us before, they could do so again.'

'They helped us because we and those who followed us – now dead – were a distraction for the Quartet,' Magda said. 'We're of no use to them now.' She looked long and hard at Avon. 'I don't suppose you would give us Orac, so that we could be of use to them?'

Grant snorted. 'If it didn't suit his purpose, Avon wouldn't give you the time of day.'

Magda drew a small handgun from a pocket. 'This might persuade him.'

Grant was startled. Avon was stock still, his eyes on the gun.

'You'd have to kill him,' Grant said hurriedly, 'If you do that, Orac won't function.'

'So I understand, from what I overheard of your little conversation. But a computer analyst could make Orac do something.'

Avon eased himself away from the flight console.

'You don't believe I'll shoot you, do you?' Magda said icily.

'Well now, if someone's pointing a loaded gun at me and threatening to kill, I'm inclined to take their word for it.'

'I don't want to kill you.'

'Then don't.'

'But I will, if it's the only way to get hold of Orac.'

'It's the only way.'

Grant, who had backed away, watched the two of them anxiously. He was beginning to perspire and his breathing was uneven. For a split second, his apparent distress distracted Magda. A split second was all Avon needed. He leapt forward, knocked Magda's gun hand aside and punched her in the face. The gun went off as she hit the ground, semi-conscious.

'She really meant to do it,' Grant gasped.

Avon knelt and cradled Magda in his arms.

Grant's eyes latched on to the gun on the floor.

'Don't even think about it,' Avon said, without looking.

Magda moaned and Avon wiped her brow. Her eyes fluttered open. 'I'd forgotten how hard you can hit,' she whispered.

Avon lifted her to her feet. He glanced at Grant. 'Are you all right?'

Grant raised an eyebrow. 'I get a little nervous around guns.'

'You could have fooled me,' Avon said, as he stooped, picked up the handgun and tucked it into his belt. He helped Magda to a chair.

Orac grunted before saying, 'The Dragon ship has opened a communication channel.'

'Let's hear what they have to say,' Avon instructed.

Fu Ti's voice came over the speakers. 'First of all, Avon, I apologise for any inconvenience we may have caused you. You will understand, of course, that it was necessary to attempt to capture you and Orac magnetically. In my position, I feel, you would have done the same. Perhaps with a more satisfactory result... I trust there are no hard feelings between us?'

'None at all,' Avon said.

Fu Ti chuckled. 'May I offer you any assistance as recompense?'

Avon looked at Grant and Magda. 'There are two former

associates of mine here. It would be kind of you to offer them some of your generous hospitality, before escorting them to a safe place.'

Magda seemed about to protest, but thought better of it. Grant merely shrugged.

'It is the least I can do,' Fu Ti said. 'But what about you, Avon?'

'I'll be just fine. Thank you anyway.'

Fu Ti sighed. 'I will despatch a pod to collect your former associates. It will be necessary to attach it to the hull of your ship, your docking area being a little cluttered.'

'Once more, thank you!'

'Doubtless, our paths shall cross again,' Fu Ti said.

The communication channel shut down.

'Orac seems to function independently of you,' Grant said curiously.

'Yes it does. But it won't do anything specific, unless I instruct it to.'

Magda stood and moved next to Grant. 'Do we really have to go?' she asked.

'The Dragon pod will attach itself so that it covers the dock doors. You can board it that way,' Avon said, the tone of his voice chilly.

'How can we be certain that our "friends" won't harm us?' Grant asked.

'Nothing is certain. But Fu Ti is a man of his word.'

Grant sighed. 'All right, we'll go.' He took Magda's hand and led her from the flight deck.

Before following, Avon said, 'Cover me, Orac.'

'Don't I always?'

Xian had flown the pod. She stepped into the docking area of the former Alien Grey spacecraft and glanced disapprovingly at the wreckage strewn about it. 'You were lucky to get out of that,' she said. Turning to Grant and Magda, she added, 'Be so kind as to get aboard.'

Without a word, Grant did as instructed. Magda, after some hesitation, followed suit.

'Love's labour's lost – is that it?' Xian said to Avon.

'There's no love lost,' he replied.

Xian smiled. 'What will you do? Where will you go?'

'I'll go somewhere I've never been before. I'm not sure what I'll do.'

'Like the ageing lion, you'll search for a place to die.'

'That's not exactly what I have in mind.'

Xian smiled again. 'I think it would be entertaining to accompany you. But, alas, I have other things to do.' She frowned. 'You know, of course, that for as long as you have Orac, the Quartet, the Cathay Empire and, I suspect, many others will continue to pursue you.'

'I know.'

'Well, we've chased away the Alien Greys – so they shouldn't bother you.'

'Thank you.'

Xian lifted a bag that she had placed on the floor when alighting from her pod. 'There are a few things in here that might be of use to yo. With the compliments of Fu Ti.'

Avon's mouth twitched. It might have been a smile. Then again, it might not.

Xian replaced the bag on the floor, came very close to Avon and kissed him.

'Do the few things of use to me include a tracking device?' he asked.

'But of course!' Xian laughed.

'Secure the docking doors and get us out of here, Orac,' Avon said, as he returned to the flight deck.

'Do you have a course in mind?'

'No. Why don't you choose?'

'We'll re-enter secure Quartet air space, then.'

'Why that air space?'

'Because, Avon, you have unfinished business there.'

'What might that be?'

'You don't want to die with a whimper – you want to go out with a bang. You want to blow up the Base!'

PART FOUR
The End

The *Claw* was the biggest and best-protected warship in the Empire of Cathay's space fleet. It was shaped like a right-hand fist, with four long talons thrusting forwards and a smaller one to the left of them – this latter being a detachable fast attack fighter named, unsurprisingly, the *Thumb*. The tips, or nails, of the talons housed laser weaponry, the 'knuckles' of the spaceship featured cannon and locked-off heavy machine guns that could rotate and, therefore, challenge any predator, from whichever direction it might choose to attack. Its fuel-rod power was contained in the rear section of the fist, as were generators that provided light and energy to pump water from huge barrels, as well as temperature control and air filters.

It was not dissimilar to the Quartet's Base. But whereas the Base had been designed to remain static, the *Claw* was a third its size, highly manoeuvrable, and could reach top speed fast. It would prove to be a formidable opponent of anything other than a mass attack. As an extra precaution, it was accompanied by a much smaller warship – that was now commanded by Li Lang's replacement, Kai Kim. Whilst its exterior was forbidding, sections of its interior provided luxurious accommodations for the empress and her entourage.

The Quartet's space cruiser, though well-armed and armoured, was dwarfed by the impressive *Claw* and Pandora Ess experienced a shiver of apprehension as her spacecraft settled into a trough below it. A strengthened metal cylinder slowly emerged from the larger ship and locked on to the observation deck of the *Pandora*. (Though sometimes cruel, always ruthless and determined and fixated on the accumulation of power, the doctor was not without vanity and had 'permitted' a sycophantic supplicant to name the ship after her.) Once firmly in position, a panel of the cylinder slid open and Pandora Ess entered into a slightly cramped, but comfortably outfitted, interior pod which, in the manner of an elevator, raised her to a reception area within the *Claw*.

She was greeted there by a stunningly beautiful young Eurasian woman, clad in black silk, emblazoned with the ubiquitous red dragon. The woman bowed. Pandora Ess merely nodded.

The woman smiled and retreated towards an ornately decorated door.

The door opened, she stepped aside, and Pandora Ess entered a replica of what might have been an elegant room in a palace in Beijing. The Empress of Cathay, dressed in a long, silk, emerald-green gown turned to greet her. This time, it was Pandora Ess who bowed and the empress who merely nodded.

'My dear Pandora!' said Empress Kwai Shi Yan. 'It has been far too long since we last greeted each other. I am so very pleased that we are able to remedy that situation.' She smiled shyly. 'Particularly at this interesting time for both of us.'

'I also am very pleased,' Pandora Ess said, and the two women embraced.

The Eurasian opened a bottle of champagne and, breaking apart, both women took a glass.

'This is an excellent wine, I feel sure you will agree,' said Kwai Shi Yan. 'I learnt to appreciate it whilst enjoying a brief acquaintanceship with the late Servalan.' She raised her glass. 'A toast to the dear departed.'

When they had completed the toast, the Eurasian refilled their glasses. 'This is Lauren,' said the Empress. 'She is my constant companion and I would trust her with my life. There are so few about whom one can say that – as I am sure you are aware.'

'I am aware,' Pandora Ess replied. 'You are very fortunate.'

'Lauren is the product of a liaison between a handsome, if dissolute, Caucasian and a cousin of mine. Alas, both are now deceased and I have taken her under my wing, so to speak.'

'To be under the wing of the Dragon Empress must be a great privilege.'

Kwai Shi Yan chuckled. 'Lauren is deaf and dumb. This has its disadvantages and its advantages,' she said coolly.

'How then do you communicate?'

'Oh, Lauren reads lips in several languages. Would you care for more champagne?'

Though wary of becoming inebriated in the presence of her hostess – a hostess who, she understood, could be as cunning and unpredictable as herself – a refusal would be impolite, so she held out her glass.

'I must thank you for revealing Li Lang's treachery to me,' Kwai Shi Yan said. 'In him, my trust was misplaced. But the matter has been dealt with.' She sipped champagne then added, 'I am sorry, if only to a degree, to learn of the demise of Gregor Steiner. Whilst he caused some harm to my people and was, I believe, a despicable hedonist, he was a formidable adversary and as such commanded respect. How did he die?'

'I am afraid he was over-enthusiastic in matters sexual. He put his heart and soul into it. I cannot account for his soul, but his heart gave up on him.'

Kwai Shi Yan laughed. 'Your other colleague,' she said sombrely, 'you will be sad – or should that be glad? – to hear, suffered a dreadful accident. I was really quite fond of Eugene Furneaux.' She sniffed, as if holding back a tear.

'What happened exactly?'

'Oh, his spacecraft blew up,' she smiled. 'There were no survivors.'

'Well,' said Pandora Ess, also smiling, 'that leaves only one fly in our ointment, doesn't it?'

'How is the lovely Gabriella?'

The 'lovely' Gabriella was in a foul mood. She did not react kindly to taking instruction from Sarin, who claimed to speak with the authority of Pandora Ess. News had just reached the Base that the Alien Grey, Egil Nacre, had failed to assist the Huntress in the assassination of Avon and the acquisition of Orac. Not only that, Adonis – on whom she had become dependent and had confided in perhaps more than she should – was preparing to leave her.

'You need to give this up now,' Sarin was saying. 'The terrorist has got the better of you yet again.'

'He needs killing!' Gabriella said through gritted teeth, fighting back tears of frustration.

'I'll grant you that. But you should leave it to those who have a chance of success.'

'Name them!'

'Cathay is good at this sort of thing.'

Gabriella snorted in disgust. 'They've been helping him. If they were going to kill him, they'd have done it by now.'

'They'll have held off because like you – like everyone else – they want to get their hands on the computer.'

'What makes you think they don't want to now?'

Sarin smiled secretively before saying, 'The game is changing, Gabriella. Steiner's dead and I'm only awaiting confirmation of Furneaux's demise.'

Gabriella's eyes widened. 'Doctor Ess is moving a lot faster than I anticipated,' she said quietly.

'She has ensured that the Quartet is now defunct. So, long live the Duet!'

'How long will it live, Sarin?' Gabriella said.

Sarin shrugged. 'It'll live for as long as Doctor Ess wants it to.'

Gabriella became very still. 'When she doesn't want it to, when she decides to go solo, what's supposed to happen to me?'

'What I meant was,' Sarin said hastily, 'it'll last until she gets too old or too weary, or both – or until she dies. Then you will be the one to go solo, as her natural successor.'

Gabriella smiled. 'You got out of that one rather well.'

Sarin grinned sheepishly. 'I don't have her full confidence, but I'm under the impression that that is her vision.'

'Why has Adonis been replaced by you?' Gabriella asked peremptorily.

'She needs him. He's been by her side for a long time. It was a sign of her respect for you that she loaned him out.'

Gabriella gave that some thought. 'You do realise, don't you,' she said finally, 'that I have control of the Base? If at some time Pandora Ess should lose that respect for me, I can be a very dangerous enemy.'

'That's why she holds you close,' Sarin said mischievously.

'I think there's more to you than meets my eye,' Gabriella said, after an ominous pause.

Sarin inclined his head. 'I'm here to serve you and to ensure that the Base remains secure. Without it, the Duet might not live very long. The Cathay Empire is making inroads into your power sources. It already has Earth, the Martian Territories and many other less significant areas of influence. It's flexing its Dragon wings and it might very well think of going after Iphigenia. The power of the Base will make it think twice.'

Gabriella smiled contentedly. 'That puts me in a very strong position, doesn't it?'

'Yes it does.'

'And that's why you are here, with fighter craft and a few soldiers. To make sure I don't abuse my power to Doctor Ess's detriment.' She laughed. 'My people could destroy your little expeditionary force in minutes.' She snapped her fingers.

'That's probably true.'

A thought struck Gabriella. 'But you who are here to serve me would assassinate me, if Pandora Ess told you to. Am I right?'

Sarin smiled a cold smile. 'That's supposing Adonis does not assassinate Pandora Ess first.'

Gabriella looked stunned.

'We are able, upon occasion and with certain restrictions, to achieve stealth mode for many of our spacecraft,' Kwai Shi Yan said, as she extracted the meat from a lobster claw. 'But not as efficiently as the Orac computer,' she added. 'This, of course, is one of the reasons we are eager to acquire it. However, Avon seems to be living a charmed life and protects it with an almost religious fervour,' she sighed. 'The time may have come when we should consider abandoning our pursuit and destroy it – and that terrorist with it. What do you think?'

After a brief hesitation, Pandora Ess said, 'It is my understanding that you have had a number of opportunities to do that very thing. Instead, you seem to have aided and abetted the terrorist.'

'Ah well, you see, aiding and abetting, as you so charmingly put it, was our way of getting close to him, in the hope that he might drop his guard and leave himself, and the computer, vulnerable. The tactic, in my opinion, is to be preferred to the use of brute force.'

'But now, you have changed your mind?'

'Let us be candid with one another, Pandora. We have sought to gain control of Orac so that one or other of us would gain an advantage – as we proceed together to absolute power.' The empress's eyes glistened. 'Both of us desired the proverbial "ace up the sleeve" – just in case our togetherness might wither and die and we turn against each other. As a gesture of good faith, it occurs to me that we should agree to the computer's destruction, thus denying ourselves any temptation to renege on our agreement to share that absolute power. What are your thoughts on the matter?'

Again, Pandora Ess hesitated. 'It is Gabriella who has seemed set on acquiring Orac,' she said at last.

'I am not so naïve as to be unaware that you have encouraged her,' Kwai Shi Yan said acidly. 'But I forgive you, as I hope you will forgive me,' she added, smiling a killer smile.

Pandora Ess swallowed hard. 'I agree that we should destroy the Orac computer,' she said.

'Oh, I'm so pleased,' the Empress gushed. 'I was dreading the possibility that we might fall out over what is such a minor matter in the vast scheme of things.'

Pandora Ess hardly thought that Orac was a minor consideration, but she let it go. 'How will the destruction be achieved?' she asked.

The empress leaned forward and spoke in what Pandora Ess considered to be an unnecessarily conspiratorial whisper. 'By aiding and abetting Avon, we are able to keep track of him. Hitherto, we helped him to stay alive so that he might lead us to Orac. But now that we have agreed to destroy the machine, we'll help him to die instead. That should soothe Gabriella?'

'Gabriella will be pleased, yes.'

'I have something that may also soothe you.'

'What might that be?'

'*General* Fu Ti – I have recently promoted him – is currently playing host to Magda Lens and the dissident, Del Grant. It would be my pleasure to instruct him to execute them in our traditional fashion.'

Pandora Ess frowned. 'It is my understanding that Lens

murdered Servalan and Grant has eluded capture for far too long. Servalan would be disinclined to allow them to die swiftly and I, in memory of her, feel the same.'

'Oh well, in that case, why don't we hand them over to Gabriella's torturers at the Base?'

'That would be satisfactory.'

'Consider it done.'

'Was it not Fu Ti who assisted the woman to escape Gabriella's clutches on a previous occasion?' Pandora Ess asked slyly.

The empress was unfazed. 'That was another tactical move. She was to be used as bait for Avon. It worked – up to a point. The woman was beguiled into placing her trust in Fu Ti and Avon, now seemingly uninterested, has returned her to his care. In so doing, Avon was a little distracted and the tracking device to which I have previously referred was planted on him.'

'Will it be Fu Ti who will destroy him – and Orac?'

'Yes, with the assistance of the warship currently shadowing the *Claw*. Kai Kim, the warship's new commander, will ensure that Fu Ti will not lose heart and fail to complete the mission. She will also bring proof of the destruction.'

Pandora Ess nodded and smiled her approval.

'Now there are more serious matters we need to discuss,' Kwai Shi Yan said.

'What was in the bag?' Orac asked.

'Fuel rods, some canned food, bullets,' Avon replied. 'But I can't find any tracking device.'

'That is because it is on, or rather in, your person.'

'What do you mean?'

'I have gathered that you feel some affection for the woman called Xian,' Orac said disapprovingly. 'Doubtless, you permitted her to kiss you – as a fond farewell.'

'I had forgotten what a puritan you are, Orac.'

'Well, did you?'

'She kissed me, yes.'

'That explains it then.'

'Kindly explain it to me.'

'In the act of kissing, Xian placed the tiniest of soft metal trackers in your mouth. It is no bigger than a full stop at the end of a sentence.'

'I was unaware that such a device existed.'

'Our "friends" are highly skilled and resourceful.'

'Oh well, it'll come out in the wash.'

'It has adhered to your palate.'

Avon frowned. 'How do I get rid of it?'

'A laser beam can disintegrate it.'

'A laser beam in my mouth?'

'It would be a tricky operation, unless skilfully carried out.'

'And you have that skill, Orac. Is that right?'

'You know I do.'

Avon paused for thought. 'Where do we find the laser?'

Orac sighed with irritation. 'You fitted one to me as a security device. Clearly, you have forgotten. Your forgetfulness as you age is becoming more than just occasional.'

'Well, you'll always be here to remind me of anything I've overlooked.'

'The laser is embedded in my interior. Should anyone other than you attempt to interfere with my circuitry, the laser would activate and blind them. Something you omitted to mention to Del Grant when describing how I function.'

'Am I that cruel, Orac?'

'There are those who are crueller.'

'I think we'll leave it for the time being.'

'You are afraid?'

'Fear is the key to my survival.' Avon thought for a moment. 'Alter course. If the Dragons want to track us, we'll lead them a merry dance. Let's take them into the Beyond.'

Kwai Shi Yan did not waste any time. She issued instructions for Kai Kim to fly her warship to rendezvous with that of Fu Ti and order him to deliver Grant and Magda into the hands of Gabriella. Then, both warships should seek out and eliminate Avon and Orac.

Kai Kim was somewhat bemused by this last instruction –

as, she supposed, might be Fu Ti – but it was not for her to reason why.

'What are your long term plans for Gabriella?' the empress enquired of Pandora Ess, as she sipped more champagne.

'She could prove to be of some use to us. After all, Servalan's plan was that Gabriella should be a major player in the expansion of Quartet power. I see no reason why we should not utilise her talents for our benefit. But it will be necessary to curb her ambition and reduce her influence over the Base.'

'What if that cannot be done?'

'Then it may prove necessary to delete her from our plan.'

'That will not be easy. Not while she commands the loyalty of the Base.'

'I have already made certain arrangements that could make it easier. But I am hopeful that she will come to heel and serve us well. We need the Base as a springboard into the Beyond, for reasons of which you must be aware.'

'I am aware.'

The two women became solemn.

'What is the Empire's fuel situation?' Pandora Ess asked.

The empress sighed. 'Not dissimilar to yours, I imagine. It is estimated to become a severe problem for us within the year.'

'You are right, it is the same with us. We must lose no time in invading the Beyond. Fuel seems plentiful enough there.'

'Let us hope our expedition doesn't turn out as badly as the Federation's abortive attempt to invade.'

'We are better equipped. The warlords will not be expecting us. Besides, we have no choice. Without their fuel resources, we will come to nothing. I don't intend to allow that to happen.'

'My dear Pandora, neither do I!'

'They're not following,' Orac said. 'What's the point of planting a tracking device and not using it?'

'Fu Ti promised to take Grant and Magda to a place of safety. The Dragon ship will follow once he's done that.'

'Do you really think so?'

'Fu Ti is an honourable man.'

'But his superiors may not be.'

Avon pondered the remark. 'Where is he now?'

'The warship is stationary.'

'That's odd.'

'Not if he's waiting for something – or somebody.'

Avon began to pace the flight deck. 'All right, shut down all engines. We'll wait and see if you're right.'

'If I am, you might not like the look of the "something or somebody". We might have to run away again!'

'We can go into stealth mode.'

'Whilst not as efficiently as I can manage it – so can they!'

Avon stopped pacing. 'Why haven't they done it before?'

'I cannot answer that.'

'Speculate!'

Orac was silent for a full minute. 'Stealth requires the usage of a great deal of fuel,' it said at last. 'It could be that the Dragon ship needs to conserve it.'

'If that were so, Fu Ti would hardly be likely to supply us with fuel rods, would he?'

'He did that in an effort to gain your trust, in the hope that you might lower your guard and leave me vulnerable. A few fuel rods would be a small price to pay for me.'

It was Avon's turn to be silent.

'It occurs to me,' Orac said, 'that Earth might be experiencing a fuel shortage. It's happened before!'

Avon frowned. 'If that's true, it might explain why Fu Ti told me the Empire wasn't ready to go against the Quartet – and why he only gave limited assistance to Grant and Magda.'

'Why don't I look at the Empire of Cathay's computers?' Orac said. 'It might be possible to find an answer.'

'You can do that? Why haven't you done it before?'

'You never asked me to.'

'Tell me, Sarin,' Gabriella cooed, as she wiped perspiration from his brow – the result of recent exertions – 'is there some kind of palace coup in the offing that I know nothing of?'

Sarin, who had been dozing, opened one eye. 'There might be,' he said.

Gabriella kissed him lightly on the lips. 'Would you care to enlighten me?'

'Is that why you've brought me into your bed? Is your aim to learn something from pillow talk?'

Gabriella laughed. 'It's been done before,' she said coquettishly.

Sarin sighed. 'Steiner and Furneaux are dead. Other than you, there is no brake on Pandora Ess's ambition. It might be necessary to curb that ambition at source.'

'I too am ambitious.'

'Rest assured, Doctor Ess will do her utmost to curb that!'

Gabriella climbed off the bed and stretched her naked body, well aware of the effect it was having on her recent conquest. 'How will she go about it?'

'She'll offer you a deal. Settle for second best and eventually take over or...' He felt there was no need to finish the sentence.

'You'll kill me?'

'I want to end up on the winning side. Right now, Doctor Ess is in pole position.' Sarin frowned. 'I think she has another, secret, agenda but I can't figure it out.'

'Well, if you can't, who can?'

'Adonis might.'

'Ah! So, his returning to her side and reassuming his role as her confidant could play to your advantage. I'm assuming you also have ambition.'

'It could play to our advantage!'

'You are ambitious then?'

'I'm happy to stay in the background and merely help to shape events.'

Gabriella returned to the bed and lay on top of him. 'It doesn't matter to you in whose shadow you might be?' she whispered.

Sarin smiled. 'After this,' he stroked her skin, 'I think I might prefer it to be yours.'

'If I accept Doctor Ess's terms, you get the best of both worlds.'

'It's more than just worlds we are playing for, Gabriella!'

*

Magda had asked to meet with Fu Ti and had been granted an audience.

'I was wondering why we have stopped?' she said.

Fu Ti smiled, in avuncular fashion. 'I am in receipt of a brief signal and am obliged to await the accompaniment of another Dragon warship. Its commander, who happens to be my niece, will bring instructions from the empress.'

Magda frowned. 'Might not these instructions have been communicated electronically?'

'Electronic communications, unless brief, may be intercepted,' Fu Ti replied. 'My empress has a fear of such insecurity. It may be irrational, but "better safe than sorry" is, I believe, an appropriate phrase.'

Magda looked towards Xian, who was sitting in a corner of the cabin, pretending not to eavesdrop.

Reacting to her penetrating gaze, Xian said, 'Avon's spacecraft is also motionless. Perhaps he is loath to tear himself away from you.'

Magda scowled.

'He is probably wondering the same as you,' Fu Ti interjected, 'and is awaiting developments.'

'He might be in for a bit of shock then,' Xian said lightly. 'Saint George only slew one dragon. He would have been reluctant to take on two.'

Magda chose to ignore her. 'Where is it that you will be taking us?'

Fu Ti pursed his lips. 'That has yet to be decided,' he said.

'But it will be a safe place?' Magda asked suspiciously.

'I have given my word.'

'What if your empress instructs you to break it?'

Fu Ti looked sorrowful.

The *Pandora* took its leave of the *Claw*. Kwai Shi Yan, through a window that was a powerful telescope, watched it go. She turned to Sun Cheng and his aide, Tung Ma.

'You have both done well,' she said.

Sun Cheng was expressionless. Tung Ma smiled.

'But you must do even better,' the empress continued. 'Whilst I do not entirely dislike Pandora Ess, I do distrust her. But we are in a situation when sure and certain enemies must collude – if only for the time being. We are ill equipped to enter the Beyond alone, this apart from the fact that the Base, a formidable obstacle, stands in our way.' She smiled humourlessly. 'I have my doubts regarding Pandora's ability to restrain Gabriella. From what I have heard, the young woman is ambitious – and she is made of stuff stern enough to spur her on.' She shrugged. 'Still, we have no alternative but to support Pandora's initiative. For the time being. Would you agree, Sun Cheng?'

'I would. In due course, we will be able to dispense with the aid of the Quartet – or whatever it calls itself now. But, given the severity of the fuel crisis we both face, we must be patient. After all, a half of everything is to be preferred to all of nothing for the time being.'

'You are very wise, Sun Cheng,' the empress said graciously. 'Kai Kim is fully aware of what must be done regarding the terrorist and the computer?'

'She is. Before Tung Ma and I transferred to the *Claw*, my instructions to her were explicit.'

Kwai Shi Yan smiled – this time with a hint of genuine humour. 'Pandora and I have agreed that they must be destroyed. I am indifferent to the fate of the terrorist, but the computer is another matter.'

'It will appear that they have been destroyed,' Sun Cheng said solemnly.

'You are certain that our experts can adapt Orac to our purposes?'

'The experts are certain.'

'Pandora will require proof of the destruction. Proof that we know to be false. How will this false proof manifest itself?'

'General Fu Ti holds the dissidents Grant and Lens. They will witness the apparent destruction. They will then be handed over to the commander of the Base. Under interrogation, however intense, they will swear to what they have seen.'

Sun Cheng permitted himself a slight smile.

'We are masters of deception,' he added.

The empress nodded approvingly.

'There is one small matter of concern,' Sun Cheng said. 'General Fu Ti is an honourable man and might be reluctant to break his word to the dissidents and by so doing, instead of offering sanctuary, deliver them to their tormentors.'

'Fu Ti will do as he is told!' the empress snapped.

'But if he does not?'

'Kai Kim will ensure that he does.'

'Kai Kim is his close relative.'

There was an ominous silence.

'Do you have any suggestions, Sun Cheng?'

'In order to ensure Fu Ti's compliance, I would suggest that we despatch Tung Ma in the fast fighter – the *Thumb*. Tung Ma should carry your authority to, if necessary, force him to obey or suffer the consequences.'

Kwai Shi Yan's eyes widened. 'You mean execute Fu Ti?'

'Only if absolutely necessary. He must not be allowed to spoil the master plan. Perhaps you may have forgotten that Fu Ti – and Li Lang before him – liaised with the terrorist, Avon, and there may be a residue of mutual respect, even admiration.'

'Li Lang was a traitor.'

'Li Lang was beguiled into a form of treason. We would not wish the same for Fu Ti.'

After a pause, the empress smiled upon Tung Ma. 'You will have my written authority, as well as command of the *Thumb*.'

Avon had dismantled a gun and was cleaning it when Orac appeared to clear its throat, before saying, 'The Cathay computers are devilishly difficult to hack.'

'But you've done it anyway.'

'Well yes, but only up to a point. There seems to be some kind of a blackout in their systems. That tells us they've got something to hide.'

'What have you found out?'

'With the exception of the Cathay space fleet, there is

fuel rationing throughout Earth and the Empire's other territories.'

'So you were right.'

'It is not often that I am wrong,' Orac said petulantly. 'But it does not necessarily follow that the Empire is running out of fuel.'

'Doesn't it?'

'Well, let us say we should entertain the possibility.'

'Let's entertain it, by all means,' Avon said, re-assembling the gun. 'What about the Quartet?'

'What about it?'

'Come on, Orac! You've hacked into its computers as well, haven't you?'

Orac sulked for a moment. 'It was equally difficult but yes, I have,' it said. 'The Quartet is definitely running out of fuel.'

'The mines of Uranus and its satellites can't have dried up, can they?'

'They can. They are currently working at less than half capacity.'

'Well, well, well! So where are they going to replenish their stocks?'

'Guess!'

'Where we replenished ours?'

'You're a good guesser, Avon.'

'So, both the Quartet and the Cathay Empire will need to enter the Beyond.' Avon smiled slightly. 'The Federation tried that and it didn't work out too well.'

'But the combined strength of the Quartet and the Empire could, and almost certainly would, produce a happier outcome,' Orac said.

'Not for the warlords in the Beyond.'

'We could warn them.'

'I'm not too popular there. They'd probably shoot me before I could open my mouth.'

'There is that.'

'What do you suggest?' Avon asked.

'All I can suggest is that if I happened to be you, and I thank the computer gods that I am not, I'd risk it anyway. We're going to need fuel rods, sooner rather than later, and the Beyond is the only place we're going to get them.'

'You mean enter the Beyond in stealth mode, raid a warlord's fuel dump, then run for it?'

'You did it on Xerxes.'

'I had a little help.'

'You've got me,' Orac said plaintively.

Pandora Ess was in her study on Iphigenia, trying to make sense of several maps of the Beyond. Adonis made a silent entrance so that it was a moment or two before she noticed him.

'I can't make head or tail of these,' she said irritably.

'There is really no need,' Adonis said quietly. 'Our computer program, linked with that of Cathay, will show you the way.'

'By the tone of your voice, it would seem that you find my links distasteful,' Pandora Ess said, still irritable.

'Joining forces with the Empire of Cathay could prove to be a dangerous liaison.'

'But I have no choice, Adonis. The fuel situation is becoming critical.'

'You do have a choice. You can choose to go into the Beyond without Cathay.'

Pandora Ess laughed disparagingly. 'And while I am there, the Empire wreaks havoc throughout the Quartet's territories. It's inevitable, once I turn my back.'

'That may not be necessarily so.'

Pandora Ess sighed. 'All right. Kindly enlighten me.'

Adonis sat on the edge of the desk upon which the maps were set. He brushed them to one side. 'You cannot trust Kwai Shi Yan. Why then are you allowing her safe passage past the Base? We should go into the Beyond without her, take what fuel we need and rely on the Base's strength to keep her out. You will return in a much more powerful position, so that the Empress of Cathay will then bow to you, rather than the other way around, as seems to be the case now.'

'I kowtow to no-one,' Pandora Ess said emphatically.

Adonis smiled. 'That's more like it,' he said.

'But there is still the danger that we will be attacked. Oh, I understand Kwai Shi Yan would steer clear of the Base, but Iphigenia would be vulnerable and...' the Doctor's voice tailed away.

'Iphigenia would put up spirited resistance. The late General Steiner's forces would not succumb easily, now that they owe their allegiance to you,' Adonis smiled again. 'And I must disagree with you as to the likelihood of an attack. Think about it.'

'You think I haven't?' Pandora Ess interjected.

'Of course you have,' Adonis said soothingly, 'but you are overcomplicating the situation. Why would Cathay launch an offensive?'

'Kwai Shi Yan would be infuriated if I prevented her from entering the Beyond and acquiring the fuel her Empire so desperately needs. She would react accordingly.'

'But to what effect? She'd be fighting a war that, in the long term, she couldn't win. Sooner, rather than later, the shortage of fuel would diminish her Empire. In order to save it, she would have to come, cap in hand, to you. You would hold all the cards. The Empire of Cathay would become a vassal of the Empire of Pandora Ess. That's your ultimate aim, isn't it?'

After a long pause, Pandora Ess said, 'Like a spoilt child who cannot have her way, Kwai Shi Yan would hit out blindly. There would be much in the way of destruction.'

'Once again, I must disagree,' Adonis said. 'Those surrounding her would recognise the writing on the wall if she were to react so violently. It would not be in their interests to allow her to do so.'

'They would remove her?'

'Permanently! It is what I, or Sarin, or Gabriella for that matter, would do in a similar situation.'

Pandora Ess smiled shyly. 'You would do that to me?'

Adonis flinched. Then he stood. 'We are not talking about you,' he said quietly.

Pandora Ess studied him carefully. 'What are your suggested variations to my plan?'

'You could send a small task force into the Beyond. Ignore the larger, better protected sources of crystal fuel and hit the most vulnerable. Hit it hard and fast and get out. I need hardly remind you that the terrorist, Avon, did it and is still causing us problems.'

'Why didn't I think of that?'

'It might be because you are too focused on building your empire and contemplating including the Beyond in it,' Adonis said, warming to his subject. 'You seem to be seeking some kind of reparation for the Federation's ignominious defeat at the hands of its warlords. You don't need the Beyond – it's a dreadful place anyway. You do need its fuel resources. From time to time, you send in a force and take what you need. The warlords aren't fools – they won't want another fight. Providing you put any thoughts of conquest on one side, they'll see sense and, in time, come to an arrangement. You will give them a little of what they want – and they'll give us a lot of what we want.'

'Who might "us" be?'

'Us would be you, of course, and your faithful servant!' Adonis executed a mock bow.

Pandora Ess laughed. 'And which is the most vulnerable source of fuel in the Beyond?'

'It's a small, poorly policed, execrably ruled planet called Xerxes.'

'Return to Xerxes?' Avon said. 'I must be out of my mind.'

'The other fuel sources are too well protected,' said Orac.

'I would remind you that there's a nasty piece of work on Xerxes who would joyfully gut me.'

'You got away from Alaric before – you can do it again.'

'I admire your confidence in me.'

'What else are you going to do? Sit around twiddling your thumbs, waiting for death?'

'Well, if you put it that way...'

'We need to leave now. I have just recognised the approach of another Dragon warship. One is acceptable. Two, worrisome.'

'They're preparing to enter the Beyond in force?'

'It's a possibility.'

'It's time to go then.'

'I said that! We need to get into the Beyond before them.'

'It's getting out of the Beyond that bothers me.'

'Are we going, or not?'

'Start engines, hit full speed, then enter stealth mode. Take me to Xerxes, Orac,' Avon said.

'He's on the move,' Xian muttered.

'Track him!' said Fu Ti.

'I don't think I really need to. I'd already guessed he would be heading into the Beyond.'

'Why do you think he's chosen this moment to leave?'

'It might have something to do with the fact that Kai Kim's warship is about to join us.'

The two Dragon warships were stationary, side by side. Very slowly, the newly arrived spacecraft edged closer to Fu Ti's. A large cylinder protruded from it and locked on to the parallel ship.

After a few minutes, Kai Kim emerged onto its flight deck and was greeted formally by Fu Ti. She might be his niece, but she now outranked him. Both Fu Ti and Xian bowed. Having returned the courtesy, as protocol required, Kai Kim smiled and embraced her uncle. She nodded agreeably at Xian.

'Did I detect the rapid departure of an alien spacecraft?' she enquired.

'It's an Alien Grey ship,' Xian replied, 'requisitioned – if that's the word – by the terrorist, Avon.'

'I don't need to ask you if you have a placed a tracker on it, do I?' Kai Kim said, still smiling.

'He's at full speed now. The course set is Four Five One Zero. I don't need the tracker to be able to tell you that his ultimate destination is a poor excuse for a planet, called Xerxes. He's been there before.'

'Why is he going there?'

Xian smiled. 'He needs fuel and, as he won't be getting any

more from us, he'll get it there. Xerxes is poor in every other respect, except that.'

Kai Kim frowned prettily. 'The empress will be displeased if he eludes us.'

Fu Ti cast a worried glance in Xian's direction. Returning his attention to his niece he asked, 'Has there been a change in policy? Are we to follow and attack?'

'The empress requests the death of the terrorist and that we secure the computer, Orac.'

Xian laughed, which brought another frown from Kai Kim – this one not at all pretty.

'We attempted to fulfil those instructions,' Fu Ti said meekly.

'And you failed,' said Kai Kim. 'That is why I am here. Failure is no longer an option.'

'Then we had better get after him,' Xian said, breaking an awkward silence. But nobody moved.

'What the hell was that?' Avon said, as he picked himself up from the floor of the flight deck.

'The George spacecraft is under rocket attack,' Orac spluttered. 'We have been hit just astern of the engine room.'

'You didn't see it coming?'

'I regret not. Preparing for stealth mode at high speed distracted me.' Orac seemed most apologetic.

'Are the engines still functioning?'

'Yes – and we are in stealth.'

'Alter course right away, and alter it again and again every two minutes. We'll zigzag our way out of this.'

'Course has been altered and speed maintained.'

'Can you identify the attacker?'

'It is a fast attack fighter with Dragon markings.'

'How well armed is it?'

'It will take me a little time to scan it.'

'Make it as little time as possible.'

Avon paced anxiously for a few moments.

'The fighter is a Predator-class Dragon,' Orac said quickly. 'It carries six rockets – three are nuclear-tipped – and three heavy cannon, as well as two machine guns. There is a crew of ten. Four of them are elite troops. It is known as the *Thumb* and is usually attached to the Empire of Cathay's flagship, the *Claw*.'

'The *Thumb*, the *Claw*? I've never heard of them.'

'Well, they have definitely heard of you.'

'Can we take on this *Thumb*?'

'We are heavily outgunned so the answer is no. Evasion is the only course open to us.'

'They could have blown us out of the sky,' Avon said thoughtfully, 'but they didn't, and I wonder why not.'

'Overcoming any modesty, I would suggest they did not wish to harm me,' Orac said.

Avon laughed without much humour. 'It would appear that they are stepping up their attempts to get hold of you.'

'And kill you in the process.'

'They haven't done too well so far, have they? But we'll need to step up our attempts to foil them.'

'They know where we're going. Even if they don't, they can track us.'

Avon swore.

'I cannot remove the tracker unless we are stationary and undisturbed,' Orac said.

'I should have let you do it when we were hanging around checking on Fu Ti.'

'Yes, you should.'

'Tell me, if the *Thumb* is a fast attack fighter, what's its range?' Avon asked, ignoring Orac's critical tone.

'That's a good question.'

'How about coming up with an answer?'

'It will have to break contact and return to its mothership, or a Dragon warship, within seven minutes.'

'Well, that's good news.'

'The bad news is that it is closing fast and, despite our attempts to evade it, is preparing another attack.'

'I'm beginning to get it,' Avon said. 'Whoever is in charge of the *Thumb* is trying to cripple us. What's the betting another rocket is aimed at our engines?'

'It's on its way.'

'Halve engine speed and drop,' Avon instructed. 'How can they see us when we're in stealth mode?'

'They are also in stealth.'

The former Alien Grey spacecraft plummeted. But it was too late. The *Thumb*'s rocket had locked on and struck its target. Once again, the impact threw Avon to the floor, as the ship stalled its fall before coming to a stop. It hung in space, like a bird with a broken wing.

'Were you aware?' Fu Ti asked.

Kai Kim bit her lip. 'No.'

'It would seem the empress was determined Avon wouldn't get away this time,' said Xian. 'She didn't trust us to do the job, so she sent the *Thumb*. How disappointing.'

'There is no question of disappointment,' Kai Kim said sharply. 'The terrorist is at our mercy.'

'I meant...'

'I know what you meant.'

Xian was about to respond but was distracted. 'There is a communication from the *Thumb*,' she said.

'Put it on speaker.'

'I bring greetings from Empress Kwai Shi Yan,' said the voice of Tung Ma. 'Upon my arrival in this area, I noticed that the terrorist's spacecraft was leaving the area whilst two Dragon warships sat idly by.' His tone was contemptuous. 'Needless to say,' he continued, 'I took action and the spacecraft is now crippled and useless. I will board it, acquire the Orac computer and eliminate any who oppose me.'

'Upon what authority do you do this?' Kai Kim asked.

'I do so upon the authority of the empress.'

'Avon will destroy the computer before you get to it.'

'Not if I destroy him first,' was Tung Ma's reply. 'It is necessary that I act quickly, as I require replenishment of fuel. You will kindly approach my position and support me.' The speaker cut out.

'Well,' sighed Xian, 'let's hope he's more fortunate than Micah. He couldn't get Orac, even when Avon wasn't there.'

'We will manoeuvre our respective warships as Tung Ma has requested,' Kai Kim said authoritatively.

'I think it was something more than a request,' said Xian.

Kai Kim gave her a spiteful look before leaving the flight deck.

'You should take care, my dear,' Fu Ti said quietly. 'My niece has much power within our Empire.'

'But not, it would seem, as much as Tung Ma.'

Fu Ti shook his head. 'This is the work of Sun Cheng. First, he rids himself of a rival in Li Lang. Secondly, he persuades the empress to permit Tung Ma to usurp Kai Kim's authority. I wonder what his third move might be.'

Xian said nothing.

'I am very sorry, Avon,' Orac said.

'There's no need to apologise. I'm as much to blame for getting us into this situation. Question is, how do we get out of it?'

'I fear we are lost.'

'There's no need to be fearful.' Avon began laying out an assortment of weapons.

'They will send a boarding party.'

'I'm sure they will. I suspect they're launching a pod about now.'

'They are.'

'Well, our docking facility is a little cluttered. They're going to have to struggle through the wreckage and then move along the corridor to this flight deck. They'll proceed with caution, not knowing what to expect.'

'They'll be expecting you.'

'I don't intend to disappoint them.'

'We are at a considerable disadvantage. You and I must face at least four well-armed, hardened troopers and there's a Dragon fighter bristling with weaponry, about to be joined by two Dragon warships, backing them up.'

Avon racked a pump-action shotgun. 'I'd say that makes the odds about even, wouldn't you?'

*

The *Thumb*'s pod approached the stricken spacecraft. Noticing that its docking area was half-wrecked, the pilot slowed and prepared to attach itself to the side of the ship.

Four elite troopers led by Tung Ma left the pod and made their way gingerly through the wreckage until they reached the corridor that would lead them to the heart of the ship. Except one of the troopers didn't make it. As he trod on a concealed spring, a sharpened spike of metal, horizontal on the floor, straightened to the vertical and plunged into his abdomen. Impaled, he cried out in the agony of death.

Tung Ma and the others froze by the exit from the dock. After a moment, having received whispered instructions, one of the troopers stepped into the corridor and unpinned a smoke grenade. As he threw it, a shotgun blast lifted him off his feet and slammed him into a wall. His corpse slid down the wall into a sitting position, its passage assisted by the slipperiness of blood and visceral matter. The corridor filled with acrid smoke.

A third trooper, using the smoke as concealment and hugging the wall opposite to that which his slain comrade leaned upon, made his way along the corridor, a four-barrelled shotgun, loaded with spread shot, at the ready.

After a brief interval, Tung Ma and the other trooper followed. They reached the open door to the flight deck without incident. The smoke beginning to clear, they could see that, apart from a small, strange looking machine perched at eye level on a plinth, the deck was unattended. The two troopers took up defensive positions, their keen eyes seeking any hint of danger.

Tung Ma approached the machine and stared at it. 'So you are the famous Orac,' he whispered. He leaned forward to take a closer look. At which point the internal laser Avon had planted as a security device activated and seared Tung Ma's face. He staggered back, blinded and howling with pain, before sinking to the floor, mewling and puking.

One of the troopers sprang to his aid. As he did so, Avon emerged from the rear of the flight console and emptied a clip of Nine7 bullets into his back. The remaining trooper turned swiftly and opened fire, but Avon had ducked out of sight. The trooper warily approached the console. The muzzle of his weapon touched it and an electrical charge, identical to that which had killed the Alien Grey, Zed, did the same for him. Avon, careful not to touch the console himself, re-emerged and made his way to the whimpering Tung Ma. Avon slid a fresh clip into the Nine7 and put him out of his misery with a bullet in the back of his head.

'Well, I'm not very impressed, are you?' Orac said.

'These are just cannon fodder,' Avon said, 'The real cannon are out there.' He gestured in the general direction of the pod dock. 'Have you scanned their pod?'

'Yes. There remains its pilot.'

'Is he armed?'

'Yes, of course he is.'

'I'm just checking.' Avon knelt by a fallen trooper and extracted a gas canister from his clothing. 'I'll go and pay him a visit.'

Bypassing the sprawled corpse of the trooper in the corridor, Avon entered the pod dock and was confronted by the standing body – supported by the vertical spike through it – of the first to die. He skirted it, searching the floor for another spring that he had set. Finding it, he knelt down and disabled it. He then turned his attention to the pod attached to the George spacecraft. In order to complete the manoeuvre of attachment, the pilot would have had to reverse before locking off the magnetic suction pads. That meant, as he was situated on the forward, space-side of the machine, he was unlikely to be aware of what had happened to his passengers.

Avon placed the smoke canister on the floor and pulled a thin metal garrotte from his belt. He entered the pod. The pilot was conveniently leaning forward, checking instruments, when Avon slipped the garrotte over his head, tightened it and sliced it into his throat. He lifted the pilot from his seat and dragged him into the dock. Returning, he checked the instruments, especially the fuel gauge.

Satisfied, he made his way back to the flight deck.

'Now might be a good time to remove the tracker in my mouth,' he said nonchalantly.

Orac grunted.

'We are stationary and undisturbed,' Avon said, as he leaned towards the computer. 'I'll adjust the strength of the laser to minimum and you can get on with it. You will take care, won't you? I don't want to end up like our uninvited guests.'

'Have you dealt with the pilot?'

'I wouldn't be here if I hadn't.' Avon made the adjustment to the laser beam.

'Open your mouth,' Orac said. 'Think of me as a dentist.'

Avon made a face. 'I'd rather not.' But he opened his mouth and leaned further forward.

'Oh, this is a very pretty little thing,' Orac said. 'Close your eyes and think of something else.'

Avon obeyed the instruction. There was a hissing sound, followed by a tingling sensation in the roof of his mouth.

'Don't move,' Orac said. Then, in a triumphant tone, it exclaimed, 'Got it!'

Avon backed away, rubbing his jaw.

'That wasn't too bad, was it?'

Avon licked the roof of his mouth. Apart from a slight hint of metal, he tasted nothing. 'Not bad at all,' he said.

'What happens now?'

'We fly the Dragon pod out of here.'

'That won't get us very far.'

'It'll get us far enough. We're on the very edge of the Beyond, almost in Alien Grey territory. We'll land on the first planetoid we get to and borrow another of their spacecraft. Before you ask, I've checked the pod 's instruments and it has the range and sufficient fuel. The planetoid I have in mind is Grey Two.'

'Of course, you've been here before, haven't you?'

'Well, sort of. Then we'll go to Xerxes, as you've suggested, get what we need and then go where we want.'

'May I remind you that you are just as unpopular with Alien Greys as you are with Cathay, the Quartet and anyone else you care to name?'

'Given our present situation, there isn't an alternative, is there?'

Orac sighed. 'You do know the Dragons will come after us?'

'That's the beauty of my plan.'

'Oh, you have a plan?'

'With the Dragons following on, the Greys will think they could be in trouble. Don't forget, the pod has Dragon insignia. They're more than likely to accede to my request, just to get rid of us – and the warships.'

'It's not a very good plan.'

'Well, since it's the only one we've got, we better put it into action before the Dragons work out what's happened here.'

Orac sighed again. 'I must say, Avon, there's never a dull moment with you is there?'

'The tracker has gone down,' Xian said, a hint of sorrow in her voice.

'That does not necessarily mean that Avon is dead,' Fu Ti commented. 'He may have been clever enough to remove it.'

Xian brightened a little. 'Are you always this optimistic?'

'I am being realistic. Optimism as to the fate of someone my empress has marked for death is not in my remit.'

There was a tinkling sound from the Dragon ship's flight console. 'There is a message,' Xian said, truly sorrowful now.

'Put it on the speaker, if you will.'

'I cannot. The message is from the pod and we have no speaker contact with it.'

'Then read it to me.'

'It says: "I have the computer and have placed explosives in strategic positions on board the terrorist spacecraft. It will be necessary for both Dragon warships and the *Thumb* to stay clear of imminent explosions. I shall manoeuvre the pod accordingly."'

Fu Ti closed his eyes for a moment, as if in silent prayer.

'Shall I instruct Micah to bring the dissidents to the flight deck to witness this destruction?' Xian asked.

'It is the empress's wish.'

*

The Dragon ships halted their progress towards the stricken, soon to be destroyed, spacecraft. The *Thumb* withdrew towards them. The pod detached from the wrecked docking area and began to move in an arc that, perhaps to a discerning and suspicious eye, would only seem to be creating distance between it and the attendant flotilla.

It began to increase speed even as George, after what seemed to be a giant intake of breath, erupted into a sea of flame. Shock waves reached as far as the Dragons, but the pod avoided them as it sped away.

'I wanted to do that a long time ago,' Micah said, as he stood beside Grant and Magda, with Fu Ti and Xian slightly behind them, watching the spectacle on a telescopic screen. 'Finally, the warlock is dead,' he added.

'As is, in a sense, Orac,' Fu Ti said, quietly but firmly.

'What made you decide you didn't want it?' Grant asked.

Fu Ti shrugged, 'It was not my decision, but that of a higher power.'

Magda fainted.

'You had better take her below,' Fu Ti said. No-one moved. 'Micah. You will do as I say.'

Reluctantly, Micah assisted Grant, in half walking, half carrying Magda from the flight deck.

Left alone with Xian, Fu Ti breathed a great sigh. Xian was watching the screen. As the flames died and smoke cleared – debris scattering away – she said, 'The pod is moving away from us at great speed.'

'How can that be? Tung Ma should be returning with his prize.'

'It's gone,' Xian whispered to herself. 'We've lost him.'

Fu Ti's eyes anxiously searched the screen then narrowed. He turned to Xian. 'In what script was the message?' he asked, a degree of anxiety still to the fore.

'It was in Cantonese,' Xian said, smiling. 'Avon's knowledge of the language would appear to be not so rusty, after all.'

By the time the representatives of the Empire of Cathay had

swallowed their embarrassment and loss of face – yet again – and set off in pursuit, Avon and Orac were into the Beyond and well on the way to the planetoid Grey Two.

'Kill the dissidents!' Micah shouted, spittle forming at the corners of his mouth.

'What good would that do?' said Xian, almost indifferently.

'They are needed alive, so that they may persuade Gabriella on the Base that Avon and Orac are no more – as promised by our Empress,' Fu Ti said calmly.

'But Avon is still making fools of us,' Micah said petulantly.

Fu Ti continued in his calm, measured tone. 'Grant and Lens don't know that. They will report what they have seen. They can do no more or less.'

'Look at the big picture, Micah,' Xian said. 'If your small mind can encompass it.'

Micah turned on her in fury and raised his hand to hit her. But she was as quick. Avoiding the intended blow, she kicked him in the most vulnerable parts of his anatomy. Micah doubled up in pain.

Fu Ti winced. 'We really mustn't fight amongst ourselves,' he said soothingly.

Xian seemed unconcerned. 'What are your orders now?'

'I await confirmation. I would remind you that they will be our orders, not mine alone. And they will be obeyed,' Fu Ti said – unyielding instead of emollient.

Micah, having recovered, made another move towards Xian. So she kicked him again and he went down. 'If he's the best the Empire can offer,' she said derisively, 'it's no wonder Avon has been able to give us the run-around.'

Helping a sickly looking Micah to his feet, Fu Ti said, 'You know, Micah, she might have a point.'

Pandora Ess was alone in her room, gazing at herself in a mirror. She had neither agreed to, nor disagreed with, Adonis's proposal to launch an expedition to Xerxes, without consulting Kwai Shi Yan. Something was nagging at her. How had he known about her negotiations with the empress? She had deliberately loaned him to Gabriella so that she – Pandora

– could execute her plans in the utmost secrecy. Not even Sarin could know. Or could he?

She began to remove the thick make-up that hid the many tiny, only partially healed scars on her face – scars earned in the early service of her then idol, Servalan. It hid a lot of other things – including sometimes conflicting emotions. Adonis and Sarin were essential to her plans. Or were they? She shook her head. She could manage without them. Then, any triumph would be hers and hers alone. Again, she shook her head.

'Don't be stupid,' she muttered to herself.

Her problem, she realised, was that she could not trust anybody. She could use them, of course, to help her achieve her aims, but she needed to beware any possible treachery. After all, she reasoned, had she not been treacherous in arranging for the deaths of her rivals – Steiner and Furneaux and others before them? Might not Sarin and Adonis – not to mention Gabriella – take a leaf out of her book and, tutored by the mistress of deceit, use her own methods against her? What if she was being paranoid? What if Sarin and Adonis were her genuine admirers – even worshippers? She could never be certain though, could she? At all times, she would need to watch her back – physically, as well as metaphorically. She turned sharply, sensing another presence in the room. But there was no-one.

She sighed theatrically. Then she assumed a stern expression. She knew what she wanted, and how she had schemed for decades and she was now on the brink... the brink of what? She frowned slightly, which puckered the scars on her face. She was on the brink of becoming the supreme power throughout the known galaxies.

Even Servalan, despite her single-minded determination, cruelty and ruthless exploitation of others, had not matched the doctor's achievements. She smiled a little and gazed once more into the mirror. Unsmiling eyes gazed back at her. What would happen when the supreme power she craved was in her grasp, she thought? What could she do with it? With whom could she share it? There would be nothing she could do – and no-one to share it.

*

The empress did not know (and Sun Cheng was not going to tell her) that the mission to capture Orac and kill Avon had ended in failure. As far she was concerned, the matter had been settled to her satisfaction and she would continue to deceive Pandora Ess under the assumption that possession of Orac would yield her a significant advantage over her.

Sun Cheng did inform Lauren and instructed her to contact his agent, embedded in the power structure of what was no longer a quartet. Lauren, the trusted confidante of Kwai Shi Yan, was in reality a sleeper, placed in proximity to the Empress by Sun Cheng whilst he was preparing to come out of the shadows of power in Cathay and assume it himself. She communicated with the agent in coded Russian, the language of her Caucasian father.

Adonis cursed when he received it. Avon was either very clever, or very lucky – perhaps a combination of the two. The fact remained, however, that Orac was out of reach, and that adversely affected his plans. Plans that had been mapped out over some years, whilst he had kept a low profile within the Quartet. He had secured for himself a degree of influence, his fellow conspirator, Sun Cheng, having done likewise in the Empire of Cathay. Had Orac been taken, or destroyed, those plans would have accelerated to fruition. Adonis cursed again. That his scheming could be endangered by the interference of an ageing bandit was infuriating!

A contingency plan was clearly needed, but Lauren's missive had given no guidance as to what was to be done. It would seem that Sun Cheng was in a quandary and prepared to allow him, Adonis, to take the lead.

'Well, so be it,' he thought.

'Are the Dragons still on our tail?' Avon asked.

'If they are, they are a long way behind,' Orac said. 'We are almost at Grey Two and there is an Alien Grey fighter coming to greet us.'

'I see it.' Avon tensed. 'Scan it.'

'It is a refurbished Federation long-range attack fighter. It carries two hellfire rockets, two heavy machine guns and has a crew of one.'

Avon was surprised. 'A crew of just one, you say?'

'It's a cyborg.'

'Well now, that's a piece of good fortune. I'm assuming you can interfere with its workings and confuse its controller.'

'You know I can. I am already in the process of doing so.'

'Bring the Grey's spacecraft to a standstill. Then we'll go alongside.'

'You expect a lot of me, don't you?'

'You usually deliver.'

'The cyborg is impotent and I have control of the fighter,' Orac said smugly.

'Thank you! We'll lock on to it and I'll go aboard.'

'Locking procedure is under way.'

The Dragon pod aligned itself with the Grey spaceship and there was a sharp thud as it connected.

'Stabilise air pressure, then open its entrance hatch.'

'It's done.'

'Very well – open our hatch and I'll go and take a look.'

'Beware the cyborg,' Orac said, 'its controller will have switched on its safety device. I can tell you that it is an electrical circuit. It is similar to that which we used to eliminate our enemies when on the George spaceship.'

Avon was already gone.

'Do be careful,' Orac muttered.

The interior of the Alien Grey ship was almost identical to that of the previous spacecraft that Avon had purloined. A little smaller perhaps, with no computer controls other than those contained within the cyborg, static in the pilot seat.

Avon approached the cyborg with the exquisite care that Orac had urged upon him. He studied it – searching for a way to disarm the electrical circuit that would surely kill him if he didn't. He quickly spotted a thin wire protruding minutely from the cyborg's metal neck and smiled grimly – that old trick. He searched again, not daring to touch the inert figure. It took him quite a while to find another wire that was almost identical to the first. Which one would spring the trap, and which was the genuine article? He pondered his dilemma. The first wire was fairly easily detectable, which would suggest that a clever fixer would, by making it so, likely persuade anyone attempting to interfere with the cyborg to dismiss it as too obvious a trap and assume that the second wire was the one to cut. Only someone with a devious mind would not be fooled and cut the first wire.

Avon had a devious mind – he cut the first wire. Then he removed the cyborg from its position and settled into the pilot's seat himself. He checked all instruments and was pleased to note that the fighter was fuelled and that all armaments were well maintained. Satisfied, he returned to the pod and lifted Orac. 'We have a new spaceship that will get us to Xerxes in no time,' he said.

Having deposited Orac on the fighter's flight deck, Avon dragged the cyborg on to the pod. He re-fused the wire that he had cut, coiled another wire around the cyborg's neck and attached it to the pod's drive mechanism. He set the automatic pilot and returned to the Alien Grey ship.

'Cut us loose, Orac,' he said, somewhat breathlessly. Orac did as instructed and the two spacecraft separated. The pod began to move towards the surface of the planetoid, Grey Two.

'That worked out rather well,' Avon said, 'the Greys practically gifted this fighter to us. They've saved us the trouble of having to go and get it.'

'One day, your luck will run out,' Orac said dryly. 'Why get rid of the pod?'

'Where there's one attack fighter, there's likely to be two. The second will be after us any time now. I've fixed it so the pod will slow its progress – maybe permanently.'

'You're right,' Orac said, 'another fighter is on its way. It's almost parallel with the pod.'

There was a sudden explosion and a bright light illuminated the darkness.

After a pause, Orac said, 'Well, I suppose that lets the Alien Greys know that you didn't much appreciate them setting the Huntress on you, or trying to blow us up when we were escaping Abyss.'

Avon shrugged.

Adonis replied to Lauren's message, suggesting that Sun Cheng be informed of a slight alteration to their master plan and that he should follow the example that he – Adonis – was about to set. He sent another communication to Sarin on the Base and then went in search of Pandora Ess. He found her in her sleeping quarters. She looked drawn and tired.

Smiling slightly, she said, 'I am taking your suggestion under consideration, Adonis. But I need to sleep. You understand, I'm sure.'

Adonis almost pitied her, as she sat on her bed, looking for all the worlds like a child bereft.

'Of course I do,' he said, smiling in return. But, shutting the bedroom door behind him, he advanced towards her. She frowned in annoyance. Before she could speak again, Adonis hit her hard in her scarred face and she fell backwards. Adonis climbed on top of her and, selecting a pillow, covered the scars with it.

Pandora Ess squirmed and fought for her life. But Adonis was much stronger than he looked and, literally, had the upper hand.

It took only a few minutes for Pandora Ess to suffocate. Adonis, panting from his effort, slid off the bed and surveyed his work. He leaned over Pandora Ess's body and checked for a pulse. Finding none, he covered the lifeless form with a sheet and left the room, locking the door. He glanced at the guard who was supposedly responsible for Pandora Ess's safety and smiled sheepishly. The guard nodded. Adonis had attended Pandora Ess in her bedroom before, so no suspicion was aroused.

Adonis sent another encoded message to Lauren which read in translation, '*Stage one completed. Stage two?*' Then he sent another two messages. One was to Sarin on the Base.

Sarin got the message, in more ways than one. He sighed.

He had held Pandora Ess in some esteem and had hoped it would not be necessary to end her life so prematurely. She had schemed and fought and, he felt, deserved to see some reward for her efforts. Still, he had suspected a hidden agenda and, now that he had learned from Adonis what her agenda had been, he understood that there was no choice but to eliminate her from the game.

Sarin had suffered at the hands of Cathay and could not – would not – tolerate Pandora Ess's secret association with them. Adonis clearly felt the same way and had acted accordingly. Now it was up to him, Adonis and, perhaps, Gabriella to proceed. What Sarin did not know was that Adonis had his own agenda that included Cathay. What Sarin did not know was going to hurt him.

On board the *Claw*, the deaf mute, Lauren, held a consultation with Sun Cheng. They communicated, as always, in sign language. Lauren asked what Adonis meant by stage two?

Sun Cheng smiled and drew a finger across his throat. Lauren recoiled.

Sun Cheng took her in his arms and attempted to soothe her fears by stroking her hair, her face and her neck.

Breaking away from him, Lauren seemed mollified. She signed, 'When?'

Sun Cheng signed back, 'Not until I tell you, but be ready.'

Stage three was already under way.

'Adonis has discovered that Doctor Ess was in collusion with the Cathay Empire,' Sarin was saying, 'It was her intention to cut you out of the game – and me for that matter. According to Adonis, she was going to allow a space fleet to enter the Beyond, without interference from you. She would accompany that fleet, gather enough fuel rods to last a decade and then return to take the Base away from you. Always providing you weren't prepared to bow to the Cathay Empress and Pandora Ess herself. I don't think you would have been.'

Gabriella looked paler than usual. 'I find all that hard to believe,' she said quietly.

'And so did I. But Adonis has convinced me.'

'You used the past tense when referring to Pandora.'

'She's dead.'

Gabriella emitted a short gasp. 'How did she die?'

'She ran out of breath.' Sarin smiled at his cruel joke.

Gabriella stared at him. 'What happens now?'

'We send a raiding party into the Beyond to gather fuel and then lock ourselves up in the Base – and prepare to be attacked.'

'There must be other routes Cathay could take to enter the Beyond.'

'Indeed there are. But passing close by the Base is the safest and fastest of them.'

'They could also send a raiding party. They don't need to go in strength.'

'Oh, but they do. They go in in strength and come out even stronger. They then turn on us.' Sarin scowled. 'Doctor Ess didn't believe that dividing our forces and effectively neutering the Base would tempt them to do that. She was blinded by her ambition and succumbed to their "honourable" promises.' He spat on the floor.

'She was not such a fool.'

'It would appear that she was. But you are not, and neither am I.'

'We can defend the Base?'

'Oh yes! Forewarned is forearmed. We have to thank Adonis for quite a lot.'

Gabriella looked momentarily sorrowful. 'Pandora and he were once close.'

'If they hadn't been, he wouldn't have been able to get even closer and stop her.'

'He now claims to be devoted to me,' Gabriella said shyly.

'He's proved it, hasn't he?'

'I suppose so.'

'We need to get a move on,' Sarin said. 'I'll lead the raid. You shore up the defences here. When the space fleet of Cathay shows up... Well, we have a better chance of beating them than we would have had if Doctor Ess was still in charge.'

'What is Adonis doing?'

Sarin was disconcerted by the sudden change of tack. 'I expect he's preparing to defend Iphigenia. That's where Cathay will go when we've frustrated them here,' he said, not particularly convincingly.

'So many schemes, so many games,' Gabriella said. 'And most of them coming to nothing.'

'Well this is the big game,' Sarin said tightly. 'It's a game we cannot afford to lose.'

'Then we had better start playing it, hadn't we?' Gabriella smiled beatifically.

'We are in receipt of fresh commands from the *Claw*,' Kai Kim announced, the loudspeaker making her sound stiff and formal. 'There will be no further pursuit of the terrorist. Fu Ti will proceed to the Base in all haste and deliver the dissidents to Gabriella Travis. He will then withdraw to a safe distance and await the *Claw*. I am to enter the Beyond and proceed with caution towards the island planet known as Xerxes. The *Claw* and Fu Ti and I will later rendezvous in its vicinity.'

'Who has issued these commands?' Fu Ti asked politely, suspecting he already knew the answer to the question.

'Supreme Commander Sun Cheng.'

Fu Ti smiled, somewhat wearily.

'The *Thumb* will return to the *Claw*,' Kai Kim continued. 'There is a request that Xian assume command of it.'

'Not a command to assume command, but merely a request,' Fu Ti said sarcastically. 'Who has issued this request?'

'The request comes from the personal aide to the empress. Lauren Adonis.'

Avon was gently caressing the sniper rifle that he had taken off the Huntress on Abyss. 'This is quite something,' he said. 'Given Xerxes's fascination with fine guns, it might go some way to getting us the fuel we need, without confrontation.'

'You don't really believe that?' Orac said disparagingly.

'I concede that I'm going to have to get past Alaric first.'

'How are you going to do that?'

'I'll think of something.'

'You could shoot him with the rifle. That should convince Xerxes that it's a gun worth having.'

Avon stifled a laugh. 'We've got a problem, haven't we?' he said rather more seriously.

'We've got more than one. A Dragon warship has just crossed into the Beyond and it's on course for Xerxes.'

Avon looked startled. 'I thought they'd given up the chase?'

'Well, you'll need to think again,' Orac said. Then, after a brief pause, 'Of course, it could be – indeed it's most likely – that the Dragon is going to Xerxes for the fuel it needs. The island planet is an easier target than a lot of others.' Before Avon could say anything, Orac continued. 'There's something else. Two attack fighters, bearing Quartet insignia, are fast approaching Xerxes on its far side.'

'Well now, this could prove to be interesting.'

'It is highly likely,' Orac said, 'that we may be observers at a conflict in which, unusually, we will have no part to play. Until, of course, there is a victor, and to the victor will go the spoils.'

'Thus presenting us with an opportunity to sneak in while the conflict is under way and no-one is looking out for us and grab the spoils for ourselves,' Avon said.

'It really is an almost perfect opportunity to acquire the fuel rods we need,' Orac said, almost enthusiastically.

'It's called a blindside hit and run.'

'And you are very good at those, aren't you, Avon?'

As the Quartet's fighters curved into Xerxes's atmosphere, Sarin was stunned to be confronted by the Dragon warship of Kai Kim.

At the same time, Xerxes's protection spacecraft launched an attack. This turned out to be not a good idea. Though probably capable of giving Sarin a good fight, they were no match for the superior firepower of the Dragon and were quickly eliminated from the fray – limping to the surface of the island planet.

Sarin took evasive action, flying as low as he dared, at high speed. His accompanying fighter, slow to react to the Dragon threat, was caught by a savage burst of fire and, reduced to a fireball, crashed to the ground.

Whilst this seriously damaging warfare was going on, Orac had placed the Grey spacecraft in stealth mode, in a strategic position on the blind side of the fight. Flying a minute, cramped heliplane, Avon came into land behind the bunker that he knew housed the required crystal fuel rods.

Armed with a handgun, the Huntress's sniper rifle and with a large leather bag with a thin metal lining, he took cover and surveyed the Xerxes compound. There was chaos. One of the Xerxes fighters had crumpled in a heap within it and was on fire. Xerxes's men were running around like headless chickens. This suited Avon just fine.

Keeping close to the walls of the bunker and avoiding the light from the burning fighter as best he could, he reached its entrance. He blew off the locks with a burst from a Nine7 – there was so much going on, no-one heard or observed him do it – and went inside. He picked up several racks of fuel rods and tipped them into the bag. Satisfied that he had all he could carry, he returned to the bunker entrance and, through the scope of the rifle, scanned the compound.

There, in his sights, trying to restore some sense of order was Alaric. Avon didn't hesitate, that was not his style. He took the shot and a high velocity bullet burst Alaric's skull. Not wasting time, Avon scurried back to the heliplane, threw the bag on board and scrambled after it.

The plane lifted into blackness, streaked with red, and Orac guided it into its holding bay, before, still in stealth mode, lifting the Grey ship up and away.

Avon had been on the surface of Xerxes for exactly seven minutes.

The jet heliplane with Dragon markings settled in Xerxes's compound, narrowly avoiding wreckage and other debris. Flanked by two sturdy warriors, Kai Kim alighted and, carefully skirting Alaric's corpse, walked towards a cringing Louis, Xerxes's surviving wife. Machine guns on the plane covered the disarmed remnants of Xerxes's forces. Louis managed to get a grip on himself and, after bowing low, offered to surrender to the Empire of Cathay.

'That won't be necessary,' Kai Kim said. 'We are not at war. What happened here was unfortunate and I am sorry for your losses.'

Louis smiled ingratiatingly and executed another bow. 'My husband, Xerxes, is unwell. Otherwise he would have greeted you. He sends his apologies.'

Kai Kim raised an eyebrow. 'His apologies are accepted,' she said graciously. 'The reason for this visit is that my empress has authorised me to request that you furnish me with crystal fuel rods. Under normal circumstances, there would have been reimbursement but, given that you launched an unwarranted attack on my Dragon ship, I feel certain that you would prefer to offer them as a gift.' She smiled icily.

'But of course,' Louis said, pointing to the bunker.

One of Kai Kim's guards set off towards it.

'We will not denude your supply entirely,' Kai Kim said, still gracious. 'Once I am in possession of the rods, I will withdraw my forces and leave you in peace.'

Louis was about to utter an obsequious reply when there was an explosion at the entrance to the bunker and the guard, covered in blue flame, threw himself to the ground, shrieking in agony.

The other guard rushed over to him, but he was too late. He surveyed the wrecked bunker. Turning to Kai Kim – who was pale with shock – he muttered the word, 'Nitroglycerin.'

Having secured the small rotary heliplane, Avon entered the flight deck, carrying the heavy bag containing fuel rods.

'Something wicked this way comes,' Orac said, with just a suggestion of humour.

Avon smiled grimly. 'I figured that phial of nitro would come in handy,' he said.

'And you disposed of Alaric. I said you would have to kill him. Although, it would seem, it might not have been essential.'

'I had him in my sights. It seemed like too good an

opportunity to miss.' Avon began to unpack the bag.

'And you never miss good opportunities. You will need to insert fuel rods, we are running low,' Orac said. 'How many did you get?'

'We have twenty-seven.'

'That's an odd number.'

'Yes, it is.' Avon replaced the rods in the bag, moved to a hatch below and behind the pilot's seat, and dropped through it. He returned within a minute.

'Where are we going?' Orac asked, with a hint of trepidation.

Avon sighed. 'I'll leave that up to you.'

'Might I suggest somewhere quiet and out of the way, at least for the time being?'

'Like I said, Orac, it's your call.' Avon sank wearily into the pilot seat.

Gabriella sat in a chair sipping champagne. Del Grant, his arms twisted behind his back by two of her eunuch bodyguards, had been forced to kneel at her feet.

'I'm inclined to believe you,' Gabriella waved her glass at an attendant, who refilled it, 'but it might be in your interest to try and convince me that my father's murderer is no longer alive – not to mention that Orac has been destroyed.'

'I have no reason to lie. I saw the ship explode, as did Magda.'

'Hmm. She is receiving treatment but... Well, to be honest, she is not in the best of health.'

'She's hardly likely to be any better once you've finished with her.'

Gabriella threw her drink in Grant's face. Once again, the attendant refilled it. An officer entered the room. Commander Hermann was about Gabriella's age but, though handsome enough, there was an obvious coarseness about him. Despite this, she had entertained him – and he her – in her bed. Gabriella could not be accused of being undemocratic when it came to her choice of lovers.

'The Dragon ship has withdrawn, as Fu Ti promised,' he

said. 'I learned from one of his men that he awaits the arrival of the *Claw*.'

Gabriella looked at him sharply then smiled. 'Is there anything else?'

'Sarin is returning empty handed. He ran into trouble with another Dragon warship.'

The smile slipped. 'What of Magda Lens?' Gabriella asked.

Hermann glanced at Grant. 'She died under interrogation.'

'You son of a bitch,' Grant said, spitting the words. A eunuch slapped him into silence.

'She confirmed what he has said,' Hermann added.

Gabriella stood and gazed down at Grant. 'She killed Servalan,' she said. 'It was inevitable that, in due time, she would pay the price.'

'I would have killed Servalan, if I'd had the chance,' Grant said through gritted teeth.

Gabriella kicked him, so that he toppled to the floor. 'And you too will pay the price. Take him away.'

'Do you wish his death?' said Hermann.

'Of course I do, but tell the interrogators to take their time.' She turned away, to be served more champagne.

After a nod from Hermann, eunuchs dragged Grant out of the room.

'Sarin has failed, you say?'

'Yes.'

Gabriella sighed. 'Well, you know what to do.'

Hermann touched her lightly on the arm.

Without looking at him, Gabriella said, 'Later, Hermann.'

Kwai Shi Yan, Empress of Cathay, had been in festive mood. She and Sun Cheng and the lovely Lauren had enjoyed a celebratory dinner – celebrating the mythical capture of Orac – and, to tell the truth, the empress had drunk a little too much. She did not demur, therefore, when Sun Cheng suggested she might care to retire. As he made the suggestion, he caught the eye of the Eurasian and gave an almost imperceptible nod. He received a slight smile in return.

Once in her lavish bedroom, the empress stripped herself

of her clothes and turned to face her trusted confidante. Very slowly, and enticingly, Lauren undressed. The two naked women came together and embraced. Kwai Shi Yan turned her back, so that she might enjoy the sensation of Lauren caressing her breasts, as had occurred on many a previous occasion. Instead, Lauren's hands closed round her throat and squeezed hard.

The empress's eyes bulged and her face began to turn blue, as she fought for breath. She struggled and squirmed – much as Pandora Ess had done, when another Adonis had smothered the life out of her – but the younger woman was very strong and Kwai Shi Yan did not take long to die. Lauren lowered the naked corpse to the floor. She dressed, then dragged the body to the bed and lifted it, with some little difficulty, so that it lay, as if asleep, upon it. She covered it with a silk sheet and left the room.

Sun Cheng sent a coded message to Adonis which read, in translation: '*Stage two is complete.*'

Where most people find it difficult to play a double game, Adonis was attempting a triple and proving to be quite adept – up to a point. The problem he faced, although he didn't realise it yet, was that, if playing with partners, it was necessary to believe they would not take it upon a whim to switch sides and thus betray you.

So far, all was going to plan. Adonis's relationship with Pandora Ess had been a good one. Until, that is, he reached the conclusion that, like Servalan before her, she was 'losing the plot'. He had offered her the chance to dispense with Cathay's influence and seize the grand prize for herself, but her previous seemingly unstoppable momentum had stalled and it appeared her confidence was on the wane. She had become uneasy at the prospect of wearing the crown. That was intolerable as far as Adonis was concerned. Her indecisiveness was a sin, which forbade redemption. As far as Pandora Ess was concerned it was game over. Thus, Stage one needed to be set in motion.

Sun Cheng, in the second game, was behaving well. But

then, Adonis had back-up, in the shape of his half-sister, Lauren. They shared the same father but, whereas Lauren's mother had been beautiful and tall, his had been relatively plain and short, and had suffered debilitating illnesses prior to his birth. He bore no resentment and had quickly realised that Lauren was a perfect tool in the manufacture of his ambition. He had ensured that she achieved an influential position in the emerging Empire of Cathay. This had not been too difficult. Sun Cheng – until his recent elevation to supreme commander – had supervised ground forces and, in the course of his duties, had kept a watchful eye on their reluctant ally, Russia. It was here that he had first met Adonis, a native of the vast, if crumbling, state, and had been smitten by his half-sister. It was but a small step to her becoming Sun Cheng's mistress and a willing pawn in the long term plot hatched by the two men. A plot, not just to take over the world, but all galaxies known and, as yet, unknown. Unless, that is, Adonis could forge a better deal with Pandora Ess.

The third game player was the unpredictable Gabriella. At the same time as communicating with Sarin on the Base, Adonis had sent her a message, issuing vital instructions. If she carried them out, all well and good but, if she did not – well, the best-laid plans of the little man might go awry. There was also the slight problem of Avon, and his wonder computer. But what could Avon hope to achieve against the might of Cathay and, for that matter, what was left of the Quartet, even supposing he chose to challenge them? Adonis brushed aside the thought. Gabriella was now the key to the realisation of his aspirations. And Gabriella, he understood only too well, was prone to whimsy.

Adonis believed he had been chosen. By whom, or what, he didn't know, and didn't care to know. Emerging at last from the shadows and assuming the mantle of power, it was sufficient unto the day that he was possessed of a fierce determination and blessed with the ability to inspire most of those, if not all, he needed to bend to his will. His speech to the Quartet troops on Niobe and Iphigenia was masterful. After solemnly announcing the death of Pandora Ess from a brain tumour, he quickly whipped the crowd into a frenzy of chauvinism – the last refuge of a scoundrel – and extracted from it a sworn allegiance to Gabriella Travis, at whose side he, Adonis, would humbly serve as she completed the late Doctor's grand design. Of course, he did not fail to emphasise the treasures and pleasures that lay in store for each and every one who chose to follow Gabriella and, by implication, him.

Exhausted by his recent efforts but confident that he was in command of the situation, Adonis delayed putting stage three into action. He would have been better advised to recall the phrase 'he who hesitates is lost'. To lose one, even two, games could be described as unfortunate. To lose all three would be the result of incompetence. That can end in tragedy.

The whimsical Gabriella, however, was ensuring that all was going according to the plan. When the dejected Sarin returned to the Base, Hermann arrested him and charged him with treason, citing him as an accomplice in the deaths of General Steiner and Pandora Ess. A swiftly assembled kangaroo court confirmed the charge and condemned him to death, a sentence that was equally swiftly carried out.

Instead of fortifying the Base, as she had promised the now-dead man, Gabriella offered to open its facilities to the new leader of the Cathay Empire and to assist the invasion of the Beyond.

Sun Cheng had learned of Kai Kim's disaster on Xerxes. After spending a little time with the glamorous Base commander, he accepted with alacrity when she made him an offer it would be difficult to refuse.

The *Claw*, in tandem with the warship of Fu Ti, set course for the territories of the Alien Greys. They were preceded by the *Thumb*, now commanded by Xian at the request of Lauren Adonis.

Gabriella was pleased with herself. The punishment of the incompetent Egil Nacre for failing her in the matter of Avon and Orac was overdue. It was only then, relishing once more her power as commander of the Base, that she issued commands for Base fortification.

Sun Cheng didn't know it yet, but while Gabriella had allowed him passage into the Beyond, she was going to make it extremely difficult for him to get out if he reneged on their new deal.

She was playing Adonis's game, but by her rules – and strictly to her own advantage.

Avon awakened with a start. 'How long have I been out?'

'You have been in the arms of Morpheus for almost twelve hours,' Orac said.

Avon took a deep breath and released it.

'Considering the effects your recent exertions have had upon you – and, let's face it, you're not getting any younger – sleep was essential,' Orac announced.

'Where are we exactly?'

'It is not possible to be exact.'

'Might you come up with an educated guess?'

'We are alone in space between the Base and Iphigenia.'

'Thank you.' Avon rose and took a bottle of water from a cooler. He drank greedily. 'What have you been doing all this time, Orac?' he asked.

'Oh, I've been doing this and that.'

'Tell me about "this". Then you can tell me about "that".'

'"This" is the situation as far as the Empire of Cathay and the fractured Quartet are concerned. The *Claw* and two other Dragon warships have entered the Beyond, courtesy of the commander of the Base, and are about to inflict some harm on the Alien Grey leader – Egil Nacre, of less than fond memory – whilst relieving him of his stash of crystal fuel rods. "That" is all.'

'Are you sure about that?'

Orac seemed to hesitate. 'The Base has issued a number of disturbing pictures. You won't care to see them, but I think you probably should.'

'Show them on the screen.' Avon sat in the pilot's seat.

The pictures duly appeared. They showed the wracked naked bodies of three humans, suspended from meat hooks.

'The third person is, or was, called Sarin,' Orac said

tonelessly. 'Sarin was a high-ranking, somewhat talented, military subordinate to General Steiner – cast in the mould of Travis – and, latterly, owed his allegiance to Gabriella. The other two you will recognise.'

Avon's face was a mask. 'I recognise them,' he said, so quietly that it was almost a thought, rather than a statement.

'The pictures are designed to deter those who would go against Gabriella.'

'You mean me.'

'And others like you, although they are likely to be very few.'

Avon leaned forward to take a closer look at the pictures. 'Magda and Grant were tortured,' he said, almost to himself.

'Does that observation mean you are deterred?'

'I am angry,' Avon said mildly.

'Oh dear,' Orac stuttered. 'I don't like it when you're angry. And those against whom your anger is directed will like it even less.'

'How secure is the Base?'

'It is a fortress. And I know you'd like to blow it up but, given its current high state of alert, any attempt to do so would be unwise.'

'How secure is Iphigenia?'

'Well, now you come to mention it, it's not very. There are all sorts of goings on elsewhere and, as a result, the planet has been denuded of most of its protection.'

'Is that a fact?'

'It is.'

Avon left the pilot seat and stood gazing at Orac.

'I feel sorry for you, Avon,' Orac said at length.

'You're not supposed to have feelings, let alone express them.'

Orac went on, 'The only man to gain your hard-earned respect betrayed you – or so you thought – so you killed him. The only woman you ever loved betrayed you – or so you thought – so you killed her. Thus, you have lost all faith in humanity and stand alone, except for me. And I am nothing but a machine. You are a dead man walking. You have no-one to turn to and nowhere to go. If these are not sufficient reasons for feeling sorry for you, I don't know what are.'

Avon turned away. 'Your sentimentality is beginning to irritate me,' he said.

'Anger has given way to mere irritation?'

'I didn't say that. And you're wrong. I may not have anyone to turn to, but I do have somewhere to go.'

'You want me to set a course for Iphigenia?'

'How did you guess?'

'It wasn't a guess, and we are already on our way. I know you too well, Avon. It is payback time, isn't it?'

Avon smiled and, if it could, Orac would probably have done the same.

Adonis had taken control of General Steiner's warship. Now, accompanied by four long range attack spacecraft, with two hundred elite troops, it entered the Base's airspace.

'Supreme Commander Adonis requests permission to land,' Hermann informed Gabriella.

Gabriella smiled to herself. 'Tell him he'll be very welcome, but to come alone.'

'He won't like that.'

'What he likes, or dislikes, is a matter of indifference to me. Is everything prepared?'

'As you instructed. Defence shields are in position, all big guns are locked and loaded and aircraft are in a state of readiness.'

'Target Adonis's warship. We may need to take it out,' Gabriella said wistfully as if deciding which dress she might care to wear for dinner and which should be discarded.

'There are attack fighters and many troops,' Hermann said.

'Troops are useless, unless they're on the ground. With the flagship gone, the fighters will be vulnerable.'

'I thought Adonis was on our side?'

'You think too much, Hermann. When the time comes, just do as I say.' Gabriella moved towards him and kissed him lightly on the mouth. She smiled seductively, and Hermann tried to take her in his arms. 'Later, Hermann,' Gabriella said.

Adonis was not best pleased, but decided he had no alternative but to acquiesce to Gabriella's demand and arrive on the Base alone. A pod transported him.

'*Supreme Commander* Adonis is it now? We're getting a little above ourselves, aren't we?' Gabriella said coolly.

'With Pandora Ess gone, someone had to assume that title,' Adonis replied insouciantly.

'With Pandora Ess gone, I am the sole survivor of the Quartet hierarchy. Ergo, I am the Supreme Commander.'

Adonis stiffened. 'I was under the impression that you and I are allies,' he said cautiously.

Gabriella smiled. 'I don't think so. But you are my faithful accomplice, are you not?' The smile froze on her lips. 'As you once were to Pandora.'

Adonis licked his lips, a nervous contrast to Gabriella's smile.

'It would seem, though,' Gabriella continued, 'that you proved to be faithless to her. I am wondering, therefore, if I have been mistaken in placing my faith in you.'

'It has always been the plan to eliminate Pandora and replace her with you.'

'It may always been your plan, *Supreme Commander* Adonis,' Gabriella said contemptuously. 'My plan has been, and is, somewhat different.'

Adonis was becoming very nervous now. 'Are you suggesting that you may wish to dispense with my services?' he asked.

Gabriella laughed. 'I know full well that you have been playing your games quite expertly for a very long time, but it is the endgame that counts. And this is the end for you, no longer my friend.'

Adonis was stunned. 'I underestimated you,' he said hoarsely.

'Yes. It's a not-uncommon mistake.'

During the long silence that ensued, as the two protagonists stared at each other, Adonis began to reassume his dignity and confidence. 'I think it likely that you may have underestimated me,' he said.

'Oh, you mean that you have a back-up plan. You can throw in your lot with the Empire of Cathay.' Gabriella shrugged. 'I think that opportunity may have eluded you.'

'How is that so?'

'I have had a visit from the *Claw* and its estimable commander, Sun Cheng. We got on surprisingly well.' She smiled dazzlingly.

'I have already "thrown in my lot", as you put it, with Sun Cheng,' Adonis said, not too confidently.

'I think you'll find he has thrown it out,' Gabriella said.

'I have worked for many years with him,' Adonis said.

'You have both played a very good game together, but Sun Cheng has chosen to swap partners. Without Pandora Ess to turn to, you're now on your own.'

Adonis forced a smile. 'I think you may be playing a game with me. Sun Cheng would not abandon me – after all that I have done.'

'Perhaps that's why he has abandoned you. You did too much – and went too far.'

'It is you who have gone too far, Gabriella. You seem to have overlooked the fact that I have a considerable force at my disposal.' Adonis was gaining confidence now.

Gabriella yawned. 'But that force is not with you, is it? You are here alone.'

Adonis was aghast. 'I trusted you,' he whispered.

'I can't help feeling that was a mistake.'

Adonis was beginning to perspire. 'If you harm me, my men will take their revenge.'

'Oh, I don't think so. Not when they find out that it was you who murdered their heroine – Doctor Ess. The same Doctor Ess who taught me all I know and groomed me so that I could assume the power that I now enjoy. Power that I intend to exercise to the full.'

'Sun Cheng will betray you as he has betrayed me,' said Adonis, desperately.

Gabriella shrugged. 'Should he do so — and you could be right — I have arrangements in place to counteract such a betrayal. I control the Base. You don't.'

'You're going to kill me?'

'Why would I do that?'

Adonis was startled, if relieved. 'But if you do not, now that we are enemies, I will haunt you, like the terrorist, Avon.'

'Avon has a computer called Orac. You don't. You won't be too threatening a ghost.' Gabriella turned away and waved her hand dismissively. 'You can go now.'

Adonis hesitated. 'You're almost as bad as your dead father,' he said spitefully.

Unperturbed, Gabriella said, 'You told me once that you admired him.'

Adonis, quivering with anger, made a move towards her, but two muscular eunuchs appeared, as if from nowhere, and stood in his way.

'You should leave now,' Gabriella said, not unkindly. 'Try and be a good loser, won't you.'

The two eunuchs escorted Adonis from the room.

Hermann came out of the shadows and watched them go. 'Why not kill him?' he asked.

'That matter is in hand. I presume you've let it be known how Doctor Ess met her death, and that Adonis is culpable.'

'The word is out.'

'Then when he dies there will be few to mourn him.'

'What about the terrorist he mentioned? The dissidents, even under torture, swore that they saw him die.'

'They were misled. My new friend and ally, Sun Cheng, informs me that he is still alive.'

'He could cause problems then.'

Gabriella laughed drily. 'He's caused quite a few already. But by airing the pictures of his tortured and dead comrades, I may have encouraged him to try and cause me another. If I'm right, he'll be making a fatal mistake.'

Hermann didn't look too convinced.

*

Sun Cheng had been much taken with Gabriella Travis. Not only was she beautiful, but also she was clever. Also, she was not unrealistic about the likely future power structures governing Earth and other galaxies, as her proposition to him revealed.

It was quite simple. She was prepared to stand aside and permit the Empire of Cathay to expand as far and as wide as it desired. She would control the Base, possess Iphigenia and its satellite Niobe as well as the many moons of Uranus – these latter, although present production was spectacularly low, would be the Base's main crystal fuel suppliers. She would share future largesse with Cathay in return for a small share of the Empire's fuel collection in the Beyond.

Of course, Adonis would have to go. Sun Cheng shook his head in admiration of her political common sense. He smiled to himself. In truth, as Gabriella had indicated, what real use was Adonis, now that he, Sun Cheng, was so close to achieving his ends? In further truth, he was beginning to tire of Adonis's half-sister, Lauren, and had more or less replaced her with the less temperamental Xian. No-one knew, of course, but Xian had acted as his spy on Fu Ti.

Fu Ti was the only one he feared as a likely rival for power within the Cathay Empire, which was why he had insisted they should enter the Beyond together and had, in Lauren's name, recalled Xian and given her command of the *Thumb*. Sun Cheng had every intention of returning from the Beyond, but he hoped and expected that Fu Ti would not. He shivered with self-congratulation. Li Kang and the Empress Kwai Shi Yan were obstacles already removed from his path. Very soon, Fu Ti would follow them.

Manoeuvring others to dispose of his opponents was, he considered, sheer brilliance on his part. He had covered his tracks so well that no-one could accuse him of complicity in those dispositions. True, Li Lang, an honourable man, had taken his own life, but Lauren had murdered the empress and, if all went according to his plan, he would expose her, put her on trial and, regretfully, oversee her execution. Then, once Fu Ti had been put in harm's way and suffered at the hands of those from whom they were extracting vital fuel supplies, or so it would seem, the people would clamour for him to become their supreme leader.

At first, he would appear to be modest about his worthiness and talents. Like Caesar so many centuries ago, he would refuse the crown – only to finally, if reluctantly, accept it. He would become emperor out of a sense of duty to the people. Again like Caesar, he would distribute some wealth amongst them – the only difference being that when Caesar's wealth was distributed he was dead. Sun Cheng would be very much alive.

Supreme Being of the Galactic Empire of Cathay... Not bad for a poor boy from the slums of Shanghai.

Gabriella, Hermann at her side, watched through a telescopic window as the pod carrying Adonis towards his warship began to slow and veer from side to side, as if losing power – which indeed it was. The contaminated crystal rods Gabriella had caused to be inserted in its fuel injection system were doing their work. Hermann gasped as the pod stalled and slowly, like an autumn leaf, fell away into oblivion. He fancied he could hear Adonis's screams.

Gabriella snapped her fingers and a eunuch was immediately at her side, pouring champagne into an elegant glass.

'The Quartet warship may attack,' Hermann ventured tentatively.

'I am mistress of the Quartet,' Gabriella said savagely. Then she smiled. 'Besides, our big guns are trained on it, are they not?'

'Yes, as you instructed.'

'Well then, if it starts to move, blow it out of the sky. If it doesn't, communicate with its commandant and invite him to dinner. We can discuss future arrangements.'

Having failed to enlist support from the bandit clans of the Beyond, Egil Nacre, disrespected leader of Alien Greys, was in a quandary.

All too aware of the approach of the *Claw* and attendant

.

warships, he had to decide to fight alone, come to some kind of rapprochement with the invaders – or run.

He dismissed the first option. The devil Avon and his confounded computer had robbed him of significant air power. He cursed the terrorist in many tongues. If he were to run, he would be abandoning his people. Given that they already held him in low esteem, he might instead redeem himself by remaining. Reluctantly, he decided upon this course and entered into negotiations.

Thus, without firing a shot, Sun Cheng acquired the bulk of the Alien Grey crystal fuel rod stores. Though satisfactory and securing some admiration from his followers, it was disappointing, insomuch as an opportunity to dispose of Fu Ti in combat was lost.

Wary of the watching clans, he commanded the orderly withdrawal of Cathay forces from the Beyond. He had got what he had come for. Although it might be necessary to return in the future for more, he was aware that many small fighting craft could damage the seemingly mighty *Claw*. Discretion, therefore, was the better part of his valour.

However, another method of removing Fu Ti from his path would need to be sought. But that lay ahead. For the time being, all seemed well with the worlds of Sun Cheng.

Fully aware of her lover's intention to remove Fu Ti from his equation, Xian was relieved when the older man survived the foray into the Beyond. She had grown to like him, even admire him, and did not believe that he was egotistical enough to imagine he could, or should, usurp Sun Cheng's newly acquired power. Paranoia is the bane of those who succeed, by fair means or foul, at the expense of others, so she understood Cheng's fears. Nevertheless, she was disapproving of his intended means to overcome them.

The arrest of Lauren Adonis for murder of the empress was announced as the *Claw* left the Beyond. It was followed by Lauren's speedy trial and execution – by the sword hand of Sun Cheng himself no less. This did nothing to dispel Xian's doubts as to the wisdom of forming a liaison with him. When he grew tired of her, would she be the next to lose her head? She had already noticed how enamoured he had become of Gabriella Travis. That would be a conflation that could lead to hell and Xian had no intention of visiting that place prematurely. She shivered.

Then, as she recalled her brief encounter with Avon – a happening never revealed to Sun Cheng – she smiled slightly. Avon was a rogue, of course, much older than she, and wearily treading the path to dusty death. But there was something about him that was appealing, despite her intuition that he harboured a death wish. His paradoxical ambition, for the moment, seemed to be to postpone that inevitability for as long as possible. It was his misfortune that so many connived to thwart that ambition. Still, he was proving highly skilled in avoiding the Grim Reaper and appeared to enjoy pitting his wits against enemies, real or imagined.

She wondered if she might be safer with him than with Sun Cheng. But then, he had already rejected her offer to accompany him on his adventures and, should their paths cross again, he would be deeply suspicious of her motives should she renew that offer.

She shook herself out of what she considered to be a foolish reverie. The Cathay flotilla was approaching the Base and, as commander of the *Thumb*, she was leading the way. The siren, Gabriella, was calling.

The Grey spacecraft, in stealth mode, drifted into Iphigenia's atmosphere. There was no sign of any active aerial defence and Orac set the Grey down in a small hollow exactly one kilometre from the palace of Pandora Ess, close to the edge of the lake that fronted it. The computer scanned it.

'How far did you say, Orac?' Avon asked, somewhat bemused by the fact that he glimpsed the waters of the lake through sparse trees that guarded the hollow ground.

'Exactly one klick as the crow flies.'

'I'm not a crow. How do I get to the palace?'

'You have three choices. You can skirt the lake on foot, you can try and steal a boat or you can swim.'

'Is that the best you can do?'

'One of the three is the best you can do.'

Avon frowned. 'Well, I may not need to go there.'

'You will if you intend to burgle their arsenal. It lies directly underneath it.'

'Are you sure?'

'Of course I'm sure. My scanning technique is beyond reproach.'

'That's a dangerous place to keep an armoury.'

'It does mean that the military within and surrounding the palace have easy and quick access to weapons.'

Avon thought for a moment. 'Where is the military?'

'It would seem that their guard is down. Some sort of party – more like an orgy – is taking place within. When the cat's away, the mice will be sure to play,' Orac said, its voice streaked with puritanism.

'How do I get in?'

'You want to join the orgy?'

'You're being too flippant here, Orac. How do I get into the basement?'

'There are two entrances. The armoury is accessible from the main hall and by means of a short passage. The door opening into this latter is set into a stone wall overlooking the gardens on the left hand side of the building.'

'Well now, that would seem the way to go.'

'That would be my advice.'

Avon shivered. 'I'm getting a dread sense of déjà vu,' he said quietly.

'Oh, I shouldn't worry. You've done this sort of thing before. On Xerxes, for example.'

'I got lucky. And I seem to remember you telling me that my luck may run out sooner than I might like.'

'It's just a question of when,' Orac said, tartly.

'That's a big boost to my confidence.'

'Well, are you going to sit here shivering, or get on with it?'

Avon checked a Nine7 and stuck it in his belt. He hefted the bag that he had carried on Xerxes and headed for the exit.

'Stay alert, Orac. We may have to leave in a hurry.'

*

There was a celebration of sorts on the Base, although rather more refined than the 'orgy' on Iphigenia. The exquisitely gowned and bejewelled Gabriella was the perfect hostess to Sun Cheng, Fu Ti, Kai Kim and Xian – the commanders of the four Dragon warships currently orbiting her Base. Hermann was in attendance, so there were six who dined at table, served, as always, by silent eunuchs.

Champagne flowed freely, as did idle conversation. Serious discussion did not occur until all had eaten their fill and were sipping liqueurs, as well as tasting a range of differently sourced coffees.

Gabriella, Xian noticed, had drunk sparingly – as had she. Sun Cheng, on the other hand, had imbibed freely and Fu Ti, Kai Kim, even Hermann, had failed to keep up with him. All were agreed that Lauren Adonis and her half-brother had suffered deservedly for murder and treachery and that the premature demise of Empress Kwai Shi Yan was a tragedy. There was even some sympathy for the late Pandora Ess. But there was no mention of Eugene Furneaux, General Steiner, Li Lang, or any others who had fallen by the wayside.

Gabriella selected a cheroot and Hermann lit it for her. She blew a smoke ring. 'Am I to understand that you have acquired sufficient fuels for your immediate needs?' she asked graciously.

Sun Cheng's response was an inebriated belch, so it was left to Fu Ti to answer her. The Alien Greys of Egil Nacre had stockpiled crystal rods and, having relieved them of a very large quantity, there would be sufficient fuel, after the promised division of the spoils, to sustain Cathay for six Earth months, he assured her.

Gabriella raised an eyebrow. 'That's not very long, is it?'

Fu Ti nodded. 'It will be necessary to acquire further supplies,' he said, adding, 'but as we understand it, the mines on the moons of Uranus are, albeit slowly, increasing production and you have generously offered to share such as may be surplus to your needs with the Empire.'

Gabriella nodded in return. 'That is our agreement.'

She frowned prettily. 'I trust Egil Nacre received his just deserts?'

It was Kai Kim who responded. 'He is a pathetic semblance of a man,' she said, 'hardly worthy of consideration. It is my impression that his people will deal with him in their own inimitable fashion.'

Gabriella decided she would have to be satisfied with that. 'What news of the terrorist, Avon?' she smiled. 'He seems to have caused you much loss of face.'

After a pause, Xian said, 'As he would seem to have caused you.'

Gabriella's eyes flashed with anger.

Fu Ti quickly interjected, 'He is gone away, no-one knows where. There is no guarantee of course, but it is likely we have heard the last of him.'

Xian permitted herself a sly smile.

Gabriella shrugged. 'I would prefer it if he were dead and the computer that is assisting him to stay alive were destroyed.'

Fu Ti gave a sympathetic nod. Xian and Kai Kim remained silent. Sun Cheng belched again and Hermann plied him with more drink.

There was a semi-conscious drunk lying directly in front of the entrance to the Iphigenia armoury. Avon broke his neck with a savage chop of his hand and stepped over him. There was a panel attached to the heavy metal door that required the entry of a code to open it. Avon mouthed a curse and drew his Nine7 with a view to blowing off the lock. Thinking better of it – the less attention he attracted, the better – he took a gamble and punched in the letters that spelt 'Quartet'. The door opened!

Once inside, Avon proceeded along the passage described by Orac until he reached a flight of steps. He descended in darkness until his feet stood on firm, flat ground. He felt along a wall, found a switch and turned on a light. He was now looking upon what some might describe as terrorist heaven. There were racks of all sorts of guns – rifles, handguns, shotguns and laser guns. There were boxes of grenades, mortar shells and other explosive devices. In addition, there was a box containing a number of crystal rods. What then caught his eye was a metal box that, when he touched it, was ice cold. He opened it, to reveal half a dozen neatly arranged phials of nitroglycerin.

He set the box on one side, selected a couple of new Nine7's and a fine, sawn off, three-barrelled shotgun and placed them, together with ammunition, in his bag, along with the fuel rods. Getting ready to leave, he then spied something that made him smile – coils of plastic explosive. He selected a coil and, after a quick search, found a detonator. He looked around. There was a door at the far end of the armoury – a faint hum emanating from beyond it. Once again, there was coded entry. Once again, Avon punched in 'Quartet' and the door opened. Once again, he smiled. This was a room that contained generating equipment for the palace above. He selected a gas-fired generator and draped the plastic explosive over it. He set the detonator's timer for one hour then returned to the armoury. He carefully removed a phial of nitroglycerin from the icebox and placed it close by a pile of mortar shells.

Gathering up his spoils, he left by the way he had come in. The dead drunk was still there. From within the palace, which was ablaze with light – light that did not extend to where he skulked in shadow – Avon could hear loud music, raucous laughter and screams of orgiastic pleasure. He shook his head, contemptuous of the lack of security surrounding what was, after all, the heart of Iphigenia.

Within a short time, he had returned to the Grey spacecraft – a ghostly outline in stealth mode – and was guided by a tiny winking light to its entrance hatch.

'You were quick this time,' Orac said.

Avon placed the box of nitro below the pilot's seat and covered it with a thick cloth. He stored his other ill-gotten gains on a rack. 'We need to get out of here,' he said hoarsely.

'Is the balloon about to go up?' Orac said sarcastically.

'You could say that.'

'I just did.'

'Let's go, Orac.'

The computer duly obliged and the Grey ship lifted off from Iphigenia.

As it almost reached the extent of the planet's atmosphere, there was a spectacular series of explosions – although Avon couldn't hear them – and a firework display brilliantly lit the deep darkness. Through the telescopic observation window, the palace could be seen to be disintegrating, its walls falling to the ground in slow motion, a raging fire replacing its interior.

'That's some balloon,' Orac said admiringly. 'You don't do things by half measures do you?'

Avon was silent, his face distorted by reverse telescopic images of destruction playing upon it.

'Are you satisfied now?' Orac asked tentatively. 'Or do you still want to blow up the Base?'

'I'll think about it.'

'Yes, well while you're doing that, I think I'll remove us from hereabouts with some dispatch. The troops on Iphigenia's satellite are springing into action.'

'Springing?'

'Well, staggering. Those who are relatively sober, that is.'

'It's time to go then.'

'We're on our way. Question is, Avon – where to?'

'I'll think about it.'

Orac sighed in frustration.

Fu Ti and Kai Kim had returned to their respective warships and Xian to the *Thumb* when they heard the news of Iphigenia. Gabriella, having been less than satisfied by a drunken Sun Cheng, was in bed with him when she was informed.

Fu Ti shook his head and smiled, Kai Kim shook hers and frowned.

Xian threw back her head and laughed. 'Oh Avon, what a piece of work you are!' she exclaimed.

Gabriella let out a shriek of fury.

Sun Cheng belched.

'Is anybody after us?' Avon asked.

'Everybody's after us,' Orac said irritably.

'I mean as of right now.'

'I know what you mean. An attack fighter made a half-hearted attempt at pursuit, but he's given up on us.'

'Would that everybody else might do the same.'

'I doubt they ever will.'

There was a momentary silence between man and machine.

'After your antics on Iphigenia,' Orac said at last, almost sorrowfully, 'I would imagine they'll throw everything at you, always assuming they can find you.'

'Who are "they"?'

'The "everybody" you just mentioned. I think I've already given you a list.'

'So, where do we go where they can't find me?'

'I've been thinking about that.'

'Would you care to share your thoughts?'

'We should go to the last place they would expect you to go: planet Earth.'

Though startled, Avon said, with a hint of admiration, 'You're a genius, Orac.'

'I thought that went without saying?'

Avon stretched and flexed his muscles. 'All right then, set a course.'

'I already have.'

'Why am I not surprised?' Then, after a pause, Avon added, 'Let's go home.'

Orac seemed to laugh – and Avon smiled.

AVAILABLE FROM BIG FINISH...

PART 1 OF THE LUCIFER TRILOGY:

LUCIFER
BY PAUL DARROW

*Many legends surround the aftermath of the collapse of the
Federation, including the fate of Kerr Avon...*

What happened to Avon after the death of Blake and the
crew of the Scorpio? Paul Darrow's vivid re-imagining picks
up Avon's story at the final moments of the final episode
of *Blake's 7* and follows him on his fight for survival, this
time with no crew and no ship to help him. The adventure
continues years later as Avon, now an old man, finds himself
a key player in the game of power politics being played out
on a grand scale by the Quartet – four ruthless leaders in
an uneasy alliance, who govern the world in place of the
Federation. Old enemies resurface and dangerous new ones
appear as the time comes for old scores to finally be settled...

ALSO AVAILABLE AS AN AUDIOBOOK
READ BY PAUL DARROW

AVAILABLE FROM BIG FINISH BOOKS

AVAILABLE AS CD OR DOWNLOAD

THE LIBERATOR CHRONICLES

THE LIBERATOR CHRONICLES: Vol 1
The Turing Test by Simon Guerrier
Solitary by Nigel Fairs
Counterfeit by Peter Anghelides

THE LIBERATOR CHRONICLES: Vol 2
The Magnificent Four by Simon Guerrier
False Positive by Eddie Robson
Wolf by Nigel Fairs

THE LIBERATOR CHRONICLES: Vol 3
The Armageddon Storm – Parts One, Two and Three
by Cavan Scott and Mark Wright

THE LIBERATOR CHRONICLES: Vol 4
Promises by Nigel Fairs
Epitaph by Scott Harrison
Kerr by Nick Wallace

THE LIBERATOR CHRONICLES: Vol 5
Logic by Simon Guerrier
Risk Management by Una McCormack
Three by James Goss

THE LIBERATOR CHRONICLES: Vol 6
Incentive by Peter Anghelides
Jenna's Story by Steve Lyons
Blake's Story by Mark Wright and Cavan Scott

THE LIBERATOR CHRONICLES: Vol 7
Spy by Simon Guerrier
Disorder by Eddie Robson
The Hard Road by James Swallow

THE LIBERATOR CHRONICLES: Vol 8
President by Simon Guerrier
The Sea of Iron by Marc Platt
Spoils by James Goss

AVAILABLE AS CD OR DOWNLOAD

THE CLASSIC AUDIO ADVENTURES

1.1. *Fractures* by Justin Richards

1.2. *Battleground* by Andrew Smith

1.3. *Drones* by Marc Platt

1.4. *Mirror* by Peter Anghelides

1.5. *Cold Fury* by Mark Wright and Cavan Scott

1.6. *Caged* by Mark Wright and Cavan Scott